Saunterings

Charles Dudley Warner

Contents

SAUNTERINGS

BY

Charles Dudley Warner

SAUNTERINGS
By Charles Dudley Warner

MISAPPREHENSIONS CORRECTED

I should not like to ask an indulgent and idle public to saunter about with me under a misapprehension. It would be more agreeable to invite it to go nowhere than somewhere; for almost every one has been somewhere, and has written about it. The only compromise I can suggest is, that we shall go somewhere, and not learn anything about it. The instinct of the public against any thing like information in a volume of this kind is perfectly justifiable; and the reader will perhaps discover that this is illy adapted for a text-book in schools, or for the use of competitive candidates in the civil-service examinations.

Years ago, people used to saunter over the Atlantic, and spend weeks in filling journals with their monotonous emotions. That is all changed now, and there is a misapprehension that the Atlantic has been practically subdued; but no one ever gets beyond the "rolling forties" without having this impression corrected.

I confess to have been deceived about this Atlantic, the roughest and windiest of oceans. If you look at it on the map, it does n't appear to be much, and, indeed, it is spoken of as a ferry. What with the eight and nine days' passages over it, and the laying of the cable, which annihilates distance, I had the impression that its tedious three thousand and odd miles had been, somehow, partly done away with; but they are all there. When one has sailed a thousand miles due east and finds that he is then nowhere in particular, but is still out, pitching about on an uneasy sea, under an inconstant sky, and that a thousand miles more will not make any perceptible change, he begins to have some conception of the unconquerable ocean. Columbus rises in my estimation.

I was feeling uncomfortable that nothing had been done for the memory of Christopher Columbus, when I heard some months ago that thirty-seven guns had been fired off for him in Boston. It is to be hoped that they were some satisfaction to him. They were discharged by countrymen of his, who are justly proud that he should have been able, after a search of only a few weeks, to find a land where the hand-organ had never been heard. The Italians, as a people, have not profited much by this discovery; not so much, indeed, as the Spaniards, who got a reputation by it which even now gilds their decay. That Columbus was born in Genoa entitles the Italians to celebrate the great achievement of his life; though why they should discharge exactly thirty-seven guns I do not know. Columbus did not discover the United States: that we partly found ourselves, and partly bought, and gouged the Mexicans out of. He did not even appear to know that there was a continent here. He discovered the West Indies, which he thought were the East; and ten guns would be enough for them. It is probable that he did open the way to the discovery of the New World. If he had waited, however, somebody else would have discovered it,-- perhaps some Englishman; and then we might have been spared all the old French and Spanish wars. Columbus let the Spaniards into the New World; and their civilization has uniformly been a curse to it. If he had brought Italians, who neither at that time showed, nor since have shown, much inclination to come, we should have had the opera, and made it a paying institution by this time. Columbus was evidently a person who liked to sail about, and did n't care much for consequences.

Perhaps it is not an open question whether Columbus did a good thing in first coming over here, one that we ought to celebrate with salutes and dinners. The Indians never thanked him, for one party. The Africans had small ground to be gratified for the market he opened for them. Here are two continents that had no use for him. He led Spain into a dance of great expectations, which ended in her gorgeous ruin. He introduced tobacco into Europe, and laid the foundation for more tracts and nervous diseases than the Romans had in a thousand years. He introduced the potato into Ireland indirectly; and that caused such a rapid increase of population, that the great famine was the result, and an enormous emigration to New York-- hence Tweed and the constituency of the Ring. Columbus is really responsible for New York. He is responsible for our whole tremendous experiment of democracy, open to all comers, the best three in five to win. We cannot yet tell how it is coming out, what with the foreigners and the communists and the women. On our great stage we are playing a piece of mingled tragedy and comedy, with what denouement we cannot yet say. If it comes out well, we ought to erect a monument to Christopher as high as the one at Washington expects to be; and we presume it is well to fire a salute occasionally to keep the ancient mariner in mind while we are trying our great experiment. And this reminds me that he ought to have had a naval salute.

There is something almost heroic in the idea of firing off guns for a man who has been stone-dead for about four centuries. It must have had a lively and festive sound in Boston, when the meaning of the salute was explained. No one could hear those great guns without a quicker beating of the heart in gratitude to the great discoverer who had made Boston possible. We are trying to "realize" to ourselves the importance of the 12th of October as an anniversary of our potential existence. If any one wants to see how vivid is the gratitude to Columbus, let him start out among our business-houses with a subscription-paper to raise money for powder to be exploded in his honor. And yet Columbus was a well-meaning man; and if he did not discover a perfect continent, he found the only one that was left.

Columbus made voyaging on the Atlantic popular, and is responsible for much of the delusion concerning it. Its great practical use in this fast age is to give one an idea of distance and of monotony.

I have listened in my time with more or less pleasure to very rollicking songs about the sea, the flashing brine, the spray and the tempest's roar, the wet sheet and the flowing sea, a life on the ocean wave, and all the rest of it. To paraphrase a land proverb, let me write the songs of the sea, and I care not who goes to sea and sings 'em. A square yard of solid ground is worth miles of the pitching, turbulent stuff. Its inability to stand still for one second is the plague of it. To lie on deck when the sun shines, and swing up and down, while the waves run hither and thither and toss their white caps, is all well enough to lie in your narrow berth and roll from side to side all night long; to walk uphill to your state-room door, and, when you get there, find you have got to the bottom of the hill, and opening the door is like lifting up a trap-door in the floor; to deliberately start for some object, and, before you know it, to be flung against it like a bag of sand; to attempt to sit down on your sofa, and find you are sitting up; to slip and slide and grasp at everything within reach, and to meet everybody leaning and walking on a slant, as if a heavy wind were blowing, and the laws of gravitation were reversed; to lie in your berth, and hear all the dishes on the cabin-table go sousing off against the wall in a general smash; to sit at table holding your soup-plate with one hand, and watching for a chance to put your spoon in when it comes high tide on your side of the dish; to vigilantly watch, the lurch of the heavy dishes while holding your glass and your plate and your knife and fork, and not to notice it when Brown, who sits next you, gets the whole swash of the gravy from the roast-beef dish on his light-colored pantaloons, and see the look of dismay that only Brown can assume on such an occasion; to see Mrs. Brown advance to the table, suddenly stop and hesitate, two waiters rush at her, with whom she struggles wildly, only to go down in a heap with them in the opposite corner; to see her partially recover, but only to shoot back again through her state-room door, and be seen no more;--all this is quite pleasant and refreshing if you are tired of land, but you get quite enough of it in a couple of weeks. You become, in time, even a little tired of the Jew who goes about wishing "he vas a veek older;" and the eccentric man, who looks at no one, and streaks about the cabin and on deck, without any purpose, and plays shuffle-board alone, always beating himself, and goes on the deck occasionally through the sky-light instead of by the cabin door, washes himself at the salt-water pump, and won't sleep in his state-room, saying he is n't used to sleeping in a bed,--as if the hard narrow, uneasy shelf of a berth was anything like a bed!--and you have heard at last pretty nearly all about the officers, and their twenty and thirty years of sea-life, and every ocean and port on the habitable globe where they have been. There comes a day when you are quite ready for land, and the scream of the "gull" is a welcome sound.

Even the sailors lose the vivacity of the first of the voyage. The first two or three days we had their quaint and half-doleful singing in chorus as they pulled at the ropes: now they are satisfied with short ha-ho's, and uncadenced grunts. It used to be that the leader sang, in ever-varying lines of nonsense, and the chorus struck in with fine effect, like this:

"I wish I was in Liverpool town.

Handy-pan, handy O!
O captain! where 'd you ship your crew
Handy-pan, handy O!
Oh! pull away, my bully crew,
Handy-pan, handy O!"

There are verses enough of this sort to reach across the Atlantic; and they are not the worst thing about it either, or the most tedious. One learns to respect this ocean, but not to love it; and he leaves it with mingled feelings about Columbus.

And now, having crossed it,--a fact that cannot be concealed,--let us not be under the misapprehension that we are set to any task other than that of sauntering where it pleases us.

PARIS AND LONDON
SURFACE CONTRASTS OF PARIS AND LONDON

I wonder if it is the Channel? Almost everything is laid to the Channel: it has no friends. The sailors call it the nastiest bit of water in the world. All travelers anathematize it. I have now crossed it three times in different places, by long routes and short ones, and have always found it as comfortable as any sailing anywhere, sailing being one of the most tedious and disagreeable inventions of a fallen race. But such is not the usual experience: most people would make great sacrifices to avoid the hour and three quarters in one of those loathsome little Channel boats,--they always call them loathsome, though I did n't see but they are as good as any boats. I have never found any boat that hasn't a detestable habit of bobbing round. The Channel is hated: and no one who has much to do with it is surprised at the projects for bridging it and for boring a hole under it; though I have scarcely ever met an Englishman who wants either done,--he does not desire any more facile communication with the French than now exists. The traditional hatred may not be so strong as it was, but it is hard to say on which side is the most ignorance and contempt of the other.

It must be the Channel: that is enough to produce a physical disagreement even between the two coasts; and there cannot be a greater contrast in the cultivated world than between the two lands lying so close to each other; and the contrast of their capitals is even more decided,--I was about to say rival capitals, but they have not enough in common to make them rivals. I have lately been over to London for a week, going by the Dieppe and New Haven route at night, and returning by another; and the contrasts I speak of were impressed upon me anew. Everything here in and about Paris was in the green and bloom of spring, and seemed to me very lovely; but my first glance at an English landscape made it all seem pale and flat. We went up from New Haven to London in the morning, and feasted our eyes all the way. The French foliage is thin, spindling, sparse; the grass is thin and light in color--in contrast. The English trees are massive, solid in substance and color; the grass is thick, and green as emerald; the turf is like the heaviest Wilton carpet. The whole effect is that of vegetable luxuriance and solidity, as it were a tropical luxuriance, condensed and hardened by northern influences. If my eyes remember well, the French landscapes are more like our own, in spring tone, at least; but the English are a revelation to us strangers of what green really is, and what grass and trees can be. I had been told that we did well to see England before going to the Continent, for it would seem small and only pretty afterwards. Well, leaving out Switzerland, I have seen nothing in that beauty which satisfies the eye and wins the heart to compare with England in spring. When we annex it to our sprawling country which lies out-doors in so many climates, it will make a charming little retreat for us in May and June, a sort of garden of delight, whence we shall draw our May butter and our June roses. It will only be necessary to put it under glass to make it pleasant the year round.

When we passed within the hanging smoke of London town, threading our way amid numberless railway tracks, sometimes over a road and sometimes under one, now burrowing into the ground, and now running along among the chimney-pots,--when we came into the pale light and the thickening industry of a London day, we could but at once contrast Paris. Unpleasant weather usually reduces places to an equality of disagreeableness. But Paris, with its wide streets, light, handsome houses, gay windows and smiling little parks and fountains, keeps up a tolerably pleasant aspect, let the weather do its worst. But London, with its low, dark, smutty brick houses and insignificant streets, settles down hopelessly into the dumps when the weather is bad. Even with the sun doing its best on the eternal cloud of smoke, it is dingy and gloomy enough, and so dirty, after spick-span, shining Paris. And there is a contrast in the matter of order and system; the lack of both in London is apparent. You detect it in public places, in crowds, in the streets. The "social evil" is bad enough in its demonstrations in Paris: it is twice as offensive in London. I have never seen a drunken woman in Paris: I saw many of them in the daytime in London. I saw men and women fight in the streets,--a man kick and pound a woman; and nobody interfered. There is a brutal streak in the Anglo-Saxon, I fear,--a downright animal coarseness, that does not exhibit itself the other side of the Channel. It is a proverb, that the London policemen are never at hand. The stout fellows with their clubs look as if they might do service; but what a contrast they are to the Paris sergents de ville! The latter, with his dress-coat, cocked hat, long rapier, white gloves, neat, polite, attentive, alert,--always with the manner of a jesuit turned soldier,--you learn to trust very much, if not respect; and you feel perfectly secure that he will protect you, and give you your rights in any corner of Paris. It does look as if he might slip that slender rapier through your body in a second, and pull it out and wipe it, and not move a muscle; but I don't think he would do it unless he were directly ordered to. He would not be likely to knock you down and drag you out, in mistake for the rowdy who was assaulting you.

A great contrast between the habits of the people of London and Paris is shown by their eating and drinking. Paris is brilliant with cafes: all the world frequents them to sip coffee (and too often absinthe), read the papers, and gossip over the news; take them away, as all travelers know, and Paris would not know itself. There is not a cafe in London: instead of cafes, there are gin-mills; instead of light wine, there is heavy beer. The restaurants and restaurant life are as different as can be. You can get anything you wish in Paris: you can live very cheaply or very dearly, as you like. The range is more limited in London. I do not fancy the usual run of Paris restaurants. You get a great deal for your money, in variety and quantity; but you don't exactly know what it is: and in time you tire of odds and ends, which destroy your hunger without exactly satisfying you. For myself, after a pretty good run of French cookery (and it beats the world for making the most out of little), when I sat down again to what the eminently respectable waiter in white and black calls "a dinner off the Joint, sir," with what belongs to it, and ended up with an attack on a section of a cheese as big as a bass-drum, not to forget a pewter mug of amber liquid, I felt as if I had touched bottom again,--got something substantial, had what you call a square meal. The English give you the substantials, and better, I believe, than any other people. Thackeray used to come over to Paris to get a good dinner now and then. I have tried his favorite restaurant here, the cuisine of which is famous far beyond the banks of the Seine; but I think if he, hearty trencher-man that he was, had lived in Paris, he would have gone to London for a dinner oftener than he came here.

And as for a lunch,--this eating is a fascinating theme,--commend me to a quiet inn of England. We happened to be out at Kew Gardens the other afternoon. You ought to go to Kew, even if the Duchess of Cambridge is not at home. There is not such a park out of England, considering how beautiful the Thames is there. What splendid trees it has! the horse-chestnut, now a mass of pink-and-white blossoms, from its broad base, which rests on the ground, to its high rounded dome; the haw-thorns, white and red, in full flower; the sweeps and glades of living green,--turf on which you walk with a grateful sense of drawing life directly from the yielding, bountiful earth,--a green set out and heightened by flowers in masses of color (a great variety of rhododendrons, for one thing), to say nothing of magnificent green-houses and outlying flower-gardens. Just beyond are Richmond Hill and Hampton Court, and five or six centuries of tradition and history and romance. Before you enter the garden, you pass the green. On one side of it are cottages, and on the other the old village church and its quiet churchyard. Some boys were playing cricket on the sward, and children were getting as intimate with the turf and the sweet earth as their nurses would let them. We turned into a little cottage, which gave notice of hospitality for a consideration; and were shown, by a pretty maid in calico, into an upper room,--a neat, cheerful, common room, with bright flowers in the open windows, and white muslin curtains for contrast. We looked out on the green and over to the beautiful churchyard, where one of England's greatest painters, Gains-borough, lies in rural repose. It is nothing to you, who always dine off the best at home, and never encounter dirty restaurants and snuffy inns, or run the gauntlet of Continental hotels, every meal being an experiment of great interest, if not of danger, to say that this brisk little waitress spread a snowy cloth, and set thereon meat and bread and butter and a salad: that conveys no idea to your mind. Because you cannot see that the loaf of wheaten bread was white and delicate, and full of the goodness of the grain; or that the butter, yellow as a guinea, tasted of grass and cows, and all the rich juices of the verdant year, and was not mere flavorless grease; or that the cuts of roast beef, fat and lean, had qualities that indicate to me some moral elevation in the cattle,--high-toned, rich meat; or that the salad was crisp and delicious, and rather seemed to enjoy being eaten, at least, did n't disconsolately wilt down at the prospect, as most salad does. I do not wonder that Walter Scott dwells so much on eating, or lets his heroes pull at the pewter mugs so often. Perhaps one might find a better lunch in Paris, but he surely couldn't find this one.

PARIS IN MAY--FRENCH GIRLS--THE EMPEROR AT LONGCHAMPS

It was the first of May when we came up from Italy. The spring grew on us as we advanced north; vegetation seemed further along than it was south of the Alps. Paris was bathed in sunshine, wrapped in delicious weather, adorned with all the delicate colors of blushing spring. Now the horse-chestnuts are all in bloom and so is the hawthorn; and in parks and gardens there are rows and alleys of trees, with blossoms of pink and of white; patches of flowers set in the light green grass; solid masses of gorgeous color, which fill all the air with perfume; fountains that dance in the sunlight as if just released from prison; and everywhere the soft suffusion of May. Young maidens who make their first communion go into the churches in processions of hundreds, all in white, from the flowing veil to the satin slipper; and I see them everywhere for a week after the ceremony, in their robes of innocence, often with bouquets of flowers, and attended by their friends; all concerned making it a joyful holiday, as it ought to be. I hear, of course, with what false ideas of life these girls are educated; how they are watched before marriage; how the marriage is only one of arrangement, and what liberty they eagerly seek afterwards. I met a charming Paris lady last winter in Italy, recently married, who said she had never been in the Louvre in her life; never had seen any of the magnificent pictures or world-famous statuary there, because girls were not allowed to go there, lest they should see something that they ought not to see. I suppose they look with wonder at the young American girls who march up to anything that ever was created, with undismayed front.

Another Frenchwoman, a lady of talent and the best breeding, recently said to a friend, in entire unconsciousness that she was saying anything remarkable, that, when she was seventeen, her great desire was to marry one of her uncles (a thing not very unusual with the papal dispensation), in order to keep all the money in the family! That was the ambition of a girl of seventeen.

I like, on these sunny days, to look into the Luxembourg Garden: nowhere else is the eye more delighted with life and color. In the afternoon, especially, it is a baby-show worth going far to see. The avenues are full of children, whose animated play, light laughter, and happy chatter, and pretty, picturesque dress, make a sort of fairy grove of the garden; and all the nurses of that quarter bring their charges there, and sit in the shade, sewing, gossiping, and comparing the merits of the little dears. One baby differs from another in glory, I suppose; but I think on such days that they are all lovely, taken in the mass, and all in sweet harmony with the delicious atmosphere, the tender green, and the other flowers of spring. A baby can't do better than to spend its spring days in the Luxembourg Garden.

There are several ways of seeing Paris besides roaming up and down before the blazing shop-windows, and lounging by daylight or gaslight along the crowded and gay boulevards; and one of the best is to go to the Bois de Boulogne on a fete-day, or when the races are in progress. This famous wood is very disappointing at first to one who has seen the English parks, or who remembers the noble trees and glades and avenues of that at Munich. To be sure, there is a lovely little lake and a pretty artificial cascade, and the roads and walks are good; but the trees are all saplings, and nearly all the "wood" is a thicket of small stuff. Yet there is green grass that one can roll on, and there is a grove of small pines that one can sit under. It is a pleasant place to drive toward evening; but its great attraction is the crowd there. All the principal avenues are lined with chairs, and there people sit to watch the streams of carriages.

I went out to the Bois the other day, when there were races going on; not that I went to the races, for I know nothing about them, per se, and care less. All running races are pretty much alike. You see a lean horse, neck and tail, flash by you, with a jockey in colors on his back; and that is the whole of it. Unless you have some money on it, in the pool or otherwise, it is impossible to raise any excitement. The day I went out, the Champs Elysees, on both sides, its whole length, was crowded with people, rows and ranks of them sitting in chairs and on benches. The Avenue de l'Imperatrice, from the Arc de l'Etoile to the entrance of the Bois, was full of promenaders; and the main avenues of the Bois, from the chief entrance to the race-course, were lined with people, who stood or sat, simply to see the passing show. There could not have been less than ten miles of spectators, in double or triple rows, who had taken places that afternoon to watch the turnouts of fashion and rank. These great avenues were at all times, from three till seven, filled with vehicles; and at certain points, and late in the day, there was, or would have been anywhere else except in Paris, a jam. I saw a great many splendid horses, but not so many fine liveries as one will see on a swell-day in London. There was one that I liked. A handsome carriage, with one seat, was drawn by four large and elegant black horses, the two near horses ridden by postilions in blue and silver,--blue roundabouts, white breeches and topboots, a round-topped silver cap, and the hair, or wig, powdered, and showing just a little behind. A footman mounted behind, seated, wore the same colors; and the whole establishment was exceedingly tonnish.

The race-track (Longchamps, as it is called), broad and beautiful springy turf, is not different from some others, except that the inclosed oblong space is not flat, but undulating just enough for beauty, and so framed in by graceful woods, and looked on by chateaux and upland forests, that I thought I had never seen a sweeter bit of greensward. St. Cloud overlooks it, and villas also regard it from other heights. The day I saw it, the horse-chestnuts were in bloom; and there was, on the edges, a cloud of pink and white blossoms, that gave a soft and charming appearance to the entire landscape. The crowd in the grounds, in front of the stands for judges, royalty, and people who are privileged or will pay for places, was, I suppose, much as usual,--an excited throng of young and jockey-looking men, with a few women-gamblers in their midst, making up the pool; a pack of carriages along the circuit of the track, with all sorts of people, except the very good; and conspicuous the elegantly habited daughters of sin and satin, with servants in livery, as if they had been born to it; gentlemen and ladies strolling about, or reclining on the sward, and a refreshment-stand in lively operation.

When the bell rang, we all cleared out from the track, and I happened to get a position by the railing. I was looking over to the Pavilion, where I supposed the Emperor to be, when the man next to me cried, "Voila!" and, looking up, two horses brushed right by my face, of which I saw about two tails and one neck, and they were gone. Pretty soon they came round again, and one was ahead, as is apt to be the case; and somebody cried, "Bully for Therise!" or French to that effect, and it was all over. Then we rushed across to the Emperor's Pavilion, except that I walked with all the dignity consistent with rapidity, and there, in the midst of his suite, sat the Man of December, a stout, broad, and heavy-faced man as you know, but a man who impresses one with a sense of force and purpose,--sat, as I say, and looked at us through his narrow, half-shut eyes, till he was satisfied that I had got his features through my glass, when he deliberately arose and went in.

All Paris was out that day,--it is always out, by the way, when the sun shines, and in whatever part of the city you happen to be; and it seemed to me there was a special throng clear down to the gate of the Tuileries, to see the Emperor and the rest of us come home. He went round by the Rue Rivoli, but I walked through the gardens. The soldiers from Africa sat by the gilded portals, as usual,--aliens, and yet always with the port of conquerors here in Paris. Their nonchalant indifference and soldierly bearing always remind me of the sort of force the Emperor has at hand to secure his throne. I think the blouses must look askance at these satraps of the desert. The single jet fountain in the basin was springing its highest,--a quivering pillar of water to match the stone shaft of Egypt which stands close by. The sun illuminated it, and threw a rainbow from it a hundred feet long, upon the white and green dome of chestnut-trees near. When I was farther down the avenue, I had the dancing column of water, the obelisk, and the Arch of Triumph all in line, and the rosy sunset beyond.

AN IMPERIAL REVIEW

The Prince and Princess of Wales came up to Paris in the beginning of May, from Italy, Egypt, and alongshore, stayed at a hotel on the Place Vendome, where they can get beef that is not horse, and is rare, and beer brewed in the royal dominions, and have been entertained with cordiality by the Emperor. Among the spectacles which he has shown them is one calculated to give them an idea of his peaceful intentions,-a grand review of cavalry and artillery at the Bois de Boulogne. It always seems to me a curious comment upon the state of our modern civilization, when one prince visits another here in Europe, the first thing that the visited does, by way of hospitality is to get out his troops, and show his rival how easily he could "lick" him, if it came to that.

It is a little puerile. At any rate, it is an advance upon the old fashion of getting up a joust at arms, and inviting the guest to come out and have his head cracked in a friendly way.

The review, which had been a good deal talked about, came off in the afternoon; and all the world went to it. The avenues of the Bois were crowded with carriages, and the walks with footpads. Such a constellation of royal personages met on one field must be seen; for, besides the imperial family and Albert Edward and his Danish beauty, there was to be the Archduke of Austria and no end of titled personages besides. At three o'clock the royal company, in the Emperor's carriages, drove upon the training-ground of the Bois, where the troops awaited them. All the party, except the Princess of Wales, then mounted horses, and rode along the lines, and afterwards retired to a wood-covered knoll at one end to witness the evolutions. The training-ground is a noble, slightly undulating piece of greensward, perhaps three quarters of a mile long and half that in breadth, hedged about with graceful trees, and bounded on one side by the Seine. Its borders were rimmed that day with thousands of people on foot and in carriages,--a gay sight, in itself, of color and fashion. A more brilliant spectacle than the field presented cannot well be imagined. Attention was divided between the gentle eminence where the imperial party stood,--a throng of noble persons backed by the gay and glittering Guard of the Emperor, as brave a show as chivalry ever made,--and the field of green, with its long lines in martial array; every variety of splendid uniforms, the colors and combinations that most dazzle and attract, with shining brass and gleaming steel, and magnificent horses of war, regiments of black, gray, and bay.

The evolutions were such as to stir the blood of the most sluggish. A regiment, full front, would charge down upon a dead run from the far field, men shouting, sabers flashing, horses thundering along, so that the ground shook, towards the imperial party, and, when near, stop suddenly, wheel to right and left, and gallop

back. Others would succeed them rapidly, coming up the center while their prede-
cessors filed down the sides; so that the whole field was a moving mass of splendid
color and glancing steel. Now and then a rider was unhorsed in the furious rush,
and went scrambling out of harm, while the steed galloped off with free rein. This
display was followed by that of the flying artillery, battalion after battalion, which
came clattering and roaring along, in double lines stretching half across the field,
stopped and rapidly discharged its pieces, waking up all the region with echoes, filling the plain with the smoke of gunpowder, and starting into rearing activity all the
carriage-horses in the Bois. How long this continued I do not know, nor how many
men participated in the review, but they seemed to pour up from the far end in
unending columns. I think the regiments must have charged over and over again. It
gave some people the impression that there were a hundred thousand troops on the
ground. I set it at fifteen to twenty thousand. Gallignani next morning said there
were only six thousand! After the charging was over, the reviewing party rode to
the center of the field, and the troops galloped round them; and the Emperor distributed decorations. We could recognize the Emperor and Empress; Prince Albert
in huzzar uniform, with a green plume in his cap; and the Prince Imperial, in cap
and the uniform of a lieutenant, on horseback in front; while the Princess occupied
a carriage behind them.

There was a crush of people at the entrance to see the royals make their exit.
Gendarmes were busy, and mounted guards went smashing through the crowd to
clear a space. Everybody was on the tiptoe of expectation. There is a portion of the
Emperor's guard; there is an officer of the household; there is an emblazoned carriage; and, quick, there! with a rush they come, driving as if there was no crowd,
with imperial haste, postilions and outriders and the imperial carriage. There is a
sensation, a cordial and not loud greeting, but no Yankee-like cheers. That heavy
gentleman in citizen's dress, who looks neither to right nor left, is Napoleon III.;
that handsome woman, grown full in the face of late, but yet with the bloom of
beauty and the sweet grace of command, in hat and dark riding-habit, bowing constantly to right and left, and smiling, is the Empress Eugenie. And they are gone.
As we look for something more, there is a rout in the side avenue; something is
coming, unexpected, from another quarter: dragoons dash through the dense mass,
shouting and gesticulating, and a dozen horses go by, turning the corner like a small

whirlwind, urged on by whip and spur, a handsome boy riding in the midst,--a boy in cap and simple uniform, riding gracefully and easily and jauntily, and out of sight in a minute. It is the boy Prince Imperial and his guard. It was like him to dash in unexpectedly, as he has broken into the line of European princes. He rides gallantly, and Fortune smiles on him to-day; but he rides into a troubled future. There was one more show,--a carriage of the Emperor, with officers, in English colors and side-whiskers, riding in advance and behind: in it the future King of England, the heavy, selfish-faced young man, and beside him his princess, popular wherever she shows her winning face,--a fair, sweet woman, in light and flowing silken stuffs of spring, a vision of lovely youth and rank, also gone in a minute.

These English visitors are enjoying the pleasures of the French capital. On Sunday, as I passed the Hotel Bristol, a crowd, principally English, was waiting in front of it to see the Prince and Princess come out, and enter one of the Emperor's carriages in waiting. I heard an Englishwoman, who was looking on with admiration "sticking out" all over, remark to a friend in a very loud whisper, "I tell you, the Prince lives every day of his life." The princely pair came out at length, and drove away, going to visit Versailles. I don't know what the Queen would think of this way of spending Sunday; but if Albert Edward never does anything worse, he does n't need half the praying for that he gets every Sunday in all the English churches and chapels.

THE LOW COUNTRIES AND RHINELAND
AMIENS AND QUAINT OLD BRUGES

They have not yet found out the secret in France of banishing dust from railway-carriages. Paris, late in June, was hot, but not dusty: the country was both. There is an uninteresting glare and hardness in a French landscape on a sunny day. The soil is thin, the trees are slender, and one sees not much luxury or comfort. Still, one does not usually see much of either on a flying train. We spent a night at Amiens, and had several hours for the old cathedral, the sunset light on its noble front and towers and spire and flying buttresses, and the morning rays bathing its rich stone. As one stands near it in front, it seems to tower away into heaven, a mass of carving and sculpture,--figures of saints and martyrs who have stood in the sun and storm for ages, as they stood in their lifetime, with a patient waiting. It was like a great company, a Christian host, in attitudes of praise and worship. There they were, ranks on ranks, silent in stone, when the last of the long twilight illumined them; and there in the same impressive patience they waited the golden day. It required little fancy to feel that they had lived, and now in long procession came down the ages. The central portal is lofty, wide, and crowded with figures. The side is only less rich than the front. Here the old Gothic builders let their fancy riot in grotesque gargoyles,--figures of animals, and imps of sin, which stretch out their long necks for waterspouts above. From the ground to the top of the unfinished towers is one mass of rich stone-work, the creation of genius that hundreds of years ago knew no other way to write its poems than with the chisel. The interior is very magnificent also, and has some splendid stained glass. At eight o'clock, the priests were chanting vespers to a larger congregation than many churches have on Sunday: their voices were rich and musical, and, joined with the organ notes, floated sweetly and impressively through the dim and vast interior. We sat near the great portal, and, looking down the long, arched nave and choir to the cluster of candles burning on the high altar, before which the priests chanted, one could not but remember how many centuries the same act of worship had been almost uninterrupted within, while the apostles and martyrs stood without, keeping watch of the unchanging heavens.

When I stepped in, early in the morning, the first mass was in progress. The church was nearly empty. Looking within the choir, I saw two stout young priests lustily singing the prayers in deep, rich voices. One of them leaned back in his seat, and sang away, as if he had taken a contract to do it, using, from time to time, an enormous red handkerchief, with which and his nose he produced a trumpet obligato. As I stood there, a poor dwarf bobbled in and knelt on the bare stones, and was the only worshiper, until, at length, a half-dozen priests swept in from the sacristy, and two processions of young school-girls entered from either side. They have the skull of John the Baptist in this cathedral. I did not see it, although I suppose I could have done so for a franc to the beadle: but I saw a very good stone imitation of it; and his image and story fill the church. It is something to have seen the place that contains his skull.

The country becomes more interesting as one gets into Belgium. Windmills are frequent: in and near Lille are some six hundred of them; and they are a great help to a landscape that wants fine trees. At Courtrai, we looked into Notre Dame, a thirteenth century cathedral, which has a Vandyke ("The Raising of the Cross"), and the chapel of the Counts of Flanders, where workmen were uncovering some frescoes that were whitewashed over in the war-times. The town hall has two fine old chimney-pieces carved in wood, with quaint figures,--work that one must go to the Netherlands to see. Toward evening we came into the ancient town of Bruges. The country all day has been mostly flat, but thoroughly cultivated. Windmills appear to do all the labor of the people,--raising the water, grinding the grain, sawing the lumber; and they everywhere lift their long arms up to the sky. Things look more and more what we call "foreign." Harvest is going on, of hay and grain; and men and women work together in the fields. The gentle sex has its rights here. We saw several women acting as switch-tenders. Perhaps the use of the switch comes natural to them. Justice, however, is still in the hands of the men. We saw a Dutch court in session in a little room in the town hall at Courtrai. The justice wore a little red cap, and sat informally behind a cheap table. I noticed that the witnesses were treated with unusual consideration, being allowed to sit down at the table opposite the little justice, who interrogated them in a loud voice. At the stations to-day we see more friars in coarse, woolen dresses, and sandals, and the peasants with wooden sabots.

As the sun goes to the horizon, we have an effect sometimes produced by the best Dutch artists,--a wonderful transparent light, in which the landscape looks like a picture, with its church-spires of stone, its windmills, its slender trees, and red-roofed houses. It is a good light and a good hour in which to enter Bruges, that city of the past. Once the city was greater than Antwerp; and up the Rege came the commerce of the East, merchants from the Levant, traders in jewels and silks. Now the tall houses wait for tenants, and the streets have a deserted air. After nightfall, as we walked in the middle of the roughly paved streets, meeting few people, and hearing only the echoing clatter of the wooden sabots of the few who were abroad, the old spirit of the place came over us. We sat on a bench in the market-place, a treeless square, hemmed in by quaint, gabled houses, late in the evening, to listen to the chimes from the belfry. The tower is less than four hundred feet high, and not so high by some seventy feet as the one on Notre Dame near by; but it is very picturesque, in spite of the fact that it springs out of a rummagy-looking edifice, one half of which is devoted to soldiers' barracks, and the other to markets. The chimes are called the finest in Europe. It is well to hear the finest at once, and so have done with the tedious things. The Belgians are as fond of chimes as the Dutch are of stagnant water. We heard them everywhere in Belgium; and in some towns they are incessant, jangling every seven and a half minutes. The chimes at Bruges ring every quarter hour for a minute, and at the full hour attempt a tune. The revolving machinery grinds out the tune, which is changed at least once a year; and on Sundays a musician, chosen by the town, plays the chimes. In so many bells (there are forty-eight), the least of which weighs twelve pounds, and the largest over eleven thousand, there must be soft notes and sonorous tones; so sweet jangled sounds were showered down: but we liked better than the confused chiming the solemn notes of the great bell striking the hour. There is something very poetical about this chime of bells high in the air, flinging down upon the hum and traffic of the city its oft-repeated benediction of peace; but anybody but a Lowlander would get very weary of it. These chimes, to be sure, are better than those in London, which became a nuisance; but there is in all of them a tinkling attempt at a tune, which always fails, that is very annoying.

Bruges has altogether an odd flavor. Piles of wooden sabots are for sale in front of the shops; and this ugly shoe, which is mysteriously kept on the foot, is worn by all the common sort. We see long, slender carts in the street, with one horse hitched far ahead with rope traces, and no thills or pole.

The women-nearly every one we saw-wear long cloaks of black cloth with a silk hood thrown back. Bruges is famous of old for its beautiful women, who are enticingly described as always walking the streets with covered faces, and peeping out from their mantles. They are not so handsome now they show their faces, I can testify. Indeed, if there is in Bruges another besides the beautiful girl who showed us the old council-chamber in the Palace of justice, she must have had her hood pulled over her face.

Next morning was market-day. The square was lively with carts, donkeys, and country people, and that and all the streets leading to it were filled with the women in black cloaks, who flitted about as numerous as the rooks at Oxford, and very much like them, moving in a winged way, their cloaks outspread as they walked, and distended with the market-basket underneath. Though the streets were full, the town did not seem any less deserted; and the early marketers had only come to life for a day, revisiting the places that once they thronged. In the shade of the tall houses in the narrow streets sat red-cheeked girls and women making lace, the bobbins jumping under their nimble fingers. At the church doors hideous beggars crouched and whined,--specimens of the fifteen thousand paupers of Bruges. In the fishmarket we saw odd old women, with Rembrandt colors in faces and costume; and while we strayed about in the strange city, all the time from the lofty tower the chimes fell down. What history crowds upon us! Here in the old cathedral, with its monstrous tower of brick, a portion of it as old as the tenth century, Philip the Good established, in 1429, the Order of the Golden Fleece, the last chapter of which was held by Philip the Bad in 1559, in the rich old Cathedral of St. Bavon, at Ghent. Here, on the square, is the site of the house where the Emperor Maximilian was imprisoned by his rebellious Flemings; and next it, with a carved lion, that in which Charles II. of England lived after the martyrdom of that patient and virtuous ruler, whom the English Prayerbook calls that "blessed martyr, Charles the First." In Notre Dame are the tombs of Charles the Bold and Mary his daughter.

We begin here to enter the portals of Dutch painting. Here died Jan van Eyck, the father of oil painting; and here, in the hospital of St. John, are the most celebrated pictures of Hans Memling. The most exquisite in color and finish is the series painted on the casket made to contain the arm of St. Ursula, and representing the story of her martyrdom. You know she went on a pilgrimage to Rome, with her lover, Conan, and eleven thousand virgins; and, on their return to Cologne, they were all massacred by the Huns. One would scarcely believe the story, if he did not see all their bones at Cologne.

GHENT AND ANTWERP

What can one do in this Belgium but write down names, and let memory recall the past? We came to Ghent, still a hand some city, though one thinks of the days when it was the capital of Flanders, and its merchants were princes. On the shabby old belfry-tower is the gilt dragon which Philip van Artevelde captured, and brought in triumph from Bruges. It was originally fetched from a Greek church in Constantinople by some Bruges Crusader; and it is a link to recall to us how, at that time, the merchants of Venice and the far East traded up the Scheldt, and brought to its wharves the rich stuffs of India and Persia. The old bell Roland, that was used to call the burghers together on the approach of an enemy, hung in this tower. What fierce broils and bloody fights did these streets witness centuries ago! There in the Marche au Vendredi, a large square of old-fashioned houses, with a statue of Jacques van Artevelde, fifteen hundred corpses were strewn in a quarrel between the hostile guilds of fullers and brewers; and here, later, Alva set blazing the fires of the Inquisition. Near the square is the old cannon, Mad Margery, used in 1382 at the siege of Oudenarde,--a hammered-iron hooped affair, eighteen feet long. But why mention this, or the magnificent town hall, or St. Bavon, rich in pictures and statuary; or try to put you back three hundred years to the wild days when the iconoclasts sacked this and every other church in the Low Countries?

Up to Antwerp toward evening. All the country flat as the flattest part of Jersey, rich in grass and grain, cut up by canals, picturesque with windmills and red-tiled roofs, framed with trees in rows. It has been all day hot and dusty. The country everywhere seems to need rain; and dark clouds are gathering in the south for a storm, as we drive up the broad Place de Meir to our hotel, and take rooms that look out to the lace-like spire of the cathedral, which is sharply defined against the red western sky.

Antwerp takes hold of you, both by its present and its past, very strongly. It is still the home of wealth. It has stately buildings, splendid galleries of pictures, and a spire of stone which charms more than a picture, and fascinates the eye as music does the ear. It still keeps its strong fortifications drawn around it, to which the broad and deep Scheldt is like a string to a bow, mindful of the unstable state of Europe. While Berlin is only a vast camp of soldiers, every less city must daily beat its drums, and call its muster-roll. From the tower here one looks upon the cockpit of Europe. And yet Antwerp ought to have rest: she has had tumult enough in her time. Prosperity seems returning to her; but her old, comparative splendor can never come back. In the sixteenth century there was no richer city in Europe.

We walked one evening past the cathedral spire, which begins in the richest and most solid Gothic work, and grows up into the sky into an exquisite lightness and grace, down a broad street to the Scheldt. What traffic have not these high old houses looked on, when two thousand and five hundred vessels lay in the river at one time, and the commerce of Europe found here its best mart. Along the stream now is a not very clean promenade for the populace; and it is lined with beer-houses, shabby theaters, and places of the most childish amusements. There is an odd liking for the simple among these people. In front of the booths, drums were beaten and instruments played in bewildering discord. Actors in paint and tights stood without to attract the crowd within. On one low balcony, a copper-colored man, with a huge feather cap and the traditional dress of the American savage, was beating two drums; a burnt-cork black man stood beside him; while on the steps was a woman, in hat and shawl, making an earnest speech to the crowd. In another place, where a crazy band made furious music, was an enormous "go-round" of wooden ponies, like those in the Paris gardens, only here, instead of children, grown men and women rode the hobby-horses, and seemed delighted with the sport. In the general Babel, everybody was good-natured and jolly. Little things suffice to amuse the lower classes, who do not have to bother their heads with elections and mass meetings.

In front of the cathedral is the well, and the fine canopy of iron-work, by Quentin Matsys, the blacksmith of Antwerp, some of whose pictures we saw in the Museum, where one sees, also some of the finest pictures of the Dutch school,--the "Crucifixion" of Rubens, the "Christ on the Cross" of Vandyke; paintings also by Teniers, Otto Vennius, Albert Cuyp, and others, and Rembrandt's portrait of his wife,--a picture whose sweet strength and wealth of color draws one to it with almost a passion of admiration. We had already seen "The Descent from the Cross" and "The Raising of the Cross" by Rubens, in the cathedral. With all his power and rioting luxuriance of color, I cannot come to love him as I do Rembrandt. Doubtless he painted what he saw; and we still find the types of his female figures in the broad-hipped, ruddy-colored women of Antwerp. We walked down to his house, which remains much as it was two hundred and twenty-five years ago. From the interior court, an entrance in the Italian style leads into a pleasant little garden full of old trees and flowers, with a summer-house embellished with plaster casts, and having the very stone table upon which Rubens painted. It is a quiet place, and fit for an artist; but Rubens had other houses in the city, and lived the life of a man who took a strong hold of the world.

AMSTERDAM

The rail from Antwerp north was through a land flat and sterile. After a little, it becomes a little richer; but a forlorner land to live in I never saw. One wonders at the perseverance of the Flemings and Dutchmen to keep all this vast tract above water when there is so much good solid earth elsewhere unoccupied. At Moerdjik we changed from the cars to a little steamer on the Maas, which flows between high banks. The water is higher than the adjoining land, and from the deck we look down upon houses and farms. At Dort, the Rhine comes in with little promise of the noble stream it is in the highlands. Everywhere canals and ditches dividing the small fields instead of fences; trees planted in straight lines, and occasionally trained on a trellis in front of the houses, with the trunk painted white or green; so that every likeness of nature shall be taken away. From Rotterdam, by cars, it is still the same. The Dutchman spends half his life, apparently, in fighting the water. He has to watch the huge dikes which keep the ocean from overwhelming him, and the river-banks, which may break, and let the floods of the Rhine swallow him up. The danger from within is not less than from without. Yet so fond is he of his one enemy, that, when he can afford it, he builds him a fantastic summer-house over a stagnant pool or a slimy canal, in one corner of his garden, and there sits to enjoy the aquatic beauties of nature; that is, nature as he has made it. The river-banks are woven with osiers to keep them from washing; and at intervals on the banks are piles of the long withes to be used in emergencies when the swollen streams threaten to break through.

And so we come to Amsterdam, the oddest city of all,--a city wholly built on piles, with as many canals as streets, and an architecture so quaint as to even impress one who has come from Belgium. The whole town has a wharf-y look; and it is difficult to say why the tall brick houses, their gables running by steps to a peak, and each one leaning forward or backward or sideways, and none perpendicular, and no two on a line, are so interesting. But certainly it is a most entertaining place to the stranger, whether he explores the crowded Jews' quarter, with its swarms of dirty people, its narrow streets, and high houses hung with clothes, as if every day were washing-day; or strolls through the equally narrow streets of rich shops; or lounges upon the bridges, and looks at the queer boats with clumsy rounded bows, great helms' painted in gay colors, with flowers in the cabin windows,--boats where families live; or walks down the Plantage, with the zoological gardens on the one hand and rows of beer-gardens on the other; or round the great docks; or saunters at sunset by the banks of the Y, and looks upon flat North Holland and the Zuyder Zee.

The palace on the Dam (square) is a square, stately edifice, and the only building that the stranger will care to see. Its interior is richer and more fit to live in than any palace we have seen. There is nothing usually so dreary as your fine Palace. There are some good frescoes, rooms richly decorated in marble, and a magnificent hall, or ball-room, one hundred feet in height, without pillars. Back of it is, of course, a canal, which does not smell fragrantly in the summer; and I do not wonder that William III. and his queen prefer to stop away. From the top is a splendid view of Amsterdam and all the flat region. I speak of it with entire impartiality, for I did not go up to see it. But better than palaces are the picture-galleries, three of which are open to the sightseer. Here the ancient and modern Dutch painters are seen at their best, and I know of no richer feast of this sort. Here Rembrandt is to be seen in his glory; here Van der Helst, Jan Steen, Gerard Douw, Teniers the younger, Hondekoeter, Weenix, Ostade, Cuyp, and other names as familiar. These men also painted what they saw, the people, the landscapes, with which they were familiar. It was a strange pleasure to meet again and again in the streets of the town the faces, or types of them, that we had just seen on canvas so old.

In the Low Countries, the porters have the grand title of commissionaires. They carry trunks and bundles, black boots, and act as valets de place. As guides, they are quite as intolerable in Amsterdam as their brethren in other cities. Many of them are Jews; and they have a keen eye for a stranger. The moment he sallies from his hotel, there is a guide. Let him hesitate for an instant in his walk, either to look at something or to consult his map, or let him ask the way, and he will have a half dozen of the persistent guild upon him; and they cannot easily be shaken off. The afternoon we arrived, we had barely got into our rooms at Brack's Oude Doelan, when a gray-headed commissionaire knocked at our door, and offered his services to show us the city. We deferred the pleasure of his valuable society. Shortly, when we came down to the street, a smartly dressed Israelite took off his hat to us, and offered to show us the city. We declined with impressive politeness, and walked on. The Jew accompanied us, and attempted conversation, in which we did not join. He would show us everything for a guilder an hour,--for half a guilder. Having plainly told the Jew that we did not desire his attendance, he crossed to the other side of the street, and kept us in sight, biding his opportunity. At the end of the street, we hesitated a moment whether to cross the bridge or turn up by the broad canal. The Jew was at our side in a moment, having divined that we were on the way to the Dam and the palace. He obligingly pointed the way, and began to walk with us, entering into conversation. We told him pointedly, that we did not desire his services, and requested him to leave us. He still walked in our direction, with the air of one much injured, but forgiving, and was more than once beside us with a piece of information. When we finally turned upon him with great fierceness, and told him to begone, he regarded us with a mournful and pitying expression; and as the last act of one who returned good for evil, before he turned away, pointed out to us the next turn we were to make. I saw him several times afterward; and I once had occasion to say to him, that I had already told him I would not employ him; and he always lifted his hat, and looked at me with a forgiving smile. I felt that I had deeply wronged him. As we stood by the statue, looking up at the eastern pediment of the palace, another of the tribe (they all speak a little English) asked me if I wished to see the palace. I told him I was looking at it, and could see it quite distinctly. Half a dozen more crowded round, and proffered their aid. Would I like to go into the palace? They knew, and I knew, that they could do nothing more than go to the open door, through which they would not be admitted, and that I could walk across the open square to that, and enter alone. I asked the first speaker if he wished to go into the palace. Oh, yes! he would like to go. I told him he had better go at once,--they had all better go in together and see the palace,--it was an excellent opportunity. They seemed to see the point, and slunk away to the other side to wait for another stranger.

I find that this plan works very well with guides: when I see one approaching, I at once offer to guide him. It is an idea from which he does not rally in time to annoy us. The other day I offered to show a persistent fellow through an old ruin for fifty kreuzers: as his price for showing me was forty-eight, we did not come to terms. One of the most remarkable guides, by the way, we encountered at Stratford-on-Avon. As we walked down from the Red Horse Inn to the church, a full-grown boy came bearing down upon us in the most wonderful fashion. Early rickets, I think, had been succeeded by the St. Vitus' dance. He came down upon us sideways, his legs all in a tangle, and his right arm, bent and twisted, going round and round, as if in vain efforts to get into his pocket, his fingers spread out in impotent desire to clutch something. There was great danger that he would run into us, as he was like a steamer with only one side-wheel and no rudder. He came up puffing and blowing, and offered to show us Shakespeare's tomb. Shade of the past, to be accompanied to thy resting-place by such an object! But he fastened himself on us, and jerked and hitched along in his side-wheel fashion. We declined his help. He paddled on, twisting himself into knots, and grinning in the most friendly manner. We told him to begone. "I am," said he, wrenching himself into a new contortion, "I am what showed Artemus Ward round Stratford." This information he repeated again and again, as if we could not resist him after we had comprehended that. We shook him off; but when we returned at sundown across the fields, from a visit to Anne Hathaway's cottage, we met the sidewheeler cheerfully towing along a large party, upon whom he had fastened.

The people of Amsterdam are only less queer than their houses. The men dress in a solid, old-fashioned way. Every one wears the straight, high-crowned silk hat that went out with us years ago, and the cut of clothing of even the most buckish young fellows is behind the times. I stepped into the Exchange, an immense interior, that will hold five thousand people, where the stock-gamblers meet twice a day. It was very different from the terrible excitement and noise of the Paris Bourse. There were three or four thousand brokers there, yet there was very little noise and no confusion. No stocks were called, and there was no central ring for bidding, as at the Bourse and the New York Gold Room; but they quietly bought and sold. Some of the leading firms had desks or tables at the side, and there awaited orders. Everything was phlegmatically and decorously done.

In the streets one still sees peasant women in native costume. There was a group to-day that I saw by the river, evidently just crossed over from North Holland. They wore short dresses, with the upper skirt looped up, and had broad hips and big waists. On the head was a cap with a fall of lace behind; across the back of the head a broad band of silver (or tin) three inches broad, which terminated in front and just above the ears in bright pieces of metal about two inches square, like a horse's blinders, Only flaring more from the head; across the forehead and just above the eyes a gilt band, embossed; on the temples two plaits of hair in circular coils; and on top of all a straw hat, like an old-fashioned bonnet stuck on hindside before. Spiral coils of brass wire, coming to a point in front, are also worn on each side of the head by many. Whether they are for ornament or defense, I could not determine.

Water is brought into the city now from Haarlem, and introduced into the best houses; but it is still sold in the streets by old men and women, who sit at the faucets. I saw one dried-up old grandmother, who sat in her little caboose, fighting away the crowd of dirty children who tried to steal a drink when her back was turned, keeping count of the pails of water carried away with a piece of chalk on the iron pipe, and trying to darn her stocking at the same time. Odd things strike you at every turn. There is a sledge drawn by one poor horse, and on the front of it is a cask of water pierced with holes, so that the water squirts out and wets the stones, making it easier sliding for the runners. It is an ingenious people!

After all, we drove out five miles to Broek, the clean village; across the Y, up the canal, over flatness flattened. Broek is a humbug, as almost all show places are. A wooden little village on a stagnant canal, into which carriages do not drive, and where the front doors of the houses are never open; a dead, uninteresting place, neat but not specially pretty, where you are shown into one house got up for the purpose, which looks inside like a crockery shop, and has a stiff little garden with box trained in shapes of animals and furniture. A roomy-breeched young Dutchman, whose trousers went up to his neck, and his hat to a peak, walked before us in slow and cow-like fashion, and showed us the place; especially some horrid pleasure-grounds, with an image of an old man reading in a summer-house, and an old couple in a cottage who sat at a table and worked, or ate, I forget which, by clockwork; while a dog barked by the same means. In a pond was a wooden swan sitting on a stick, the water having receded, and left it high and dry. Yet the trip is worth while for the view of the country and the people on the way: men and women towing boats on the canals; the red-tiled houses painted green, and in the distance the villages, with their spires and pleasing mixture of brown, green, and red tints, are very picturesque. The best thing that I saw, however, was a traditional Dutchman walking on the high bank of a canal, with soft hat, short pipe, and breeches that came to the armpits above, and a little below the knees, and were broad enough about the seat and thighs to carry his no doubt numerous family. He made a fine figure against the sky.

COLOGNE AND ST. URSULA

It is a relief to get out of Holland and into a country nearer to hills. The people also seem more obliging. In Cologne, a brown-cheeked girl pointed us out the way without waiting for a kreuzer. Perhaps the women have more to busy themselves about in the cities, and are not so curious about passers-by. We rarely see a reflector to exhibit us to the occupants of the second-story windows. In all the cities of Belgium and Holland the ladies have small mirrors, with reflectors, fastened to their windows; so that they can see everybody who passes, without putting their heads out. I trust we are not inverted or thrown out of shape when we are thus caught up and cast into my lady's chamber. Cologne has a cheerful look, for the Rhine here is wide and promising; and as for the "smells," they are certainly not so many nor so vile as those at Mainz.

Our windows at the hotel looked out on the finest front of the cathedral. If the Devil really built it, he is to be credited with one good thing, and it is now likely to be finished, in spite of him. Large as it is, it is on the exterior not so impressive as that at Amiens; but within it has a magnificence born of a vast design and the most harmonious proportions, and the grand effect is not broken by any subdivision but that of the choir. Behind the altar and in front of the chapel, where lie the remains of the Wise Men of the East who came to worship the Child, or, as they are called, the Three Kings of Cologne, we walked over a stone in the pavement under which is the heart of Mary de Medicis: the remainder of her body is in St. Denis near Paris. The beadle in red clothes, who stalks about the cathedral like a converted flamingo, offered to open for us the chapel; but we declined a sight of the very bones of the

Wise Men. It was difficult enough to believe they were there, without seeing them. One ought not to subject his faith to too great a strain at first in Europe. The bones of the Three Kings, by the way, made the fortune of the cathedral. They were the greatest religious card of the Middle Ages, and their fortunate possession brought a flood of wealth to this old Domkirche. The old feudal lords would swear by the Almighty Father, or the Son, or Holy Ghost, or by everything sacred on earth, and break their oaths as they would break a wisp of straw: but if you could get one of them to swear by the Three Kings of Cologne, he was fast; for that oath he dare not disregard.

The prosperity of the cathedral on these valuable bones set all the other churches in the neighborhood on the same track; and one can study right here in this city the growth of relic worship. But the most successful achievement was the collection of the bones of St. Ursula and the eleven thousand virgins, and their preservation in the church on the very spot where they suffered martyrdom. There is probably not so large a collection of the bones of virgins elsewhere in the world; and I am sorry to read that Professor Owen has thought proper to see and say that many of them are the bones of lower orders of animals. They are built into the walls of the church, arranged about the choir, interred in stone coffins, laid under the pavements; and their skulls grin at you everywhere. In the chapel the bones are tastefully built into the wall and overhead, like rustic wood-work; and the skulls stand in rows, some with silver masks, like the jars on the shelves of an apothecary's shop. It is a cheerful place. On the little altar is the very skull of the saint herself, and that of Conan, her lover, who made the holy pilgrimage to Rome with her and her virgins, and also was slain by the Huns at Cologne. There is a picture of the eleven thousand disembarking from one boat on the Rhine, which is as wonderful as the trooping of hundreds of spirits out of a conjurer's bottle. The right arm of St. Ursula is preserved here: the left is at Bruges. I am gradually getting the hang of this excellent but somewhat scattered woman, and bringing her together in my mind. Her body, I believe, lies behind the altar in this same church. She must have been a lovely character, if Hans Memling's portrait of her is a faithful one. I was glad to see here one of the jars from the marriage-supper in Cana. We can identify it by a piece which is broken out; and the piece is in Notre Dame in Paris. It has been in this church five hundred years. The sacristan, a very intelligent person, with a shaven crown and his hair cut straight across his forehead, who showed us the church, gave us much useful information about bones, teeth, and the remains of the garments that the virgins wore; and I could not tell from his face how much he expected us to believe. I asked the little fussy old guide of an English party who had joined us, how much he believed of the story. He was a Protestant, and replied, still anxious to keep up the credit of his city, "Tousands is too many; some hundreds maybe; tousands is too many."

A GLIMPSE OF THE RHINE

You have seen the Rhine in pictures; you have read its legends. You know, in imagination at least, how it winds among craggy hills of splendid form, turning so abruptly as to leave you often shut in with no visible outlet from the wall of rock and forest; how the castles, some in ruins so as to be as unsightly as any old pile of rubbish, others with feudal towers and battlements, still perfect, hang on the crags, or stand sharp against the sky, or nestle by the stream or on some lonely island. You know that the Rhine has been to Germans what the Nile was to the Egyptians,--a delight, and the theme of song and story. Here the Roman eagles were planted; here were the camps of Drusus; here Caesar bridged and crossed the Rhine; here, at every turn, a feudal baron, from his high castle, levied toll on the passers; and here the French found a momentary halt to their invasion of Germany at different times. You can imagine how, in a misty morning, as you leave Bonn, the Seven Mountains rise up in their veiled might, and how the Drachenfels stands in new and changing beauty as you pass it and sail away. You have been told that the Hudson is like the Rhine. Believe me, there is no resemblance; nor would there be if the Hudson were lined with castles, and Julius Caesar had crossed it every half mile. The Rhine satisfies you, and you do not recall any other river. It only disappoints you as to its "vine-clad hills." You miss trees and a covering vegetation, and are not enamoured of the patches of green vines on wall-supported terraces, looking from the river like hills of beans or potatoes. And, if you try the Rhine wine on the steamers, you will wholly lose your faith in the vintage. We decided that the wine on our boat was manufactured in the boiler.

There is a mercenary atmosphere about hotels and steamers on the Rhine, a watering-place, show sort of feeling, that detracts very much from one's enjoyment. The old habit of the robber barons of levying toll on all who sail up and down has not been lost. It is not that one actually pays so much for sightseeing, but the charm of anything vanishes when it is made merchandise. One is almost as reluctant to buy his "views" as he is to sell his opinions. But one ought to be weeks on the Rhine before attempting to say anything about it.

One morning, at Bingen,--I assure you it was not six o'clock,--we took a big little rowboat, and dropped down the stream, past the Mouse Tower, where the cruel Bishop Hatto was eaten up by rats, under the shattered Castle of Ehrenfels, round the bend to the little village of Assmannshausen, on the hills back of which is grown the famous red wine of that name. On the bank walked in line a dozen peasants, men and women, in picturesque dress, towing, by a line passed from shoulder to shoulder, a boat filled with marketing for Rudesheim. We were bound up the Niederwald, the mountain opposite Bingen, whose noble crown of forest attracted us. At the landing, donkeys awaited us; and we began the ascent, a stout, good-natured German girl acting as guide and driver. Behind us, on the opposite shore, set round about with a wealth of foliage, was the Castle of Rheinstein, a fortress more pleasing in its proportions and situation than any other. Our way was through the little town which is jammed into the gorge; and as we clattered up the pavement, past the church, its heavy bell began to ring loudly for matins, the sound reverberating in the narrow way, and following us with its benediction when we were far up the hill, breathing the fresh, inspiring morning air. The top of the Niederwald is a splendid forest of trees, which no impious Frenchman has been allowed to trim, and cut into allees of arches, taking one in thought across the water to the free Adirondacks. We walked for a long time under the welcome shade, approaching the brow of the hill now and then, where some tower or hermitage is erected, for a view of the Rhine and the Nahe, the villages below, and the hills around; and then crossed the mountain, down through cherry orchards, and vine yards, walled up, with images of Christ on the cross on the angles of the walls, down through a hot road where wild flowers grew in great variety, to the quaint village of Rudesheim, with its queer streets and ancient ruins. Is it possible that we can have too many ruins? "Oh dear!" exclaimed the jung-frau as we sailed along the last day, "if there is n't another castle!"

HEIDELBERG

If you come to Heidelberg, you will never want to go away. To arrive here is to come into a peaceful state of rest and content. The great hills out of which the Neckar flows, infold the town in a sweet security; and yet there is no sense of imprisonment, for the view is always wide open to the great plains where the Neckar goes to join the Rhine, and where the Rhine runs for many a league through a rich and smiling land. One could settle down here to study, without a desire to go farther, nor any wish to change the dingy, shabby old buildings of the university for anything newer and smarter. What the students can find to fight their little duels about I cannot see; but fight they do, as many a scarred cheek attests. The students give life to the town. They go about in little caps of red, green, and blue, many of them embroidered in gold, and stuck so far on the forehead that they require an elastic, like that worn by ladies, under the back hair, to keep them on; and they are also distinguished by colored ribbons across the breast. The majority of them are well-behaved young gentlemen, who carry switch-canes, and try to keep near the fashions, like students at home. Some like to swagger about in their little skull-caps, and now and then one is attended by a bull-dog.

I write in a room which opens out upon a balcony. Below it is a garden, below that foliage, and farther down the town with its old speckled roofs, spires, and queer little squares. Beyond is the Neckar, with the bridge, and white statues on it, and an old city gate at this end, with pointed towers. Beyond that is a white road with a wall on one side, along which I see peasant women walking with large baskets balanced on their heads. The road runs down the river to Neuenheim. Above it on the steep hillside are vineyards; and a winding path goes up to the Philosopher's Walk, which runs along for a mile or more, giving delightful views of the castle and the glorious woods and hills back of it. Above it is the mountain of Heiligenberg, from the other side of which one looks off toward Darmstadt and the famous road, the Bergstrasse. If I look down the stream, I see the narrow town, and the Neckar flowing out of it into the vast level plain, rich with grain and trees and grass, with many spires and villages; Mannheim to the northward, shining when the sun is low; the Rhine gleaming here and there near the horizon; and the Vosges Mountains, purple in the last distance: on my right, and so near that I could throw a stone into them, the ruined tower and battlements of the northwest corner of the castle, half hidden in foliage, with statues framed in ivy, and the garden terrace, built for Elizabeth Stuart when she came here the bride of the Elector Frederick, where giant trees grow. Under the walls a steep path goes down into the town, along which little houses cling to the hillside. High above the castle rises the noble Konigstuhl, whence the whole of this part of Germany is visible, and, in a clear day, Strasburg Minster, ninety miles away.

I have only to go a few steps up a narrow, steep street, lined with the queerest houses, where is an ever-running pipe of good water, to which all the neighborhood resorts, and I am within the grounds of the castle. I scarcely know where to take you; for I never know where to go myself, and seldom do go where I intend when I set forth. We have been here several days; and I have not yet seen the Great Tun, nor the inside of the show-rooms, nor scarcely anything that is set down as a "sight." I do not know whether to wander on through the extensive grounds, with splendid trees, bits of old ruin, overgrown, cozy nooks, and seats where, through the foliage, distant prospects open into quiet retreats that lead to winding walks up the terraced hill, round to the open terrace overlooking the Neckar, and giving the best general view of the great mass of ruins. If we do, we shall be likely to sit in some delicious place, listening to the band playing in the "Restauration," and to the nightingales, till the moon comes up. Or shall we turn into the garden through the lovely Arch of the Princess Elizabeth, with its stone columns cut to resemble tree-trunks twined with ivy? Or go rather through the great archway, and under the teeth of the portcullis, into the irregular quadrangle, whose buildings mark the changing style and fortune of successive centuries, from 1300 down to the seventeenth century? There is probably no richer quadrangle in Europe: there is certainly no other ruin so vast, so impressive, so ornamented with carving, except the Alhambra. And from here we pass out upon the broad terrace of masonry, with a splendid flanking octagon tower, its base hidden in trees, a rich facade for a background, and below the town the river, and beyond the plain and floods of golden sunlight. What shall we do? Sit and dream in the Rent Tower under the lindens that grow in its top? The day passes while one is deciding how to spend it, and the sun over Heiligenberg goes down on his purpose.

ALPINE NOTES
ENTERING SWITZERLAND BERNE
ITS BEAUTIES AND BEARS

If you come to Bale, you should take rooms on the river, or stand on the bridge at evening, and have a sunset of gold and crimson streaming down upon the wide and strong Rhine, where it rushes between the houses built plumb up to it, or you will not care much for the city. And yet it is pleasant on the high ground, where are some stately buildings, and where new gardens are laid out, and where the American consul on the Fourth of July flies our flag over the balcony of a little cottage smothered in vines and gay with flowers. I had the honor of saluting it that day, though I did not know at the time that gold had risen two or three per cent. under its blessed folds at home. Not being a shipwrecked sailor, or a versatile and accomplished but impoverished naturalized citizen, desirous of quick transit to the land of the free, I did not call upon the consul, but left him under the no doubt correct impression that he was doing a good thing by unfolding the flag on the Fourth.

You have not journeyed far from Bale before you are aware that you are in Switzerland. It was showery the day we went down; but the ride filled us with the most exciting expectations. The country recalled New England, or what New England might be, if it were cultivated and adorned, and had good roads and no fences. Here at last, after the dusty German valleys, we entered among real hills, round which and through which, by enormous tunnels, our train slowly went: rocks looking out of foliage; sweet little valleys, green as in early spring; the dark evergreens in contrast; snug cottages nestled in the hillsides, showing little else than enormous brown roofs that come nearly to the ground, giving the cottages the appearance of huge toadstools; fine harvests of grain; thrifty apple-trees, and cherry-trees purple with luscious fruit. And this shifting panorama continues until, towards evening, behold, on a hill, Berne, shining through showers, the old feudal round tower and buildings overhanging the Aar, and the tower of the cathedral over all. From the balcony of our rooms at the Bellevue, the long range of the Bernese Oberland shows its white summits for a moment in the slant sunshine, and then the clouds shut down, not to lift again for two days. Yet it looks warmer on the snow-peaks than in Berne, for summer sets in in Switzerland with a New England chill and rigor.

The traveler finds no city with more flavor of the picturesque and quaint than Berne; and I think it must have preserved the Swiss characteristics better than any other of the large towns in Helvetia. It stands upon a peninsula, round which the Aar, a hundred feet below, rapidly flows; and one has on nearly every side very pretty views of the green basin of hills which rise beyond the river. It is a most comfortable town on a rainy day; for all the principal streets have their houses built on arcades, and one walks under the low arches, with the shops on one side and the huge stone pillars on the other. These pillars so stand out toward the street as to give the house-fronts a curved look. Above are balconies, in which, upon red cushions, sit the daughters of Berne, reading and sewing, and watching their neighbors; and in nearly every window are quantities of flowers of the most brilliant colors. The gray stone of the houses, which are piled up from the streets, harmonizes well with the colors in the windows and balconies, and the scene is quite Oriental as one looks down, especially if it be upon a market morning, when the streets are as thronged as the Strand. Several terraces, with great trees, overlook the river, and command prospects of the Alps. These are public places; for the city government has a queer notion that trees are not hideous, and that a part of the use of living is the enjoyment of the beautiful. I saw an elegant bank building, with carved figures on the front, and at each side of the entrance door a large stand of flowers,--oleanders, geraniums, and fuchsias; while the windows and balconies above bloomed with a like warmth of floral color. Would you put an American bank president in the Retreat who should so decorate his banking-house? We all admire the tasteful display of flowers in foreign towns: we go home, and carry nothing with us but a recollection. But Berne has also fountains everywhere; some of them grotesque, like the ogre that devours his own children, but all a refreshment and delight. And it has also its clock-tower, with one of those ingenious pieces of mechanism, in which the sober people of this region take pleasure. At the hour, a procession of little bears goes round, a jolly figure strikes the time, a cock flaps his wings and crows, and a solemn Turk opens his mouth to announce the flight of the hours. It is more grotesque, but less elaborate, than the equally childish toy in the cathedral at Strasburg.

We went Sunday morning to the cathedral; and the excellent woman who guards the portal--where in ancient stone the Last Judgment is enacted, and the cheerful and conceited wise virgins stand over against the foolish virgins, one of whom has been in the penitential attitude of having a stone finger in her eye now for over three hundred years--refused at first to admit us to the German Lutheran service, which was just beginning. It seems that doors are locked, and no one is allowed to issue forth until after service. There seems to be an impression that strangers go only to hear the organ, which is a sort of rival of that at Freiburg, and do not care much for the well-prepared and protracted discourse in Swiss-German. We agreed to the terms of admission; but it did not speak well for former travelers that the woman should think it necessary to say, "You must sit still, and not talk." It is a barn-like interior. The women all sit on hard, high-backed benches in the center of the church, and the men on hard, higher-backed benches about the sides, inclosing and facing the women, who are more directly under the droppings of the little pulpit, hung on one of the pillars,--a very solemn and devout congregation, who sang very well, and paid strict attention to the sermon.

I noticed that the names of the owners, and sometimes their coats-of-arms, were carved or painted on the backs of the seats, as if the pews were not put up at yearly auction. One would not call it a dressy congregation, though the homely women looked neat in black waists and white puffed sleeves and broadbrimmed hats.

The only concession I have anywhere seen to women in Switzerland, as the more delicate sex, was in this church: they sat during most of the service, but the men stood all the time, except during the delivery of the sermon. The service began at nine o'clock, as it ought to with us in summer. The costume of the peasant women in and about Berne comes nearer to being picturesque than in most other parts of Switzerland, where it is simply ugly. You know the sort of thing in pictures,--the broad hat, short skirt, black, pointed stomacher, with white puffed sleeves, and from each breast a large silver chain hanging, which passes under the arm and fastens on the shoulder behind,--a very favorite ornament. This costume would not be unbecoming to a pretty face and figure: whether there are any such native to Switzerland, I trust I may not be put upon the witness-stand to declare. Some of the peasant young men went without coats, and with the shirt sleeves fluted; and others wore butternut-colored suits, the coats of which I can recommend to those who like the swallow-tailed variety. I suppose one would take a man into the opera in London, where he cannot go in anything but that sort. The buttons on the backs of these came high up between the shoulders, and the tails did not reach below the waistband. There is a kind of rooster of similar appearance. I saw some of these young men from the country, with their sweethearts, leaning over the stone parapet, and looking into the pit of the bear-garden, where the city bears walk round, or sit on their hind legs for bits of bread thrown to them, or douse themselves in the tanks, or climb the dead trees set up for their gambols. Years ago they ate up a British officer who fell in; and they walk round now ceaselessly, as if looking for another. But one cannot expect good taste in a bear.

If you would see how charming a farming country can be, drive out on the highway towards Thun. For miles it is well shaded with giant trees of enormous trunks, and a clean sidewalk runs by the fine road. On either side, at little distances from the road, are picturesque cottages and rambling old farmhouses peeping from the trees and vines and flowers. Everywhere flowers, before the house, in the windows, at the railway stations. But one cannot stay forever even in delightful Berne, with its fountains and terraces, and girls on red cushions in the windows, and noble trees and flowers, and its stately federal Capitol, and its bears carved everywhere in stone and wood, and its sunrises, when all the Bernese Alps lie like molten silver in the early light, and the clouds drift over them, now hiding, now disclosing, the enchanting heights.

HEARING THE FREIBURG ORGAN--FIRST SIGHT OF LAKE LEMAN

Freiburg, with its aerial suspension-bridges, is also on a peninsula, formed by the Sarine; with its old walls, old watch-towers, its piled-up old houses, and streets that go upstairs, and its delicious cherries, which you can eat while you sit in the square by the famous linden-tree, and wait for the time when the organ will be played in the cathedral. For all the world stops at Freiburg to hear and enjoy the great organ,--all except the self-satisfied English clergyman, who says he does n't care much for it, and would rather go about town and see the old walls; and the young and boorish French couple, whose refined amusement in the railway-carriage consisted in the young man's catching his wife's foot in the window-strap, and hauling it up to the level of the window, and who cross themselves and go out after the first tune; and the two bread-and-butter English young ladies, one of whom asks the other in the midst of the performance, if she has thought yet to count the pipes,--a thoughtful verification of Murray, which is very commendable in a young woman traveling for the improvement of her little mind.

One has heard so much of this organ, that he expects impossibilities, and is at first almost disappointed, although it is not long in discovering its vast compass, and its wonderful imitations, now of a full orchestra, and again of a single instrument. One has not to wait long before he is mastered by its spell. The vox humana stop did not strike me as so perfect as that of the organ in the Rev. Mr. Hale's church in Boston, though the imitation of choir-voices responding to the organ was very effective. But it is not in tricks of imitation that this organ is so wonderful: it is its power of revealing, by all its compass, the inmost part of any musical composition.

The last piece we heard was something like this: the sound of a bell, tolling at regular intervals, like the throbbing of a life begun; about it an accompaniment of hopes, inducements, fears, the flute, the violin, the violoncello, promising, urging, entreating, inspiring; the life beset with trials, lured with pleasures, hesitating, doubting, questioning; its purpose at length grows more certain and fixed, the bell tolling becomes a prolonged undertone, the flow of a definite life; the music goes on, twining round it, now one sweet instrument and now many, in strife or accord, all the influences of earth and heaven and the base underworld meeting and warring over the aspiring soul; the struggle becomes more earnest, the undertone is louder and clearer; the accompaniment indicates striving, contesting passion, an agony of endeavor and resistance, until at length the steep and rocky way is passed, the world and self are conquered, and, in a burst of triumph from a full orchestra, the soul attains the serene summit. But the rest is only for a moment. Even in the highest places are temptations. The sunshine fails, clouds roll up, growling of low, pedal thunder is heard, while sharp lightning-flashes soon break in clashing peals about the peaks. This is the last Alpine storm and trial. After it the sun bursts out again, the wide, sunny valleys are disclosed, and a sweet evening hymn floats through all the peaceful air. We go out from the cool church into the busy streets of the white, gray town awed and comforted.

And such a ride afterwards! It was as if the organ music still continued. All the world knows the exquisite views southward from Freiburg; but such an atmosphere as we had does not overhang them many times in a season. First the Moleross, and a range of mountains bathed in misty blue light,--rugged peaks, scarred sides, white and tawny at once, rising into the clouds which hung large and soft in the blue; soon Mont Blanc, dim and aerial, in the south; the lovely valley of the River Sense; peasants walking with burdens on the white highway; the quiet and soft-tinted mountains beyond; towns perched on hills, with old castles and towers; the land rich with grass, grain, fruit, flowers; at Palezieux a magnificent view of the silver, purple, and blue mountains, with their chalky seams and gashed sides, near at hand; and at length, coming through a long tunnel, as if we had been shot out into the air above a country more surprising than any in dreams, the most wonderful sight burst upon us,--the low-lying, deep-blue Lake Leman, and the gigantic mountains rising from its shores, and a sort of mist, translucent, suffused with sunlight, like the liquid of the golden wine the Steinberger poured into the vast basin. We came upon it out of total darkness, without warning; and we seemed, from our great height, to be about to leap into the splendid gulf of tremulous light and color.

This Lake of Geneva is said to combine the robust mountain grandeur of Luzerne with all the softness of atmosphere of Lake Maggiore. Surely, nothing could exceed the loveliness as we wound down the hillside, through the vineyards, to Lausanne, and farther on, near the foot of the lake, to Montreux, backed by precipitous but tree-clad hills, fronted by the lovely water, and the great mountains which run away south into Savoy, where Velan lifts up its snows. Below us, round the curving bay, lies white Chillon; and at sunset we row down to it over the bewitched water, and wait under its grim walls till the failing light brings back the romance of castle and prisoner. Our garcon had never heard of the prisoner; but he knew about the gendarmes who now occupy the castle.

OUR ENGLISH FRIENDS

Not the least of the traveler's pleasure in Switzerland is derived from the English people who overrun it: they seem to regard it as a kind of private park or preserve belonging to England; and they establish themselves at hotels, or on steamboats and diligences, with a certain air of ownership that is very pleasant. I am not very fresh in my geology; but it is my impression that Switzerland was created especially for the English, about the year of the Magna Charta, or a little later. The Germans who come here, and who don't care very much what they eat, or how they sleep, provided they do not have any fresh air in diningroom or bedroom, and provided, also, that the bread is a little sour, growl a good deal about the English, and declare that they have spoiled Switzerland. The natives, too, who live off the English, seem to thoroughly hate them; so that one is often compelled, in self-defense, to proclaim his nationality, which is like running from Scylla upon Charybdis; for, while the American is more popular, it is believed that there is no bottom to his pocket.

There was a sprig of the Church of England on the steamboat on Lake Leman, who spread himself upon a center bench, and discoursed very instructively to his friends,--a stout, fat-faced young man in a white cravat, whose voice was at once loud and melodious, and whom our manly Oxford student set down as a man who had just rubbed through the university, and got into a scanty living.

"I met an American on the boat yesterday," the oracle was saying to his friends, "who was really quite a pleasant fellow. He--ah really was, you know, quite a sensible man. I asked him if they had anything like this in America; and he was obliged to say that they had n't anything like it in his country; they really had n't. He was really quite a sensible fellow; said he was over here to do the European tour, as he called it."

Small, sympathetic laugh from the attentive, wiry, red-faced woman on the oracle's left, and also a chuckle, at the expense of the American, from the thin Englishman on his right, who wore a large white waistcoat, a blue veil on his hat, and a face as red as a live coal.

"Quite an admission, was n't it, from an American? But I think they have changed since the wah, you know."

At the next landing, the smooth and beaming churchman was left by his friends; and he soon retired to the cabin, where I saw him self-sacrificingly denying himself the views on deck, and consoling himself with a substantial lunch and a bottle of English ale.

There is one thing to be said about the English abroad: the variety is almost infinite. The best acquaintances one makes will be English,--people with no nonsense and strong individuality; and one gets no end of entertainment from the other sort. Very different from the clergyman on the boat was the old lady at table-d'hote in one of the hotels on the lake. One would not like to call her a delightfully wicked old woman, like the Baroness Bernstein; but she had her own witty and satirical way of regarding the world. She had lived twenty-five years at Geneva, where people, years ago, coming over the dusty and hot roads of France, used to faint away when they first caught sight of the Alps. Believe they don't do it now. She never did; was past the susceptible age when she first came; was tired of the people. Honest? Why, yes, honest, but very fond of money. Fine Swiss wood-carving? Yes. You'll get very sick of it. It's very nice, but I 'm tired of it. Years ago, I sent some of it home to the folks in England. They thought everything of it; and it was not very nice, either,--a cheap sort. Moral ideas? I don't care for moral ideas: people make such a fuss about them lately (this in reply to her next neighbor, an eccentric, thin man, with bushy hair, shaggy eyebrows, and a high, falsetto voice, who rallied the witty old lady all dinner-time about her lack of moral ideas, and accurately described the thin wine on the table as "water-bewitched"). Why did n't the baroness go back to England, if she was so tired of Switzerland? Well, she was too infirm now; and, besides, she did n't like to trust herself on the railroads. And there were so many new inventions nowadays, of which she read. What was this nitroglycerine, that exploded so dreadfully? No: she thought she should stay where she was.

There is little risk of mistaking the Englishman, with or without his family, who has set out to do Switzerland. He wears a brandy-flask, a field-glass, and a haversack. Whether he has a silk or soft hat, he is certain to wear a veil tied round it. This precaution is adopted when he makes up his mind to come to Switzerland, I think, because he has read that a veil is necessary to protect the eyes from the snow-glare. There is probably not one traveler in a hundred who gets among the ice and snow-fields where he needs a veil or green glasses: but it is well to have it on the hat; it looks adventurous. The veil and the spiked alpenstock are the signs of peril. Everybody--almost everybody--has an alpenstock. It is usually a round pine stick, with an iron spike in one end. That, also, is a sign of peril. We saw a noble young Briton on the steamer the other day, who was got up in the best Alpine manner. He wore a short sack,--in fact, an entire suit of light gray flannel, which closely fitted his lithe form. His shoes were of undressed leather, with large spikes in the soles; and on his white hat he wore a large quantity of gauze, which fell in folds down his neck. I am sorry to say that he had a red face, a shaven chin, and long side-whiskers. He carried a formidable alpenstock; and at the little landing where we first saw him, and afterward on the boat, he leaned on it in a series of the most graceful and daring attitudes that I ever saw the human form assume. Our Oxford student knew the variety, and guessed rightly that he was an army man. He had his face burned at Malta. Had he been over the Gemmi? Or up this or that mountain? asked another English officer. "No, I have not." And it turned out that he had n't been anywhere, and did n't seem likely to do anything but show himself at the frequented valley places. And yet I never saw one whose gallant bearing I so much admired. We saw him afterward at Interlaken, enduring all the hardships of that fashionable place. There was also there another of the same country, got up for the most dangerous Alpine climbing, conspicuous in red woolen stockings that came above his knees. I could not learn that he ever went up anything higher than the top of a diligence.

THE DILIGENCE TO CHAMOUNY

The greatest diligence we have seen, one of the few of the old-fashioned sort, is the one from Geneva to Chamouny. It leaves early in the morning; and there is always a crowd about it to see the mount and start. The great ark stands before the diligence-office, and, for half an hour before the hour of starting, the porters are busy stowing away the baggage, and getting the passengers on board. On top, in the banquette, are seats for eight, besides the postilion and guard; in the coupe, under the postilion's seat and looking upon the horses, seats for three; in the interior, for three; and on top, behind, for six or eight. The baggage is stowed in the capacious bowels of the vehicle. At seven, the six horses are brought out and hitched on, three abreast. We climb up a ladder to the banquette: there is an irascible French-man, who gets into the wrong seat; and before he gets right there is a terrible war of words between him and the guard and the porters and the hostlers, everybody joining in with great vivacity; in front of us are three quiet Americans, and a slim Frenchman with a tall hat and one eye-glass. The postilion gets up to his place. Crack, crack, crack, goes the whip; and, amid "sensation" from the crowd, we are off at a rattling pace, the whip cracking all the time like Chinese fireworks. The great passion of the drivers is noise; and they keep the whip going all day. No sooner does a fresh one mount the box than he gives a half-dozen preliminary snaps; to which the horses pay no heed, as they know it is only for the driver's amusement. We go at a good gait, changing horses every six miles, till we reach the Baths of St. Gervais, where we dine, from near which we get our first glimpse of Mont Blanc through clouds,--a section of a dazzlingly white glacier, a very exciting thing to the imagina-tion. Thence we go on in small carriages, over a still excellent but more hilly road, and begin to enter the real mountain wonders; until, at length, real glaciers pouring down out of the clouds nearly to the road meet us, and we enter the narrow Valley of Chamouny, through which we drive to the village in a rain.

Everybody goes to Chamouny, and up the Flegere, and to Montanvert, and over the Mer de Glace; and nearly everybody down the Mauvais Pas to the Chapeau, and so back to the village. It is all easy to do; and yet we saw some French people at the Chapeau who seemed to think they had accomplished the most hazardous thing in the world in coming down the rocks of the Mauvais Pas. There is, as might be ex-pected, a great deal of humbug about the difficulty of getting about in the Alps, and the necessity of guides. Most of the dangers vanish on near approach. The Mer de Glace is inferior to many other glaciers, and is not nearly so fine as the Glacier des Bossons: but it has a reputation, and is easy of access; so people are content to walk over the dirty ice. One sees it to better effect from below, or he must ascend it to the Jardin to know that it has deep crevasses, and is as treacherous as it is grand. And yet no one will be disappointed at the view from Montanvert, of the upper glacier, and the needles of rock and snow which rise beyond.

We met at the Chapeau two jolly young fellows from Charleston, S. C. who had been in the war, on the wrong side. They knew no language but American, and were unable to order a cutlet and an omelet for breakfast. They said they believed they were going over the Tete Noire. They supposed they had four mules waiting for them somewhere, and a guide; but they couldn't understand a word he said, and he couldn't understand them. The day before, they had nearly perished of thirst, because they could n't make their guide comprehend that they wanted water. One of them had slung over his shoulder an Alpine horn, which he blew occasionally, and seemed much to enjoy. All this while we sit on a rock at the foot of the Mauvais Pas, looking out upon the green glacier, which here piles itself up finely, and above to the Aiguilles de Charmoz and the innumerable ice-pinnacles that run up to the clouds, while our muleteer is getting his breakfast. This is his third breakfast this morning.

The day after we reached Chamouny, Monseigneur the bishop arrived there on one of his rare pilgrimages into these wild valleys. Nearly all the way down from Geneva, we had seen signs of his coming, in preparations as for the celebration of a great victory. I did not know at first but the Atlantic cable had been laid; or rather that the decorations were on account of the news of it reaching this region. It was a holiday for all classes; and everybody lent a hand to the preparations. First, the little church where the confirmations were to take place was trimmed within and without; and an arch of green spanned the gateway. At Les Pres, the women were sweeping the road, and the men were setting small evergreen-trees on each side. The peasants were in their best clothes; and in front of their wretched hovels were tables set out with flowers. So cheerful and eager were they about the bishop, that they forgot to beg as we passed: the whole valley was in a fever of expectation. At one hamlet on the mulepath over the Tete Noire, where the bishop was that day expected, and the women were sweeping away all dust and litter from the road, I removed my hat, and gravely thanked them for their thoughtful preparation for our coming. But they only stared a little, as if we were not worthy to be even forerunners of Monseigneur.

I do not care to write here how serious a drawback to the pleasures of this region are its inhabitants. You get the impression that half of them are beggars. The other half are watching for a chance to prey upon you in other ways. I heard of a woman in the Zermatt Valley who refused pay for a glass of milk; but I did not have time to verify the report. Besides the beggars, who may or may not be horrid-looking creatures, there are the grinning Cretins, the old women with skins of parchment and the goitre, and even young children with the loathsome appendage, the most wretched and filthy hovels, and the dirtiest, ugliest people in them. The poor women are the beasts of burden. They often lead, mowing in the hayfield; they carry heavy baskets on their backs; they balance on their heads and carry large washtubs full of water. The more appropriate load of one was a cradle with a baby in it, which seemed not at all to fear falling. When one sees how the women are treated, he does not wonder that there are so many deformed, hideous children. I think the pretty girl has yet to be born in Switzerland.

This is not much about the Alps? Ah, well, the Alps are there. Go read your guide-book, and find out what your emotions are. As I said, everybody goes to Chamouny. Is it not enough to sit at your window, and watch the clouds when they lift from the Mont Blanc range, disclosing splendor after splendor, from the Aiguille de Goute to the Aiguille Verte,--white needles which pierce the air for twelve thousand feet, until, jubilate! the round summit of the monarch himself is visible, and the vast expanse of white snow-fields, the whiteness of which is rather of heaven than of earth, dazzles the eyes, even at so great a distance? Everybody who is patient and waits in the cold and inhospitable-looking valley of the Chamouny long enough, sees Mont Blanc; but every one does not see a sunset of the royal order. The clouds breaking up and clearing, after days of bad weather, showed us height after height, and peak after peak, now wreathing the summits, now settling below or hanging in patches on the sides, and again soaring above, until we had the whole range lying, far and brilliant, in the evening light. The clouds took on gorgeous colors, at length, and soon the snow caught the hue, and whole fields were rosy pink, while uplifted peaks glowed red, as with internal fire. Only Mont Blanc, afar off, remained purely white, in a kind of regal inaccessibility. And, afterward, one star came out over it, and a bright light shone from the hut on the Grand Mulets, a rock in the waste of snow, where a Frenchman was passing the night on his way to the summit.

Shall I describe the passage of the Tete Noire? My friend, it is twenty-four miles, a road somewhat hilly, with splendid views of Mont Blanc in the morning, and of the Bernese Oberland range in the afternoon, when you descend into Martigny,--a hot place in the dusty Rhone Valley, which has a comfortable hotel, with a pleasant garden, in which you sit after dinner and let the mosquitoes eat you.

THE MAN WHO SPEAKS ENGLISH

It was eleven o'clock at night when we reached Sion, a dirty little town at the end of the Rhone Valley Railway, and got into the omnibus for the hotel; and it was also dark and rainy. They speak German in this part of Switzerland, or what is called German. There were two very pleasant Americans, who spoke American, going on in the diligence at half-past five in the morning, on their way over the Simplex. One of them was accustomed to speak good, broad English very distinctly to all races; and he seemed to expect that he must be understood if he repeated his observations in a louder tone, as he always did. I think he would force all this country to speak English in two months. We all desired to secure places in the diligence, which was likely to be full, as is usually the case when a railway discharges itself into a postroad.

We were scarcely in the omnibus, when the gentleman said to the conductor:

"I want two places in the coupe of the diligence in the morning. Can I have them?"

"Yah" replied the good-natured German, who did n't understand a word.

"Two places, diligence, coupe, morning. Is it full?"

"Yah," replied the accommodating fellow. "Hotel man spik English."

I suggested the banquette as desirable, if it could be obtained, and the German was equally willing to give it to us. Descending from the omnibus at the hotel, in a drizzling rain, and amidst a crowd of porters and postilions and runners, the "man who spoke English" immediately presented himself; and upon him the American pounced with a torrent of questions. He was a willing, lively little waiter, with his moony face on the top of his head; and he jumped round in the rain like a parching pea, rolling his head about in the funniest manner.

The American steadied the little man by the collar, and began, "I want to secure two seats in the coupe of the diligence in the morning."

"Yaas," jumping round, and looking from one to another. "Diligence, coupe, morning."

"I--want--two seats--in--coupe. If I can't get them, two--in--banquette."

"Yaas banquette, coupe,--yaas, diligence."

"Do you understand? Two seats, diligence, Simplon, morning. Will you get them?"

"Oh, yaas! morning, diligence. Yaas, sirr."

"Hang the fellow! Where is the office?" And the gentleman left the spry little waiter bobbing about in the middle of the street, speaking English, but probably comprehending nothing that was said to him. I inquired the way to the office of the conductor: it was closed, but would soon be open, and I waited; and at length the official, a stout Frenchman, appeared, and I secured places in the interior, the only ones to be had to Visp. I had seen a diligence at the door with three places in the coupe, and one perched behind; no banquette. The office is brightly lighted; people are waiting to secure places; there is the usual crowd of loafers, men and women, and the Frenchman sits at his desk. Enter the American.

"I want two places in coupe, in the morning. Or banquette. Two places, diligence." The official waves him off, and says something.

"What does he say?"

"He tells you to sit down on that bench till he is ready."

Soon the Frenchman has run over his big waybills, and turns to us.

"I want two places in the diligence, coupe," etc, etc, says the American.

This remark being lost on the official, I explain to him as well as I can what is wanted, at first,--two places in the coupe.

"One is taken," is his reply.

"The gentleman will take two," I said, having in mind the diligence in the yard, with three places in the coupe.

"One is taken," he repeats.

"Then the gentleman will take the other two."

"One is taken!" he cries, jumping up and smiting the table,--"one is taken, I tell you!"

"How many are there in the coupe?"

"TWO."

"Oh! then the gentleman will take the one remaining in the coupe and the one on top."

So it is arranged. When I come back to the hotel, the Americans are explaining to the lively waiter "who speaks English" that they are to go in the diligence at half-past five, and that they are to be called at half-past four and have breakfast. He knows all about it,--"Diligence, half-past four breakfast, Oh, yaas!" While I have been at the diligence-office, my companions have secured room and gone to them; and I ask the waiter to show m to my room. First, however, I tell him that we three two ladies and myself, who came together, are going in the diligence at half-past five, and want to be called and have breakfast. Did he comprehend?

"Yaas," rolling his face about on the top of his head violently. "You three gentleman want breakfast. What you have?"

I had told him before what we would I have, an now I gave up all hope of keeping our parties separate in his mind; so I said, "Five persons want breakfast at five o'clock. Five persons, five hours. Call all of them at half-past four." And I repeated it, and made him repeat it in English and French. He then insisted on putting me into the room of one of the American gentlemen and then he knocked at the door of a lady, who cried out in indignation at being disturbed; and, finally, I found my room. At the door I reiterated the instructions for the morning; and he cheerfully bade me good-night. But he almost immediately came back, and poked in his head with,--

"Is you go by de diligence?"

"Yes, you stupid."

In the morning one of our party was called at halfpast three, and saved the rest of us from a like fate; and we were not aroused at all, but woke early enough to get down and find the diligence nearly ready, and no breakfast, but "the man who spoke English" as lively as ever. And we had a breakfast brought out, so filthy in all respects that nobody could eat it. Fortunately, there was not time to seriously try; but we paid for it, and departed. The two American gentlemen sat in front of the house, waiting. The lively waiter had called them at half-past three, for the railway train, instead of the diligence; and they had their wretched breakfast early. They will remember the funny adventure with "the man who speaks English," and, no doubt, unite with us in warmly commending the Hotel Lion d'Or at Sion as the nastiest inn in Switzerland.

A WALK TO THE GORNER GRAT

When one leaves the dusty Rhone Valley, and turns southward from Visp, he plunges into the wildest and most savage part of Switzerland, and penetrates the heart of the Alps. The valley is scarcely more than a narrow gorge, with high precipices on either side, through which the turbid and rapid Visp tears along at a furious rate, boiling and leaping in foam over its rocky bed, and nearly as large as the Rhone at the junction. From Visp to St. Nicolaus, twelve miles, there is only a mule-path, but a very good one, winding along on the slope, sometimes high up, and again descending to cross the stream, at first by vineyards and high stone walls, and then on the edges of precipices, but always romantic and wild. It is noon when we set out from Visp, in true pilgrim fashion, and the sun is at first hot; but as we slowly rise up the easy ascent, we get a breeze, and forget the heat in the varied charms of the walk.

Everything for the use of the upper valley and Zermatt, now a place of considerable resort, must be carried by porters, or on horseback; and we pass or meet men and women, sometimes a dozen of them together, laboring along under the long, heavy baskets, broad at the top and coming nearly to a point below, which are universally used here for carrying everything. The tubs for transporting water are of the same sort. There is no level ground, but every foot is cultivated. High up on the sides of the precipices, where it seems impossible for a goat to climb, are vineyards and houses, and even villages, hung on slopes, nearly up to the clouds, and with no visible way of communication with the rest of the world.

In two hours' time we are at Stalden, a village perched upon a rocky promontory, at the junction of the valleys of the Saas and the Visp, with a church and white tower conspicuous from afar. We climb up to the terrace in front of it, on our way into the town. A seedy-looking priest is pacing up and down, taking the fresh breeze, his broad-brimmed, shabby hat held down upon the wall by a big stone. His clothes are worn threadbare; and he looks as thin and poor as a Methodist minister in a stony town at home, on three hundred a year. He politely returns our salutation, and we walk on. Nearly all the priests in this region look wretchedly poor,--as poor as the people. Through crooked, narrow streets, with houses overhanging and thrusting out corners and gables, houses with stables below, and quaint carvings and odd little windows above, the panes of glass hexagons, so that the windows looked like sections of honey-comb,--we found our way to the inn, a many-storied chalet, with stairs on the outside, stone floors in the upper passages, and no end of queer rooms; built right in the midst of other houses as odd, decorated with German-text carving, from the windows of which the occupants could look in upon us, if they had cared to do so; but they did not. They seem little interested in anything; and no wonder, with their hard fight with Nature. Below is a wine-shop, with a little side booth, in which some German travelers sit drinking their wine, and sputtering away in harsh gutturals. The inn is very neat inside, and we are well served. Stalden is high; but away above it on the opposite side is a village on the steep slope, with a slender white spire that rivals some of the snowy needles. Stalden is high, but the hill on which it stands is rich in grass. The secret of the fertile meadows is the most thorough irrigation. Water is carried along the banks from the river, and distributed by numerous sluiceways below; and above, the little mountain streams are brought where they are needed by artificial channels. Old men and women in the fields were constantly changing the direction of the currents. All the inhabitants appeared to be porters: women were transporting on their backs baskets full of soil; hay was being backed to the stables; burden-bearers were coming and going upon the road: we were told that there are only three horses in the place. There is a pleasant girl who brings us luncheon at the inn; but the inhabitants for the most part are as hideous as those we see all day: some have hardly the shape of human beings, and they all live in the most filthy manner in the dirtiest habitations. A chalet is a sweet thing when you buy a little model of it at home.

After we leave Stalden, the walk becomes more picturesque, the precipices are higher, the gorges deeper. It required some engineering to carry the footpath round the mountain buttresses and over the ravines. Soon the village of Emd appears on the right,--a very considerable collection of brown houses, and a shining white church-spire, above woods and precipices and apparently unscalable heights, on a green spot which seems painted on the precipices; with nothing visible to keep the whole from sliding down, down, into the gorge of the Visp. Switzerland may not have so much population to the square mile as some countries; but she has a population to some of her square miles that would astonish some parts of the earth's surface elsewhere. Farther on we saw a faint, zigzag footpath, that we conjectured led to Emd; but it might lead up to heaven. All day we had been solicited for charity by squalid little children, who kiss their nasty little paws at us, and ask for centimes. The children of Emd, however, did not trouble us. It must be a serious affair if they ever roll out of bed.

Late in the afternoon thunder began to tumble about the hills, and clouds snatched away from our sight the snow-peaks at the end of the valley; and at length the rain fell on those who had just arrived and on the unjust. We took refuge from the hardest of it in a lonely chalet high up on the hillside, where a roughly dressed, frowzy Swiss, who spoke bad German, and said he was a schoolmaster, gave us a bench in the shed of his schoolroom. He had only two pupils in attendance, and I did not get a very favorable impression of this high school. Its master quite over-came us with thanks when we gave him a few centimes on leaving. It still rained, and we arrived in St. Nicolaus quite damp.

There is a decent road from St. Nicolaus to Zermatt, over which go wagons without springs. The scenery is constantly grander as we ascend. The day is not wholly clear; but high on our right are the vast snow-fields of the Weishorn, and out of the very clouds near it seems to pour the Bies Glacier. In front are the splen-did Briethorn, with its white, round summit; the black Riffelhorn; the sharp peak of the little Matterhorn; and at last the giant Matterhorn itself rising before us, the most finished and impressive single mountain in Switzerland. Not so high as Mont Blanc by a thousand feet, it appears immense in its isolated position and its slender aspiration. It is a huge pillar of rock, with sharply cut edges, rising to a defined point, dusted with snow, so that the rock is only here and there revealed. To ascend it seems as impossible as to go up the Column of Luxor; and one can believe that the gentlemen who first attempted it in 1864, and lost their lives, did fall four thousand feet before their bodies rested on the glacier below.

We did not stay at Zermatt, but pushed on for the hotel on the top of the Riffelberg,--a very stiff and tiresome climb of about three hours, an unending pull up a stony footpath. Within an hour of the top, and when the white hotel is in sight above the zigzag on the breast of the precipice, we reach a green and widespread Alp where hundreds of cows are feeding, watched by two forlorn women,--the "milkmaids all forlorn" of poetry. At the rude chalets we stop, and get draughts of rich, sweet cream. As we wind up the slope, the tinkling of multitudinous bells from the herd comes to us, which is also in the domain of poetry. All the way up we have found wild flowers in the greatest profusion; and the higher we ascend, the more exquisite is their color and the more perfect their form. There are pansies; gentians of a deeper blue than flower ever was before; forget-me-nots, a pink variety among them; violets, the Alpine rose and the Alpine violet; delicate pink flowers of moss; harebells; and quantities for which we know no names, more exquisite in shape and color than the choicest products of the greenhouse. Large slopes are covered with them,--a brilliant show to the eye, and most pleasantly beguiling the way of its tediousness. As high as I ascended, I still found some of these delicate flowers, the pink moss growing in profusion amongst the rocks of the GornerGrat, and close to the snowdrifts.

The inn on the Riffelberg is nearly eight thousand feet high, almost two thousand feet above the hut on Mount Washington; yet it is not so cold and desolate as the latter. Grass grows and flowers bloom on its smooth upland, and behind it and in front of it are the snow-peaks. That evening we essayed the Gorner-Grat, a rocky ledge nearly ten thousand feet above the level of the sea; but after a climb of an hour and a half, and a good view of Monte Rosa and the glaciers and peaks of that range, we were prevented from reaching the summit, and driven back by a sharp storm of hail and rain. The next morning I started for the GornerGrat again, at four o'clock. The Matterhorn lifted its huge bulk sharply against the sky, except where fleecy clouds lightly draped it and fantastically blew about it. As I ascended, and turned to look at it, its beautifully cut peak had caught the first ray of the sun, and burned with a rosy glow. Some great clouds drifted high in the air: the summits of the Breithorn, the Lyscamm, and their companions, lay cold and white; but the snow down their sides had a tinge of pink. When I stood upon the summit of the Gorner-Grat, the two prominent silver peaks of Monte Rosa were just touched with the sun, and its great snow-fields were visible to the glacier at its base. The Gorner-Grat is a rounded ridge of rock, entirely encirled by glaciers and snow-peaks. The panorama from it is unexcelled in Switzerland.

Returning down the rocky steep, I descried, solitary in that great waste of rock and snow, the form of a lady whom I supposed I had left sleeping at the inn, overcome with the fatigue of yesterday's tramp. Lured on by the apparently short distance to the backbone of the ridge, she had climbed the rocks a mile or more above the hotel, and come to meet me. She also had seen the great peaks lift themselves out of the gray dawn, and Monte Rosa catch the first rays. We stood awhile together to see how jocund day ran hither and thither along the mountain-tops, until the light was all abroad, and then silently turned downward, as one goes from a mount of devotion.

THE BATHS OF LEUK

In order to make the pass of the Gemmi, it is necessary to go through the Baths of Leuk. The ascent from the Rhone bridge at Susten is full of interest, affording fine views of the valley, which is better to look at than to travel through, and bringing you almost immediately to the old town of Leuk, a queer, old, towered place, perched on a precipice, with the oddest inn, and a notice posted up to the effect, that any one who drives through its steep streets faster than a walk will be fined five francs. I paid nothing extra for a fast walk. The road, which is one of the best in the country, is a wonderful piece of engineering, spanning streams, cut in rock, rounding precipices, following the wild valley of the Dala by many a winding and zigzag.

The Baths of Leuk, or Loeche-les-Bains, or Leukerbad, is a little village at the very head of the valley, over four thousand feet above the sea, and overhung by the perpendicular walls of the Gemmi, which rise on all sides, except the south, on an average of two thousand feet above it. There is a nest of brown houses, clustered together like bee-hives, into which the few inhabitants creep to hibernate in the long winters, and several shops, grand hotels, and bathing-houses open for the season. Innumerable springs issue out of this green, sloping meadow among the mountains, some of them icy cold, but over twenty of them hot, and seasoned with a great many disagreeable sulphates, carbonates, and oxides, and varying in temperature from ninety-five to one hundred and twenty-three degrees Fahrenheit. Italians, French, and Swiss resort here in great numbers to take the baths, which are supposed to be very efficacious for rheumatism and cutaneous affections. Doubtless many of them do up their bathing for the year while here; and they may need no more after scalding and soaking in this water for a couple of months.

Before we reached the hotel, we turned aside into one of the bath-houses. We stood inhaling a sickly steam in a large, close hall, which was wholly occupied by a huge vat, across which low partitions, with bridges, ran, dividing it into four compartments. When we entered, we were assailed with yells in many languages, and howls in the common tongue, as if all the fiends of the pit had broken loose. We took off our hats in obedience to the demand; but the clamor did not wholly subside, and was mingled with singing and horrible laughter. Floating about in each vat, we at first saw twenty or thirty human heads. The women could be distinguished from the men by the manner of dressing the hair. Each wore a loose woolen gown. Each had a little table floating before him or her, which he or she pushed about at pleasure. One wore a hideous mask; another kept diving in the opaque pool and coming up to blow, like the hippopotamus in the Zoological Gardens; some were taking a lunch from their tables, others playing chess; some sitting on the benches round the edges, with only heads out of water, as doleful as owls, while others roamed about, engaged in the game of spattering with their comrades, and sang and shouted at the top of their voices. The people in this bath were said to be second class; but they looked as well and behaved better than those of the first class, whom we saw in the establishment at our hotel afterward.

It may be a valuable scientific fact, that the water in these vats, in which people of all sexes, all diseases, and all nations spend so many hours of the twenty-four, is changed once a day. The temperature at which the bath is given is ninety-eight. The water is let in at night, and allowed to cool. At five in the morning, the bathers enter it, and remain until ten o'clock,--five hours, having breakfast served to them on the floating tables, "as they sail, as they sail." They then have a respite till two, and go in till five. Eight hours in hot water! Nothing can be more disgusting than the sight of these baths. Gustave Dore must have learned here how to make those ghostly pictures of the lost floating about in the Stygian pools, in his illustrations of the Inferno; and the rocks and cavernous precipices may have enabled him to complete the picture. On what principle cures are effected in these filthy vats, I could not learn. I have a theory, that, where so many diseases meet and mingle in one swashing fluid, they neutralize each other. It may be that the action is that happily explained by one of the Hibernian bathmen in an American water-cure establishment. "You see, sir," said he, "that the shock of the water unites with the electricity of the system, and explodes the disease." I should think that the shock to one's feeling of decency and cleanliness, at these baths, would explode any disease in Europe. But, whatever the result may be, I am not sorry to see so many French and Italians soak themselves once a year.

Out of the bath these people seem to enjoy life. There is a long promenade, shaded and picturesque, which they take at evening, sometimes as far as the Ladders, eight of which are fastened, in a shackling manner, to the perpendicular rocks,--a high and somewhat dangerous ascent to the village of Albinen, but undertaken constantly by peasants with baskets on their backs. It is in winter the only mode Leukerbad has of communicating with the world; and in summer it is the only way of reaching Albinen, except by a long journey down the Dala and up another valley and height. The bathers were certainly very lively and social at table-d'hote, where we had the pleasure of meeting some hundred of them, dressed. It was presumed that the baths were the subject of the entertaining conversation; for I read in a charming little work which sets forth the delights of Leuk, that La poussee forms the staple of most of the talk. La poussee, or, as this book poetically calls it, "that daughter of the waters of Loeche," "that eruption of which we have already spoken, and which proves the action of the baths upon the skin,"--becomes the object, and often the end, of all conversation. And it gives specimens of this pleasant converse, as:

"Comment va votre poussee?"

"Avez-vous la poussee?"

"Je suis en pleine poussee"

"Ma poussee s'est fort bien passee!"

Indeed says this entertaining tract, sans poussee, one would not be able to hold, at table or in the salon, with a neighbor of either sex, the least conversation. Further, it is by grace a la poussee that one arrives at those intimacies which are the characteristics of the baths. Blessed, then, be La poussee, which renders possible such a high society and such select and entertaining conversation! Long may the bathers of Leuk live to soak and converse! In the morning, when we departed for the ascent of the Gemmi, we passed one of the bathing-houses. I fancied that a hot steam issued out of the crevices; from within came a discord of singing and caterwauling; and, as a door swung open, I saw that the heads floating about on the turbid tide were eating breakfast from the swimming tables.

OVER THE GEMMI

I spent some time, the evening before, studying the face of the cliff we were to ascend, to discover the path; but I could only trace its zigzag beginning. When we came to the base of the rock, we found a way cut, a narrow path, most of the distance hewn out of the rock, winding upward along the face of the precipice. The view, as one rises, is of the break-neck description. The way is really safe enough, even on mule-back, ascending; but one would be foolhardy to ride down. We met a lady on the summit who was about to be carried down on a chair; and she seemed quite to like the mode of conveyance: she had harnessed her husband in temporarily for one of the bearers, which made it still more jolly for her. When we started, a cloud of mist hung over the edge of the rocks. As we rose, it descended to meet us, and sunk below, hiding the valley and its houses, which had looked like Swiss toys from our height. When we reached the summit, the mist came boiling up after us, rising like a thick wall to the sky, and hiding all that great mountain range, the Vallais Alps, from which we had come, and which we hoped to see from this point. Fortunately, there were no clouds on the other side, and we looked down into a magnificent rocky basin, encircled by broken and overtopping crags and snow-fields, at the bottom of which was a green lake. It is one of the wildest of scenes.

An hour from the summit, we came to a green Alp, where a herd of cows were feeding; and in the midst of it were three or four dirty chalets, where pigs, chickens, cattle, and animals constructed very much like human beings, lived; yet I have nothing to say against these chalets, for we had excellent cream there. We had, on the way down, fine views of the snowy Altels, the Rinderhorn, the Finster-Aarhorn, a deep valley which enormous precipices guard, but which avalanches nevertheless invade, and, farther on, of the Blumlisalp, with its summit of crystalline whiteness. The descent to Kandersteg is very rapid, and in a rain slippery. This village is a resort for artists for its splendid views of the range we had crossed: it stands at the gate of the mountains. From there to the Lake of Thun is a delightful drive,--a rich country, with handsome cottages and a charming landscape, even if the pyramidal Niesen did not lift up its seven thousand feet on the edge of the lake. So, through a smiling land, and in the sunshine after the rain, we come to Spiez, and find ourselves at a little hotel on the slope, overlooking town and lake and mountains.

Spiez is not large: indeed, its few houses are nearly all picturesquely grouped upon a narrow rib of land which is thrust into the lake on purpose to make the loveliest picture in the world. There is the old castle, with its many slim spires and its square-peaked roofed tower; the slender-steepled church; a fringe of old houses below on the lake, one overhanging towards the point; and the promontory, finished by a willow drooping to the water. Beyond, in hazy light, over the lucid green of the lake, are mountains whose masses of rock seem soft and sculptured. To the right, at the foot of the lake, tower the great snowy mountains, the cone of the Schreckhorn, the square top of the Eiger, the Jungfrau, just showing over the hills, and the Blumlisalp rising into heaven clear and silvery.

What can one do in such a spot, but swim in the lake, lie on the shore, and watch the passing steamers and the changing light on the mountains? Down at the wharf, when the small boats put off for the steamer, one can well entertain himself. The small boat is an enormous thing, after all, and propelled by two long, heavy sweeps, one of which is pulled, and the other pushed. The laboring oar is, of course, pulled by a woman; while her husband stands up in the stern of the boat, and gently dips the other in a gallant fashion. There is a boy there, whom I cannot make out,--a short, square boy, with tasseled skull-cap, and a face that never changes its expression, and never has any expression to change; he may be older than these hills; he looks old enough to be his own father: and there is a girl, his counterpart, who might be, judging her age by her face, the mother of both of them. These solemn old-young people are quite busy doing nothing about the wharf, and appear to be afflicted with an undue sense of the responsibility of life. There is a beer-garden here, where several sober couples sit seriously drinking their beer. There are some horrid old women, with the parchment skin and the disagreeable necks. Alone, in a window of the castle, sits a lady at her work, who might be the countess; only, I am sorry, there is no countess, nothing but a frau, in that old feudal dwelling. And there is a foreigner, thinking how queer it all is. And while he sits there, the melodious bell in the church-tower rings its evening song.

BAVARIA.
AMERICAN IMPATIENCE

We left Switzerland, as we entered it, in a rain,--a kind of double baptism that may have been necessary, and was certainly not too heavy a price to pay for the privileges of the wonderful country. The wind blew freshly, and swept a shower over the deck of the little steamboat, on board of which we stepped from the shabby little pier and town of Romanshorn. After the other Swiss lakes, Constance is tame, except at the southern end, beyond which rise the Appenzell range and the wooded peaks of the Bavarian hills. Through the dash of rain, and under the promise of a magnificent rainbow,--rainbows don't mean anything in Switzerland, and have no office as weather-prophets, except to assure you, that, as it rains to-day, so it will rain tomorrow,--we skirted the lower bend of the lake,--and at twilight sailed into the little harbor of Lindau, through the narrow entrance between the piers, on one of which is a small lighthouse, and on the other sits upright a gigantic stone lion,--a fine enough figure of a Bavarian lion, but with a comical, wide-awake, and expectant expression of countenance, as if he might bark right out at any minute, and become a dog. Yet in the moonlight, shortly afterward, the lion looked very grand and stately, as he sat regarding the softly plashing waves, and the high, drifting clouds, and the old Roman tower by the bridge which connects the Island of Lindau with the mainland, and thinking perhaps, if stone lions ever do think, of the time when Roman galleys sailed on Lake Constance, and when Lindau was an imperial town with a thriving trade.

On board the little steamer was an American, accompanied by two ladies, and traveling, I thought, for their gratification, who was very anxious to get on faster than he was able to do,--though why any one should desire to go fast in Europe I do not know. One easily falls into the habit of the country, to take things easily, to go when the slow German fates will, and not to worry one's self beforehand about times and connections. But the American was in a fever of impatience, desirous, if possible, to get on that night. I knew he was from the Land of the Free by a phrase

I heard him use in the cars: he said, "I'll bet a dollar." Yet I must flatter myself that Americans do not always thus betray themselves. I happened, on the Isle of Wight, to hear a bland landlord "blow up" his glib-tongued son because the latter had not driven a stiffer bargain with us for the hire of a carriage round the island.

"Didn't you know they were Americans?" asks the irate father. "I knew it at once."

"No," replies young hopeful: "they didn't say GUESS once."

And straightway the fawning-innkeeper returns to us, professing, with his butter-lips, the greatest admiration of all Americans, and the intensest anxiety to serve them, and all for pure good-will. The English are even more bloodthirsty at sight of a travelere than the Swiss, and twice as obsequious. But to return to our American. He had all the railway timetables that he could procure; and he was busily studying them, with the design of "getting on." I heard him say to his companions, as he ransacked his pockets, that he was a mass of hotel-bills and timetables. He confided to me afterward, that his wife and her friend had got it into their heads that they must go both to Vienna and Berlin. Was Berlin much out of the way in going from Vienna to Paris? He said they told him it was n't. At any rate, he must get round at such a date: he had no time to spare. Then, besides the slowness of getting on, there were the trunks. He lost a trunk in Switzerland, and consumed a whole day in looking it up. While the steamboat lay at the wharf at Rorschach, two stout porters came on board, and shouldered his baggage to take it ashore. To his remonstrances in English they paid no heed; and it was some time before they could be made to understand that the trunks were to go on to Lindau. "There," said he, "I should have lost my trunks. Nobody understands what I tell them: I can't get any information." Especially was he unable to get any information as to how to "get on." I confess that the restless American almost put me into a fidget, and revived the American desire to "get on," to take the fast trains, make all the connections,--in short, in the handsome language of the great West, to "put her through." When I last saw our traveler, he was getting his luggage through the custom-house, still undecided whether to push on that night at eleven o'clock. But I forgot all about him and his hurry when, shortly after, we sat at the table-d'hote at the hotel, and the sedate Germans lit their cigars, some of them before they had finished eating, and sat smoking as if there were plenty of leisure for everything in this world.

A CITY OF COLOR

After a slow ride, of nearly eight hours, in what, in Germany, is called an express train, through a rain and clouds that hid from our view the Tyrol and the Swabian mountains, over a rolling, pleasant country, past pretty little railway station-houses, covered with vines, gay with flowers in the windows, and surrounded with beds of flowers, past switchmen in flaming scarlet jackets, who stand at the switches and raise the hand to the temple, and keep it there, in a military salute, as we go by, we come into old Augsburg, whose Confession is not so fresh in our minds as it ought to be. Portions of the ancient wall remain, and many of the towers; and there are archways, picturesquely opening from street to street, under several of which we drive on our way to the Three Moors, a stately hostelry and one of the oldest in Germany.

It stood here in the year 1500; and the room is still shown, unchanged since then, in which the rich Count Fugger entertained Charles V. The chambers are nearly all immense. That in which we are lodged is large enough for Queen Victoria; indeed, I am glad to say that her sleeping-room at St. Cloud was not half so spacious. One feels either like a count, or very lonesome, to sit down in a lofty chamber, say thirty-five feet square, with little furniture, and historical and tragical life-size figures staring at one from the wall-paper. One fears that they may come down in the deep night, and stand at the bedside,--those narrow, canopied beds there in the distance, like the marble couches in the cathedral. It must be a fearful thing to be a royal person, and dwell in a palace, with resounding rooms and naked, waxed, inlaid floors. At the Three Moors one sees a visitors' book, begun in 1800, which contains the names of many noble and great people, as well as poets and doctors and titled ladies, and much sentimental writing in French. It is my impression, from an inspection of the book, that we are the first untitled visitors.

The traveler cannot but like Augsburg at once, for its quaint houses, colored so diversely and yet harmoniously. Remains of its former brilliancy yet exist in the frescoes on the outside of the buildings, some of which are still bright in color, though partially defaced. Those on the House of Fugger have been restored, and are very brave pictures. These frescoes give great animation and life to the appearance of a street, and I am glad to see a taste for them reviving. Augsburg must have been very gay with them two and three hundred years ago, when, also, it was the home of beautiful women of the middle class, who married princes. We went to see the house in which lived the beautiful Agnes Bernauer, daughter of a barber, who married Duke Albert III. of Bavaria. The house was nought, as old Samuel Pepys would say, only a high stone building, in a block of such; but it is enough to make a house attractive for centuries if a pretty woman once looks out of its latticed windows, as I have no doubt Agnes often did when the duke and his retinue rode by in clanking armor.

But there is no lack of reminders of old times. The cathedral, which was begun before the Christian era could express its age with four figures, has two fine portals, with quaint carving, and bronze doors of very old work, whereon the story of Eve and the serpent is literally given,--a representation of great theological, if of small artistic value. And there is the old clock and watch tower, which for eight hundred years has enabled the Augsburgers to keep the time of day and to look out over the plain for the approach of an enemy. The city is full of fine bronze fountains some of them of very elaborate design, and adding a convenience and a beauty to the town which American cities wholly want. In one quarter of the town is the Fuggerei, a little city by itself, surrounded by its own wall, the gates of which are shut at night, with narrow streets and neat little houses. It was built by Hans Jacob Fugger the Rich, as long ago as 1519, and is still inhabited by indigent Roman-Catholic families, according to the intention of its founder. In the windows were lovely flowers. I saw in the street several of those mysterious, short, old women,--so old and yet so little, all body and hardly any legs, who appear to have grown down into the ground with advancing years.

It happened to be a rainy day, and cold, on the 30th of July, when we left Augsburg; and the flat fields through which we passed were uninviting under the gray light. Large flocks of geese were feeding on the windy plains, tended by boys and women, who are the living fences of this country. I no longer wonder at the number of feather-beds at the inns, under which we are apparently expected to sleep even in the warmest nights. Shepherds with the regulation crooks also were watching herds of sheep. Here and there a cluster of red-roofed houses were huddled together into a village, and in all directions rose tapering spires. Especially we marked the steeple of Blenheim, where Jack Churchill won the name for his magnificent country-seat, early in the eighteenth century. All this plain where the silly geese feed has been marched over and fought over by armies time and again. We effect the passage of, the Danube without difficulty, and on to Harburg, a little town of little red houses, inhabited principally by Jews, huddled under a rocky ridge, upon the summit of which is a picturesque medieval castle, with many towers and turrets, in as perfect preservation as when feudal flags floated over it. And so on, slowly, with long stops at many stations, to give opportunity, I suppose, for the honest passengers to take in supplies of beer and sausages, to Nuremberg.

A CITY LIVING ON THE PAST

Nuremberg, or Nurnberg, was built, I believe, about the beginning of time. At least, in an old black-letter history of the city which I have seen, illustrated with powerful wood-cuts, the first representation is that of the creation of the world, which is immediately followed by another of Nuremberg. No one who visits it is likely to dispute its antiquity. "Nobody ever goes to Nuremberg but Americans," said a cynical British officer at Chamouny; "but they always go there. I never saw an American who had n't been or was not going to Nuremberg." Well, I suppose they wish to see the oldest-looking, and, next to a true Briton on his travels, the oddest thing on the Continent. The city lives in the past still, and on its memories, keeping its old walls and moat entire, and nearly fourscore wall-towers, in stern array. But grass grows in the moat, fruit trees thrive there, and vines clamber on the walls. One wanders about in the queer streets with the feeling of being transported back to the Middle Ages; but it is difficult to reproduce the impression on paper. Who can describe the narrow and intricate ways; the odd houses with many little gables; great roofs breaking out from eaves to ridgepole, with dozens of dormer-windows; hanging balconies of stone, carved and figure-beset, ornamented and frescoed fronts; the archways, leading into queer courts and alleys, and out again into broad streets; the towers and fantastic steeples; and the many old bridges, with obelisks and memorials of triumphal entries of conquerors and princes?

The city, as I said, lives upon the memory of what it has been, and trades upon relics of its former fame. What it would have been without Albrecht Durer, and Adam Kraft the stone-mason, and Peter Vischer the bronze-worker, and Viet Stoss who carved in wood, and Hans Sachs the shoemaker and poet-minstrel, it is difficult to say. Their statues are set up in the streets; their works still live in the churches and city buildings,--pictures, and groups in stone and wood; and their statues, in all sorts of carving, are reproduced, big and little, in all the shop-windows, for sale. So, literally, the city is full of the memory of them; and the business of the city, aside from its manufactory of endless, curious toys, seems to consist in reproducing them and their immortal works to sell to strangers.

Other cities project new things, and grow with a modern impetus: Nuremberg lives in the past, and traffics on its ancient reputation. Of course, we went to see the houses where these old worthies lived, and the works of art they have left behind them,--things seen and described by everybody. The stone carving about the church portals and on side buttresses is inexpressibly quaint and naive. The subjects are sacred; and with the sacred is mingled the comic, here as at Augsburg, where over one portal of the cathedral, with saints and angels, monkeys climb and gibber. A favorite subject is that of our Lord praying in the Garden, while the apostles, who could not watch one hour, are sleeping in various attitudes of stony comicality. All the stone-cutters seem to have tried their chisels on this group, and there are dozens of them. The wise and foolish virgins also stand at the church doors in time-stained stone,--the one with a perked-up air of conscious virtue, and the other with a penitent dejection that seems to merit better treatment. Over the great portal of St. Lawrence--a magnificent structure, with lofty twin spires and glorious rosewindow is carved "The Last Judgment." Underneath, the dead are climbing out of their stone coffins; above sits the Judge, with the attending angels. On the right hand go away the stiff, prim saints, in flowing robes, and with palms and harps, up steps into heaven, through a narrow door which St. Peter opens for them; while on the left depart the wicked, with wry faces and distorted forms, down into the stone flames, towards which the Devil is dragging them by their stony hair.

The interior of the Church of St. Lawrence is richer than any other I remember, with its magnificent pillars of dark red stone, rising and foliating out to form the roof; its splendid windows of stained glass, glowing with sacred story; a high gallery of stone entirely round the choir, and beautiful statuary on every column. Here, too, is the famous Sacrament House of honest old Adam Kraft, the most exquisite thing I ever saw in stone. The color is light gray; and it rises beside one of the dark, massive pillars, sixty-four feet, growing to a point, which then strikes the arch of the roof, and there curls up like a vine to avoid it. The base is supported by the kneeling figures of Adam Kraft and two fellow-workmen, who labored on it for four years. Above is the Last Supper, Christ blessing little children, and other beautiful tableaux in stone. The Gothic spire grows up and around these, now and then throwing out graceful tendrils, like a vine, and seeming to be rather a living plant than inanimate stone. The faithful artist evidently had this feeling for it; for, as it grew under his hands, he found that it would strike the roof, or he must sacrifice something of its graceful proportion. So his loving and daring genius suggested the happy design of letting it grow to its curving, graceful completeness.

He who travels by a German railway needs patience and a full haversack. Time is of no value. The rate of speed of the trains is so slow, that one sometimes has a desire to get out and walk, and the stoppages at the stations seem eternal; but then we must remember that it is a long distance to the bottom of a great mug of beer. We left Lindau on one of the usual trains at half-past five in the morning, and reached Augsburg at one o'clock in the afternoon: the distance cannot be more than a hundred miles. That is quicker than by diligence, and one has leisure to see the country as he jogs along. There is nothing more sedate than a German train in motion; nothing can stand so dead still as a German train at a station. But there are express trains.

We were on one from Augsburg to Nuremberg, and I think must have run twenty miles an hour. The fare on the express trains is one fifth higher than on the others. The cars are all comfortable; and the officials, who wear a good deal of uniform, are much more civil and obliging than officials in a country where they do not wear uniforms. So, not swiftly, but safely and in good-humor, we rode to the capital of Bavaria.

OUTSIDE ASPECTS OF MUNICH

I saw yesterday, on the 31st of August, in the English Garden, dead leaves whirling down to the ground, a too evident sign that the summer weather is going. Indeed, it has been sour, chilly weather for a week now, raining a little every day, and with a very autumn feeling in the air. The nightly concerts in the beer-gardens must have shivering listeners, if the bands do not, as many of them do, play within doors. The line of droschke drivers, in front of the post-office colonnade, hide the red facings of their coats under long overcoats, and stand in cold expectancy beside their blanketed horses, which must need twice the quantity of black-bread in this chilly air; for the horses here eat bread, like people. I see the drivers every day slicing up the black loaves, and feeding them, taking now and then a mouthful themselves, wetting it down with a pull from the mug of beer that stands within reach. And lastly (I am still speaking of the weather), the gay military officers come abroad in long cloaks, to some extent concealing their manly forms and smart uniforms, which I am sure they would not do, except under the pressure of necessity.

Yet I think this raw weather is not to continue. It is only a rough visit from the Tyrol, which will give place to kinder influences. We came up here from hot Switzerland at the end of July, expecting to find Munich a furnace. It will be dreadful in Munich everybody said. So we left Luzerne, where it was warm, not daring to stay till the expected rival sun, Victoria of England, should make the heat overpowering. But the first week of August in Munich it was delicious weather,--clear, sparkling, bracing air, with no chill in it and no languor in it, just as you would say it ought to be on a high, gravelly plain, seventeen hundred feet above the sea. Then came a week of what the Muncheners call hot weather, with the thermometer up to eighty degrees Fahrenheit, and the white wide streets and gray buildings in a glare of light; since then, weather of the most uncertain sort.

Munich needs the sunlight. Not that it cannot better spare it than grimy London; for its prevailing color is light gray, and its many-tinted and frescoed fronts go far to relieve the most cheerless day. Yet Munich attempts to be an architectural reproduction of classic times; and, in order to achieve any success in this direction, it is necessary to have the blue heavens and golden sunshine of Greece. The old portion of the city has some remains of the Gothic, and abounds in archways and rambling alleys, that suddenly become broad streets and then again contract to the width of an alderman, and portions of the old wall and city gates; old feudal towers stand in the market-place, and faded frescoes on old clock-faces and over archways speak of other days of splendor.

But the Munich of to-day is as if built to order,--raised in a day by the command of one man. It was the old King Ludwig I., whose flower-wreathed bust stands in these days in the vestibule of the Glyptothek, in token of his recent death, who gave the impulse for all this, though some of the best buildings and streets in the city have been completed by his successors. The new city is laid out on a magnificent scale of distances, with wide streets, fine, open squares, plenty of room for gardens, both public and private; and the art buildings and art monuments are well distributed; in fact, many a stately building stands in such isolation that it seems to ask every passer what it was put there for. Then, again, some of the new adornments lack fitness of location or purpose. At the end of the broad, monotonous Ludwig Strasse, and yet not at the end, for the road runs straight on into the flat country between rows of slender trees, stands the Siegesthor, or Gate of Victory, an imitation of the Constantine arch at Rome. It is surmounted by a splendid group in bronze, by Schwanthaler, Bavaria in her war-chariot, drawn by four lions; and it is in itself, both in its proportions and its numerous sculptural figures and bas-reliefs, a fine recognition of the valor "of the Bavarian army," to whom it is erected. Yet it is so dwarfed by its situation, that it seems to have been placed in the middle of the street as an obstruction. A walk runs on each side of it. The Propylaeum, another magnificent gateway, thrown across the handsome Brienner Strasse, beyond the Glyptothek, is an imitation of that on the Acropolis at Athens. It has fine Doric columns on the outside, and Ionic within, and the pediment groups are bas-reliefs, by Schwanthaler, representing scenes in modern Greek history. The passageways for carriages are through the side arches; and thus the "sidewalk" runs into the center of the street, and foot-passers must twice cross the carriage-drive in going through the gate. Such things as these give one the feeling that art has been forced beyond use in Munich; and it is increased when one wanders through the new churches, palaces, galleries, and finds frescoes so prodigally crowded out of the way, and only occasionally opened rooms so overloaded with them, and not always of the best, as to sacrifice all effect, and leave one with the sense that some demon of unrest has driven painters and sculptors and plasterers, night and day, to adorn the city at a stroke; at least, to cover it with paint and bedeck it with marbles, and to do it at once, leaving nothing for the sweet growth and blossoming of time.

You see, it is easy to grumble, and especially in a cheerful, open, light, and smiling city, crammed with works Of art, ancient and modern, its architecture a study of all styles, and its foaming beer, said by antiquarians to be a good deal better than the mead drunk in Odin's halls, only seven and a half kreuzers the quart. Munich has so much, that it, of course, contains much that can be criticised. The long, wide Ludwig Strasse is a street of palaces,--a street built up by the old king, and regarded by him with great pride. But all the buildings are in the Romanesque style,--a repetition of one another to a monotonous degree: only at the lower end are there any shops or shop-windows, and a more dreary promenade need not be imagined. It has neither shade nor fountains; and on a hot day you can see how the sun would pour into it, and blind the passers. But few ever walk there at any time. A street that leads nowhere, and has no gay windows, does not attract. Toward the lower end, in the Odeon Platz, is the equestrian statue of Ludwig, a royally commanding figure, with a page on either side. The street is closed (so that it flows off on either side into streets of handsome shops) by the Feldherrnhalle, Hall of the Generals, an imitation of the beautiful Loggia dei Lanzi, at Florence, that as yet contains only two statues, which seem lost in it. Here at noon, with parade of infantry, comes a military band to play for half an hour; and there are always plenty of idlers to listen to them. In the high arcade a colony of doves is domesticated; and I like to watch them circling about and wheeling round the spires of the over-decorated Theatine church opposite, and perching on the heads of the statues on the facade.

The royal palace, near by, is a huddle of buildings and courts, that I think nobody can describe or understand, built at different times and in imitation of many styles. The front, toward the Hof Garden, a grassless square of small trees, with open arcades on two sides for shops, and partially decorated with frescoes of landscapes and historical subjects, is "a building of festive halls," a facade eight hundred feet long, in the revived Italian style, and with a fine Ionic porch. The color is the royal, dirty yellow.

On the Max Joseph Platz, which has a bronze statue of King Max, a seated figure, and some elaborate bas-reliefs, is another front of the palace, the Konigsbau, an
imitation, not fully carried out, of the Pitti Palace, at Florence. Between these is the
old Residenz, adorned with fountain groups and statues in bronze. On another side
are the church and theater of the Residenz. The interior of this court chapel is dazzling in appearance: the pillars are, I think, imitation of variegated marble; the sides
are imitation of the same; the vaulting is covered with rich frescoes on gold ground.
The whole effect is rich, but it is not at all sacred. Indeed, there is no church in
Munich, except the old cathedral, the Frauenkirche, with its high Gothic arches,
stained windows, and dusty old carvings, that gives one at all the sort of feeling that
it is supposed a church should give. The court chapel interior is boastingly said to
resemble St. Mark's, in Venice.

You see how far imitation of the classic and Italian is carried here in Munich;
so, as I said, the buildings need the southern sunlight. Fortunately, they get the
right quality much of the time. The Glyptothek, a Grecian structure of one story,
erected to hold the treasures of classic sculpture that King Ludwig collected, has a
beautiful Ionic porch and pediment. On the outside are niches filled with statues. In
the pure sunshine and under a deep blue sky, its white marble glows with an almost
ethereal beauty. Opposite stands another successful imitation of the Grecian style of
architecture,--a building with a Corinthian porch, also of white marble. These, with
the Propylaeum, before mentioned, come out wonderfully against a blue sky. A few
squares distant is the Pinakothek, with its treasures of old pictures, and beyond it
the New Pinakothek, containing works of modern artists. Its exterior is decorated
with frescoes, from designs by Kaulbach: these certainly appear best in a sparkling
light; though I am bound to say that no light can make very much of them.

Yet Munich is not all imitation. Its finest street, the Maximilian, built by the
late king of that name, is of a novel and wholly modern style of architecture, not an
imitation, though it may remind some of the new portions of Paris. It runs for three
quarters of a mile, beginning with the postoffice and its colonnades, with frescoes on
one side, and the Hof Theater, with its pediment frescoes, the largest opera-house in
Germany, I believe; with stately buildings adorned with statues, and elegant shops,
down to the swift-flowing Isar, which is spanned by a handsome bridge; or rather
by two bridges, for the Isar is partly turned from its bed above, and made to turn

wheels, and drive machinery. At the lower end the street expands into a handsome platz, with young shade trees, plats of grass, and gay beds of flowers. I look out on it as I write; and I see across the Isar the college building begun by Maximilian for the education of government officers; and I see that it is still unfinished, indeed, a staring mass of brick, with unsightly scaffolding and gaping windows. Money was left to complete it; but the young king, who does not care for architecture, keeps only a mason or two on the brick-work, and an artist on the exterior frescoes. At this rate, the Cologne Cathedral will be finished and decay before this is built. On either side of it, on the elevated bank of the river, stretch beautiful grounds, with green lawns, fine trees, and well-kept walks.

Not to mention the English Garden, in speaking of the outside aspects of the city, would be a great oversight. It was laid out originally by the munificent American, Count Rumford, and is called English, I suppose, because it is not in the artificial Continental style. Paris has nothing to compare with it for natural beauty,-- Paris, which cannot let a tree grow, but must clip it down to suit French taste. It is a noble park four miles in length, and perhaps a quarter of that in width,--a park of splendid old trees, grand, sweeping avenues, open glades of free-growing grass, with delicious, shady walks, charming drives and rivers of water. For the Isar is trained to flow through it in two rapid streams, under bridges and over rapids, and by willow-hung banks. There is not wanting even a lake; and there is, I am sorry to say, a temple on a mound, quite in the classic style, from which one can see the sun set behind the many spires of Munich. At the Chinese Tower two military bands play every Saturday evening in the summer; and thither the carriages drive, and the promenaders assemble there, between five and six o'clock; and while the bands play, the Germans drink beer, and smoke cigars, and the fashionably attired young men walk round and round the circle, and the smart young soldiers exhibit their handsome uniforms, and stride about with clanking swords.

We felicitated ourselves that we should have no lack of music when we came to Munich. I think we have not; though the opera has only just begun, and it is the vacation of the Conservatoire. There are first the military bands: there is continually a parade somewhere, and the streets are full of military music, and finely executed too. Then of beer-gardens there is literally no end, and there are nightly concerts in them. There are two brothers Hunn, each with his band, who, like the ancient Huns, have taken the city; and its gardens are given over to their unending waltzes, polkas, and opera medleys. Then there is the church music on Sundays and holidays, which is largely of a military character; at least, has the aid of drums and trumpets, and the whole band of brass. For the first few days of our stay here we had rooms near the Maximilian Platz and the Karl's Thor. I think there was some sort of a yearly fair in progress, for the great platz was filled with temporary booths: a circus had set itself up there, and there were innumerable side-shows and lottery-stands; and I believe that each little shanty and puppet-show had its band or fraction of a band, for there was never heard such a tooting and blowing and scraping, such a pounding and dinning and slang-whanging, since the day of stopping work on the Tower of Babel. The circus band confined itself mostly to one tune; and as it went all day long, and late into the night, we got to know it quite well; at least, the bass notes of it, for the lighter tones came to us indistinctly. You know that blurt, blurt, thump, thump, dissolute sort of caravan tune. That was it.

The English Cafe was not far off, and there the Hunns and others also made night melodious. The whole air was one throb and thrump. The only refuge from it was to go into one of the gardens, and give yourself over to one band. And so it was possible to have delightful music, and see the honest Germans drink beer, and gossip in friendly fellowship and with occasional hilarity. But music we had, early and late. We expected quiet in our present quarters. The first morning, at six o'clock, we were startled by the resonant notes of a military band, that set the echoes flying between the houses, and a regiment of cavalry went clanking down the street. But that is a not unwelcome morning serenade and reveille. Not so agreeable is the young man next door, who gives hilarious concerts to his friends, and sings and bangs his piano all day Sunday; nor the screaming young woman opposite. Yet it is something to be in an atmosphere of music.

THE MILITARY LIFE OF MUNICH

This morning I was awakened early by the strains of a military band. It was a clear, sparkling morning, the air full of life, and yet the sun showing its warm, southern side. As the mounted musicians went by, the square was quite filled with the clang of drum and trumpet, which became fainter and fainter, and at length was lost on the ear beyond the Isar, but preserved the perfection of time and the precision of execution for which the military bands of the city are remarkable. After the band came a brave array of officers in bright uniform, upon horses that pranced and curveted in the sunshine; and the regiment of cavalry followed, rank on rank of splendidly mounted men, who ride as if born to the saddle. The clatter of hoofs on the pavement, the jangle of bit and saber, the occasional word of command, the onward sweep of the well-trained cavalcade, continued for a long time, as if the lovely morning had brought all the cavalry in the city out of barracks. But this is an almost daily sight in Munich. One regiment after another goes over the river to the drill-ground. In the hot mornings I used quite to pity the troopers who rode away in the glare in scorching brazen helmets and breastplates. But only a portion of the regiments dress in that absurd manner. The most wear a simple uniform, and look very soldierly. The horses are almost invariably fine animals, and I have not seen such riders in Europe. Indeed, everybody in Munich who rides at all rides well. Either most of the horsemen have served in the cavalry, or horsemanship, that noble art "to witch the world," is in high repute here.

Speaking of soldiers, Munich is full of them. There are huge caserns in every part of the city, crowded with troops. This little kingdom of Bavaria has a hundred and twenty thousand troops of the line. Every man is obliged to serve in the army continuously three years; and every man between the ages of twenty-one and forty-five must go with his regiment into camp or barrack several weeks in each year, no matter if the harvest rots in the field, or the customers desert the uncared-for shop. The service takes three of the best years of a young man's life. Most of the soldiers in Munich are young one meets hundreds of mere boys in the uniform of officers. I think every seventh man you meet is a soldier. There must be between fifteen and twenty thousand troops quartered in the city now. The young officers are everywhere, lounging in the cafes, smoking and sipping coffee, on all the public promenades, in the gardens, the theaters, the churches. And most of them are fine-looking fellows, good figures in elegantly fitting and tasteful uniforms; but they do like to show their handsome forms and hear their sword-scabbards rattle on the pavement as they stride by. The beer-gardens are full of the common soldiers, who empty no end of quart mugs in alternate pulls from the same earthen jug, with the utmost jollity and good fellowship. On the street, salutes between officers and men are perpetual, punctiliously given and returned,--the hand raised to the temple, and held there for a second. A young gallant, lounging down the Theatiner or the Maximilian Strasse, in his shining and snug uniform, white kids, and polished boots, with jangling spurs and the long sword clanking on the walk, raising his hand ever and anon in condescending salute to a lower in rank, or with affable grace to an equal, is a sight worth beholding, and for which one cannot be too grateful. We have not all been created with the natural shape for soldiers, but we have eyes given us that we may behold them.

Bavaria fought, you know, on the wrong side at Sadowa; but the result of the war left her in confederation with Prussia. The company is getting to be very distasteful, for Austria is at present more liberal than Prussia. Under Prussia one must either be a soldier or a slave, the democrats of Munich say. Bavaria has the most liberal constitution in Germany, except that of Wurtemberg, and the people are jealous of any curtailment of liberty. It seems odd that anybody should look to the house of Hapsburg for liberality. The attitude of Prussia compels all the little states to keep up armies, which eat up their substance, and burden the people with taxes. This is the more to be regretted now, when Bavaria is undergoing a peaceful revolution, and throwing off the trammels of galling customs in other respects.

THE EMANCIPATION OF MUNICH

The 1st of September saw go into complete effect the laws enacted in 1867, which have inaugurated the greatest changes in business and social life, and mark an era in the progress of the people worthy of fetes and commemorative bronzes. We heard the other night at the opera-house "William Tell" unmutilated. For many years this liberty-breathing opera was not permitted to be given in Bavaria, except with all the life of it cut out. It was first presented entire by order of young King Ludwig, who, they say, was induced to command its unmutilated reproduction at the solicitation of Richard Wagner, who used to be, and very likely is now, a "Red," and was banished from Saxony in 1848 for fighting on the people's side of a barricade in Dresden. It is the fashion to say of the young king, that he pays no heed to the business of the kingdom. You hear that the handsome boy cares only for music and horseback exercise: he plays much on the violin, and rides away into the forest attended by only one groom, and is gone for days together. He has composed an opera, which has not yet been put on the stage. People, when they speak of him, tap their foreheads with one finger. But I don't believe it. The same liberality that induced him, years ago, to restore "William Tell" to the stage has characterized the government under him ever since.

Formerly no one could engage in any trade or business in Bavaria without previous examination before, and permission from, a magistrate. If a boy wished to be a baker, for instance, he had first to serve four years of apprenticeship. If then he wished to set up business for himself, he must get permission, after passing an examination. This permission could rarely be obtained; for the magistrate usually decided that there were already as many bakers as the town needed. His only other resource was to buy out an existing business, and this usually costs a good deal. When he petitioned for the privilege of starting a bakery, all the bakers protested. And he could not even buy out a stand, and carry it on, without strict examination as to qualifications. This was the case in every trade. And to make matters worse, a master workman could not employ a journeyman out of his shop; so that, if a journeyman could not get a regular situation, he had no work. Then there were endless restrictions upon the manufacture and sale of articles: one person could make only one article, or one portion of an article; one might manufacture shoes for women, but not for men; he might make an article in the shop and sell it, but could not sell it if any one else made it outside, or vice versa.

Nearly all this mass of useless restriction on trades and business, which palsied all effort in Bavaria, is removed. Persons are free to enter into any business they like. The system of apprenticeship continues, but so modified as not to be oppressive; and all trades are left to regulate themselves by natural competition. Already Munich has felt the benefit of the removal of these restrictions, which for nearly a year has been anticipated, in a growth of population and increased business.

But the social change is still more important. The restrictions upon marriage were a serious injury to the state. If Hans wished to marry, and felt himself adequate to the burdens and responsibilities of the double state, and the honest fraulein was quite willing to undertake its trials and risks with him, it was not at all enough that

in the moonlighted beergarden, while the band played, and they peeled the sting-
ing radish, and ate the Switzer cheese, and drank from one mug, she allowed his
arm to steal around her stout waist. All this love and fitness went for nothing in the
eyes of the magistrate, who referred the application for permission to marry to his
associate advisers, and they inquired into the applicant's circumstances; and if, in
their opinion, he was not worth enough money to support a wife properly, permission was refused for him to try. The consequence was late marriages, and fewer
than there ought to be, and other ill results. Now the matrimonial gates are lifted
high, and the young man has not to ask permission of any snuffy old magistrate to
marry. I do not hear that the consent of the maidens is more difficult to obtain than
formerly.

No city of its size is more prolific of pictures than Munich. I do not know how
all its artists manage to live, but many of them count upon the American public. I
hear everywhere that the Americans like this, and do not like that; and I am sorry to
say that some artists, who have done better things, paint professedly to suit Americans, and not to express their own conceptions of beauty. There is one who is now
quite devoted to dashing off rather lamp-blacky moonlights, because, he says, the
Americans fancy that sort of thing. I see one of his smirchy pictures hanging in a
shop window, awaiting the advent of the citizen of the United States. I trust that
no word of mine will injure the sale of the moonlights. There are some excellent
figure-painters here, and one can still buy good modern pictures for reasonable
prices.

FASHION IN THE STREETS

Was there ever elsewhere such a blue, transparent sky as this here in Munich?
At noon, looking up to it from the street, above the gray houses, the color and depth
are marvelous. It makes a background for the Grecian art buildings and gateways,
that would cheat a risen Athenian who should see it into the belief that he was restored to his beautiful city. The color holds, too, toward sundown, and seems to be
poured, like something solid, into the streets of the city.

You should see then the Maximilian Strasse, when the light floods the platz where Maximilian in bronze sits in his chair, illuminates the frescoes on the pediments of the Hof Theater, brightens the Pompeian red under the colonnade of the post-office, and streams down the gay thoroughfare to the trees and statues in front of the National Museum, and into the gold-dusted atmosphere beyond the Isar. The street is filled with promenaders: strangers who saunter along with the red book in one hand,--a man and his wife, the woman dragged reluctantly past the windows of fancy articles, which are "so cheap," the man breaking his neck to look up at the buildings, especially at the comical heads and figures in stone that stretch out from the little oriel-windows in the highest story of the Four Seasons Hotel, and look down upon the moving throng; Munich bucks in coats of velvet, swinging light canes, and smoking cigars through long and elaborately carved meerschaum holders; Munich ladies in dresses of that inconvenient length that neither sweeps the pavement nor clears it; peasants from the Tyrol, the men in black, tight breeches, that button from the knee to the ankle, short jackets and vests set thickly with round silver buttons, and conical hats with feathers, and the women in short quilted and quilled petticoats, of barrel-like roundness from the broad hips down, short waists ornamented with chains and barbarous brooches of white metal, with the oddest head-gear of gold and silver heirlooms; students with little red or green embroidered brimless caps, with the ribbon across the breast, a folded shawl thrown over one shoulder, and the inevitable switch-cane; porters in red caps, with a coil of twine about the waist; young fellows from Bohemia, with green coats, or coats trimmed with green, and green felt hats with a stiff feather stuck in the side; and soldiers by the hundreds, of all ranks and organizations; common fellows in blue, staring in at the shop windows, officers in resplendent uniforms, clanking their swords as they swagger past. Now and then, an elegant equipage dashes by,--perhaps the four horses of the handsome young king, with mounted postilions and outriders, or a liveried carriage of somebody born with a von before his name. As the twilight comes on, the shutters of the shop windows are put up. It is time to go to the opera, for the curtain rises at half-past six, or to the beer-gardens, where delicious music marks, but does not interrupt, the flow of excellent beer.

Or you may if you choose, and I advise you to do it, walk at the same hour in the English Garden, which is but a step from the arcades of the Hof Garden,--but a step to the entrance, whence you may wander for miles and miles in the most enchanting scenery. Art has not been allowed here to spoil nature. The trees, which are of magnificent size, are left to grow naturally;--the Isar, which is turned into it, flows in more than one stream with its mountain impetuosity; the lake is gracefully indented and overhung with trees, and presents ever-changing aspects of loveliness as you walk along its banks; there are open, sunny meadows, in which single giant trees or splendid groups of them stand, and walks without end winding under leafy Gothic arches. You know already that Munich owes this fine park to the foresight and liberality of an American Tory, Benjamin Thompson (Count Rumford), born in Rumford, Vt., who also relieved Munich of beggars.

I have spoken of the number of soldiers in Munich. For six weeks the Landwehr, or militia, has been in camp in various parts of Bavaria. There was a grand review of them the other day on the Field of Mars, by the king, and many of them have now gone home. They strike an unmilitary man as a very efficient body of troops. So far as I could see, they were armed with breech-loading rifles. There is a treaty by which Bavaria agreed to assimilate her military organization to that of Prussia. It is thus that Bismarck is continually getting ready. But if the Landwehr is gone, there are yet remaining troops enough of the line. Their chief use, so far as it concerns me, is to make pageants in the streets, and to send their bands to play at noon in the public squares. Every day, when the sun shines down upon the mounted statue of Ludwig I., in front of the Odeon, a band plays in an open Loggia, and there is always a crowd of idlers in the square to hear it. Everybody has leisure for that sort of thing here in Europe; and one can easily learn how to be idle and let the world wag. They have found out here what is disbelieved in America,--that the world will continue to turn over once in about twenty-four hours (they are not accurate as to the time) without their aid. To return to our soldiers. The cavalry most impresses me; the men are so finely mounted, and they ride royally. In these sparkling mornings, when the regiments clatter past, with swelling music and shining armor, riding away to I know not what adventure and glory, I confess that I long to follow them. I have long had this desire; and the other morning, determining to satisfy it, I seized my hat and went after the prancing procession. I am sorry I did. For, after trudging after it through street after street, the fine horsemen all rode through an arched gateway, and disappeared in barracks, to my great disgust; and the troopers dismounted, and led their steeds into stables.

And yet one never loses a walk here in Munich. I found myself that morning by the Isar Thor, a restored medieval city gate. The gate is double, with flanking octagonal towers, inclosing a quadrangle. Upon the inner wall is a fresco of "The Crucifixion." Over the outer front is a representation, in fresco painting, of the triumphal entry into the city of the Emperor Louis of Bavaria after the battle of Ampfing. On one side of the gate is a portrait of the Virgin, on gold ground, and on the other a very passable one of the late Dr. Hawes of Hartford, with a Pope's hat on. Walking on, I came to another arched gateway and clock-tower; near it an old church, with a high wall adjoining, whereon is a fresco of cattle led to slaughter, showing that I am in the vicinity of the Victual Market; and I enter it through a narrow, crooked alley. There is nothing there but an assemblage of shabby booths and fruit-stands, and an ancient stone tower in ruins and overgrown with ivy.

Leaving this, I came out to the Marian Platz, where stands the column, with the statue of the Virgin and Child, set up by Maximilian I. in 1638 to celebrate the victory in the battle which established the Catholic supremacy in Bavaria. It is a favorite praying-place for the lower classes. Yesterday was a fete day, and the base of the column and half its height are lost in a mass of flowers and evergreens. In front is erected an altar with a broad, carpeted platform; and a strip of the platz before it is inclosed with a railing, within which are praying-benches. The sun shines down hot; but there are several poor women kneeling there, with their baskets beside them. I happen along there at sundown; and there are a score of women kneeling on the hard stones, outside the railing saying their prayers in loud voices. The mass of flowers is still sweet and gay and fresh; a fountain with fantastic figures is flashing near by; the crowd, going home to supper and beer, gives no heed to the praying; the stolid droschke-drivers stand listlessly by. At the head of the square is an artillery station, and a row of cannon frowns on it. On one side is a house with a tablet in the wall, recording the fact that Gustavus Adolphus of Sweden once lived in it.

When we came to Munich, the great annual fair was in progress; and the large Maximilian Platz (not to be confounded with the street of that name) was filled with booths of cheap merchandise, puppet-shows, lottery shanties, and all sorts of popular amusements. It was a fine time to study peasant costumes. The city was crowded with them on Sunday; and let us not forget that the first visit of the peasants was to the churches; they invariably attended early mass before they set out upon the day's pleasure. Most of the churches have services at all hours till noon, some of them with fine classical and military music. One could not but be struck with the devotional manner of the simple women, in their queer costumes, who walked into the gaudy edifices, were absorbed in their prayers for an hour, and then went away. I suppose they did not know how odd they looked in their high, round fur hats, or their fantastic old ornaments, nor that there was anything amiss in bringing their big baskets into church with them. At least, their simple, unconscious manner was better than that of many of the city people, some of whom stare about a good deal, while going through the service, and stop in the midst of crossings and genuflections to take snuff and pass it to their neighbors. But there are always present simple and homelike sort of people, who neither follow the fashions nor look round on them; respectable, neat old ladies, in the faded and carefully preserved silk gowns, such as the New England women wear to "meeting."

No one can help admiring the simplicity, kindliness, and honesty of the Germans. The universal courtesy and friendliness of manner have a very different seeming from the politeness of the French. At the hotels in the country, the landlord and his wife and the servant join in hoping you will sleep well when you go to bed. The little maid at Heidelberg who served our meals always went to the extent of wishing us a good appetite when she had brought in the dinner. Here in Munich the people we have occasion to address in the street are uniformly courteous. The shop-keepers are obliging, and rarely servile, like the English. You are thanked, and punctiliously wished the good-day, whether you purchase anything or not. In shops tended by women, gentlemen invariably remove their hats. If you buy only a kreuzer's worth of fruit of an old woman, she says words that would be, literally translated, "I thank you beautifully." With all this, one looks kindly on the childish love the Germans have for titles. It is, I believe, difficult for the German mind to comprehend that we can be in good standing at home, unless we have some title prefixed to our names, or some descriptive phrase added. Our good landlord, who waits at the table and answers our bell, one of whose tenants is a living baron, having no title to put on his doorplate under that of the baron, must needs dub himself "privatier;" and he insists upon prefixing the name of this unambitious writer with the ennobling von; and at the least he insists, in common with the tradespeople, that I am a "Herr Doctor." The bills of purchases by madame come made out to

"Frau----, well-born." At a hotel in Heidelberg, where I had registered my name with that distinctness of penmanship for which newspaper men are justly conspicuous, and had added to my own name "& wife," I was not a little flattered to appear in the reckoning as "Herr Doctor Mamesweise."

THE GOTTESACKER AND BAVARIAN FUNERALS

To change the subject from gay to grave. The Gottesacker of Munich is called the finest cemetery in Germany; at least, it surpasses them in the artistic taste of its monuments. Natural beauty it has none: it is simply a long, narrow strip of ground inclosed in walls, with straight, parallel walks running the whole length, and narrow cross-walks; and yet it is a lovely burial-ground. There are but few trees; but the whole inclosure is a conservatory of beautiful flowers. Every grave is covered with them, every monument is surrounded with them. The monuments are unpretending in size, but there are many fine designs, and many finely executed busts and statues and allegorical figures, in both marble and bronze. The place is full of sunlight and color. I noticed that it was much frequented. In front of every place of sepulcher stands a small urn for water, with a brush hanging by, with which to sprinkle the flowers. I saw, also, many women and children coming and going with watering-pots, so that the flowers never droop for want of care. At the lower end of the old ground is an open arcade, wherein are some effigies and busts, and many ancient tablets set into the wall. Beyond this is the new cemetery, an inclosure surrounded by a high wall of brick, and on the inside by an arcade. The space within is planted with flowers, and laid out for the burial of the people; the arcades are devoted to the occupation of those who can afford costly tombs. Only a small number of them are yet occupied; there are some good busts and monuments, and some frescoes on the panels rather more striking for size and color than for beauty.

Between the two cemeteries is the house for the dead. When I walked down the long central alle of the old ground, I saw at the farther end, beyond a fountain, twinkling lights. Coming nearer, I found that they proceeded from the large windows of a building, which was a part of the arcade. People were looking in at the windows, going and coming to and from them continually; and I was prompted by curiosity to look within. A most unexpected sight met my eye. In a long room, upon elevated biers, lay people dead: they were so disposed that the faces could be seen; and there they rested in a solemn repose. Officers in uniform, citizens in plain dress, matrons and maids in the habits that they wore when living, or in the white robes of the grave. About most of them were lighted candles. About all of them were flowers: some were almost covered with bouquets. There were rows of children, little ones scarce a span long,--in the white caps and garments of innocence, as if asleep in beds of flowers. How naturally they all were lying, as if only waiting to be called! Upon the thumb of every adult was a ring in which a string was tied that went through a pulley above and communicated with a bell in the attendant's room. How frightened he would be if the bell should ever sound, and he should go into that hall of the dead to see who rang! And yet it is a most wise and humane provision; and many years ago, there is a tradition, an entombment alive was prevented by it. There are three rooms in all; and all those who die in Munich must be brought and laid in one of them, to be seen of all who care to look therein. I suppose that wealth and rank have some privileges; but it is the law that the person having been pronounced dead by the physician shall be the same day brought to the dead-house, and lie there three whole days before interment.

There is something peculiar in the obsequies of Munich, especially in the Catholic portion of the population. Shortly after the death, there is a short service in the courtyard of the house, which, with the entrance, is hung in costly mourning, if the deceased was rich. The body is then carried in the car to the dead-house, attended by the priests, the male members of the family, and a procession of torch-bearers, if that can be afforded. Three days after, the burial takes place from the dead-house, only males attending. The women never go to the funeral; but some days after, of which public notice is given by advertisement, a public service is held in church, at which all the family are present, and to which the friends are publicly invited. Funeral obsequies are as costly here as in America; but everything is here regulated and fixed by custom. There are as many as five or six classes of funerals recognized. Those of the first class, as to rank and expense, cost about a thousand guldens. The second class is divided into six subclasses. The third is divided into two. The cost of the first of the third class is about four hundred guldens. The lowest class of those able to have a funeral costs twenty-five guldens. A gulden is about two francs.

There are no carriages used at the funerals of Catholics, only at those of Protestants and Jews.

I spoke of the custom of advertising the deaths. A considerable portion of the daily newspapers is devoted to these announcements, which are printed in display type, like the advertisements of dry-goods sellers with you. I will roughly translate one which I happen to see just now. It reads, "Death advertisement. It has pleased God the Almighty, in his inscrutable providence, to take away our innermost loved, best husband, father, grandfather, uncle, brother-in-law, and cousin, Herr---, dyer of cloth and silk, yesterday night, at eleven o'clock, after three weeks of severe suffering, having partaken of the holy sacrament, in his sixty-sixth year, out of this earthly abode of calamity into the better Beyond. Those who knew his good heart, his great honesty, as well as his patience in suffering, will know how justly to estimate our grief." This is signed by the "deep-grieving survivors,"--the widow, son, daughter, and daughter-in-law, in the name of the absent relatives. After the name of the son is written, "Dyer in cloth and silk." The notice closes with an announcement of the funeral at the cemetery, and a service at the church the day after. The advertisement I have given is not uncommon either for quaintness or simplicity. It is common to engrave upon the monument the business as well as the title of the departed.

THE OCTOBER FEST THE PEASANTS AND THE KING

On the 11th of October the sun came out, after a retirement of nearly two weeks. The cause of the appearance was the close of the October Fest. This great popular carnival has the same effect upon the weather in Bavaria that the Yearly Meeting of Friends is known to produce in Philadelphia, and the Great National Horse Fair in New England. It always rains during the October Fest. Having found this out, I do not know why they do not change the time of it; but I presume they are wise enough to feel that it would be useless. A similar attempt on the part of the Pennsylvania Quakers merely disturbed the operations of nature, but did not save the drab bonnets from the annual wetting. There is a subtle connection between such gatherings and the gathering of what are called the elements,--a sympathetic connection, which we shall, no doubt, one day understand, when we have collected facts enough on the subject to make a comprehensive generalization, after Mr. Buckle's method.

This fair, which is just concluded, is a true Folks-Fest, a season especially for the Bavarian people, an agricultural fair and cattle show, but a time of general jollity and amusement as well. Indeed, the main object of a German fair seems to be to have a good time and in this it is in marked contrast with American fairs. The October Fest was instituted for the people by the old Ludwig I. on the occasion of his marriage; and it has ever since retained its position as the great festival of the Bavarian people, and particularly of the peasants. It offers a rare opportunity to the stranger to study the costumes of the peasants, and to see how they amuse themselves. One can judge a good deal of the progress of a people by the sort of amusements that satisfy them. I am not about to draw any philosophical inferences,--I am a mere looker-on in Munich; but I have never anywhere else seen puppet-shows afford so much delight, nor have I ever seen anybody get more satisfaction out of a sausage and a mug of beer, with the tum-tum of a band near, by, than a Bavarian peasant.

The Fest was held on the Theresien Wiese, a vast meadow on the outskirts of the city. The ground rises on one side of this by an abrupt step, some thirty or forty feet high, like the "bench" of a Western river. This bank is terraced for seats the whole length, or as far down as the statue of Bavaria; so that there are turf seats, I should judge, for three quarters of a mile, for a great many thousands of people, who can look down upon the race-course, the tents, houses, and booths of the fair-ground, and upon the roof and spires of the city beyond. The statue is, as you know, the famous bronze Bavaria of Schwanthaler, a colossal female figure fifty feet high, and with its pedestal a hundred feet high, which stands in front of the Hall of Fame, a Doric edifice, in the open colonnades of which are displayed the busts of the most celebrated Bavarians, together with those of a few poets and scholars who were so unfortunate as not to be born here. The Bavaria stands with the right hand upon the sheathed sword, and the left raised in the act of bestowing a wreath of victory; and the lion of the kingdom is beside her. This representative being is, of course, hollow. There is room for eight people in her head, which I can testify is a warm place on a sunny day; and one can peep out through loopholes and get a good view of the Alps of the Tyrol. To say that this statue is graceful or altogether successful would be an error; but it is rather impressive, from its size, if for no other reason. In the cast of the hand exhibited at the bronze foundry, the forefinger measures over three feet long.

Although the Fest did not officially begin until Friday, October 12, yet the essential part of it, the amusements, was well under way on the Sunday before. The town began to be filled with country people, and the holiday might be said to have commenced; for the city gives itself up to the occasion. The new art galleries are closed for some days; but the collections and museums of various sorts are daily open, gratis; the theaters redouble their efforts; the concert-halls are in full blast; there are dances nightly, and masked balls in the Folks' Theater; country relatives are entertained; the peasants go about the streets in droves, in a simple and happy frame of mind, wholly unconscious that they are the oddest-looking guys that have come down from the Middle Ages; there is music in all the gardens, singing in the cafes, beer flowing in rivers, and a mighty smell of cheese, that goes up to heaven. If the eating of cheese were a religious act, and its odor an incense, I could not say enough of the devoutness of the Bavarians.

Of the picturesqueness and oddity of the Bavarian peasants' costumes, nothing but a picture can give you any idea. You can imagine the men in tight breeches, buttoned below the knee, jackets of the jockey cut, and both jacket and waistcoat covered with big metal buttons, sometimes coins, as thickly as can be sewed on: but the women defy the pen; a Bavarian peasant woman, in holiday dress, is the most fearfully and wonderfully made object in the universe. She displays a good length of striped stockings, and wears thin slippers, or sandals; her skirts are like a hogshead in size and shape, and reach so near her shoulders as to make her appear hump-backed; the sleeves are hugely swelled out at the shoulder, and taper to the wrist; the bodice is a stiff and most elaborately ornamented piece of armor; and there is a kind of breastplate, or center-piece, of gold, silver, and precious stones, or what passes for them; and the head is adorned with some monstrous heirloom, of finely worked gold or silver, or a tower, gilded and shining with long streamers, or bound in a simple black turban, with flowing ends. Little old girls, dressed like their mothers, have the air of creations of the fancy, who have walked out of a fairy-book.

There is an endless variety in these old costumes; and one sees, every moment, one more preposterous than the preceding. The girls from the Tyrol, with their bright neckerchiefs and pointed black felt hats, with gold cord and tassels, are some of them very pretty: but one looks a long time for a bright face among the other class; and, when it is discovered, the owner appears like a maiden who was enchanted a hundred years ago, and has not been released from the spell, but is still doomed to wear the garments and the ornaments that should long ago have mouldered away with her ancestors.

The Theresien Wiese was a city of Vanity Fair for two weeks, every day crowded with a motley throng. Booths, and even structures of some solidity, rose on it as if by magic. The lottery-houses were set up early, and, to the last, attracted crowds, who could not resist the tempting display of goods and trinkets, which might be won by investing six kreuzers in a bit of paper, which might, when unrolled, contain a number. These lotteries are all authorized: some of them were for the benefit of the agricultural society; some were for the poor, and others on individual account: and they always thrive; for the German, above all others, loves to try his luck. There were streets of shanties, where various things were offered for sale besides cheese and sausages. There was a long line of booths, where images could be shot at with bird-guns; and when the shots were successful, the images went through astonishing revolutions. There was a circus, in front of which some of the spangled performers always stood beating drums and posturing, in order to entice in spectators. There were the puppet-booths, before which all day stood gaping, delighted crowds, who roared with laughter whenever the little frau beat her loutish husband about the head, and set him to tend the baby, who continued to wail, notwithstanding the man knocked its head against the doorpost. There were the great beer-restaurants, with temporary benches and tables' planted about with evergreens, always thronged with a noisy, jolly crowd. There were the fires, over which fresh fish were broiling on sticks; and, if you lingered, you saw the fish taken alive from tubs of water standing by, dressed and spitted and broiling before the wiggle was out of their tails. There were the old women, who mixed the flour and fried the brown cakes before your eyes, or cooked the fragrant sausage, and offered it piping hot.

And every restaurant and show had its band, brass or string,--a full array of red-faced fellows tooting through horns, or a sorry quartette, the fat woman with the harp, the lean man blowing himself out through the clarinet, the long-haired fellow with the flute, and the robust and thick-necked fiddler. Everywhere there was music; the air was full of the odor of cheese and cooking sausage; so that there was nothing wanting to the most complete enjoyment. The crowd surged round, jammed together, in the best possible humor. Those who could not sit at tables sat on the ground, with a link of an eatable I have already named in one hand, and a mug of beer beside them. Toward evening, the ground was strewn with these gray quart mugs, which gave as perfect evidence of the battle of the day as the cannon-balls on the sand before Fort Fisher did of the contest there. Besides this, for the amusement of the crowd, there is, every day, a wheelbarrow race, a sack race, a blindfold contest, or something of the sort, which turns out to be a very flat performance. But all the time the eating and the drinking go on, and the clatter and clink of it fill the air; so that the great object of the fair is not lost sight of.

Meantime, where is the agricultural fair and cattle-show? You must know that we do these things differently in Bavaria. On the fair-ground, there is very little to be seen of the fair. There is an inclosure where steam-engines are smoking and puffing, and threshing-machines are making a clamor; where some big church-bells hang, and where there are a few stalls for horses and cattle. But the competing horses and cattle are led before the judges elsewhere; the horses, for instance, by the royal stables in the city. I saw no such general exhibition of do mestic animals as you have at your fairs. The horses that took the prizes were of native stock, a very serviceable breed, excellent for carriage-horses, and admirable in the cavalry service. The bulls and cows seemed also native and to the manor born, and were worthy of little remark. The mechanical, vegetable, and fruit exhibition was in the great glass palace, in the city, and was very creditable in the fruit department, in the show of grapes and pears especially. The products of the dairy were less, though I saw one that I do not recollect ever to have seen in America, a landscape in butter. Inclosed in a case, it looked very much like a wood-carving. There was a Swiss cottage, a milkmaid, with cows in the foreground; there were trees, and in the rear rose rocky precipices, with chamois in the act of skipping thereon. I should think something might be done in our country in this line of the fine arts; certainly, some of the butter that is always being sold so cheap at St. Albans, when it is high everywhere else, must be strong enough to warrant the attempt. As to the other departments of the fine arts in the glass palace, I cannot give you a better idea of them than by saying that they were as well filled as the like ones in the American county fairs. There were machines for threshing, for straw-cutting, for apple-paring, and generally such a display of implements as would give one a favorable idea of Bavarian agriculture. There was an interesting exhibition of live fish, great and small, of nearly every sort, I should think, in Bavarian waters. The show in the fire-department was so antiquated, that I was convinced that the people of Munich never intend to have any fires.

The great day of the fete was Sunday, October 5 for on that day the king went out to the fair-ground, and distributed the prizes to the owners of the best horses, and, as they appeared to me, of the most ugly-colored bulls. The city was literally crowded with peasants and country people; the churches were full all the morning with devout masses, which poured into the waiting beer-houses afterward with equal zeal. By twelve o'clock, the city began to empty itself upon the Theresien meadow; and long before the time for the king to arrive--two o'clock--there were acres of people waiting for the performance to begin. The terraced bank, of which I have spoken, was taken possession of early, and held by a solid mass of people; while the fair-ground proper was packed with a swaying concourse, densest near the royal pavilion, which was erected immediately on the race-course, and opposite the bank.

At one o'clock the grand stand opposite to the royal one is taken possession of by a regiment band and by invited guests. All the space, except the race-course, is, by this time, packed with people, who watch the red and white gate at the head of the course with growing impatience. It opens to let in a regiment of infantry, which marches in and takes position. It swings, every now and then, for a solitary horseman, who gallops down the line in all the pride of mounted civic dignity, to the disgust of the crowd; or to let in a carriage, with some overdressed officer or splendid minister, who is entitled to a place in the royal pavilion. It is a people' fete, and the civic officers enjoy one day of conspicuous glory. Now a majestic person in gold lace is set down; and now one in a scarlet coat, as beautiful as a flamingo. These driblets of splendor only feed the popular impatience. Music is heard in the distance, and a procession with colored banners is seen approaching from the city.

That, like everything else that is to come, stops beyond the closed gate; and there it halts, ready to stream down before our eyes in a variegated pageant. The time goes on; the crowd gets denser, for there have been steady rivers of people pouring into the grounds for more than an hour.

The military bands play in the long interval; the peasants jabber in unintelligible dialects; the high functionaries on the royal stand are good enough to move around, and let us see how brave and majestic they are.

At last the firing of cannon announces the coming of royalty. There is a commotion in the vast crowd yonder, the eagerly watched gates swing wide, and a well-mounted company of cavalry dashes down the turf, in uniforms of light blue and gold. It is a citizens' company of butchers and bakers and candlestick-makers, which would do no discredit to the regular army. Driving close after is a four-horse carriage with two of the king's ministers; and then, at a rapid pace, six coal-black horses in silver harness, with mounted postilions, drawing a long, slender, open carriage with one seat, in which ride the king and his brother, Prince Otto, come down the way, and are pulled up in front of the pavilion; while the cannon roars, the big bells ring, all the flags of Bavaria, Prussia, and Austria, on innumerable poles, are blowing straight out, the band plays "God save the King," the people break into enthusiastic shouting, and the young king, throwing off his cloak, rises and stands in his carriage for a moment, bowing right and left before he descends. He wears to-day the simple uniform of the citizens' company which has escorted him, and is consequently more plainly and neatly dressed than any one else on the platform,--a tall (say six feet), slender, gallant-looking young fellow of three and twenty, with an open face and a graceful manner.

But, when he has arrived, things again come to a stand; and we wait for an hour, and watch the thickening of the clouds, while the king goes from this to that delighted dignitary on the stand and converses. At the end of this time, there is a movement. A white dog has got into the course, and runs up and down between the walls of people in terror, headed off by soldiers at either side of the grand stand, and finally, becoming desperate, he makes a dive for the royal pavilion. The consternation is extreme. The people cheer the dog and laugh: a white-handed official, in gold lace, and without his hat, rushes out to "shoo" the dog away, but is unsuccessful; for the animal dashes between his legs, and approaches the royal and carpeted steps. More men of rank run at him, and he is finally captured and borne away; and we all breathe freer that the danger to royalty is averted. At one o'clock six youths in white jackets, with clubs and coils of rope, had stationed themselves by the pavilion, but they did not go into action at this juncture; and I thought they rather enjoyed the activity of the great men who kept off the dog.

At length there was another stir; and the king descended from the rear of his pavilion, attended by his ministers, and moved about among the people, who made way for him, and uncovered at his approach. He spoke with one and another, and strolled about as his fancy took him. I suppose this is called mingling with the common people. After he had mingled about fifteen minutes, he returned, and took his place on the steps in front of the pavilion; and the distribution of prizes began. First the horses were led out; and their owners, approaching the king, received from his hands the diplomas, and a flag from an attendant. Most of them were peasants; and they exhibited no servility in receiving their marks of distinction, but bowed to the king as they would to any other man, and his majesty touched his cocked hat in return. Then came the prize-cattle, many of them led by women, who are as interested as their husbands in all farm matters. Everything goes off smoothly, except there is a momentary panic over a fractious bull, who plunges into the crowd; but the six white jackets are about him in an instant, and entangle him with their ropes.

This over, the gates again open, and the gay cavalcade that has been so long in sight approaches. First a band of musicians in costumes of the Middle Ages; and then a band of pages in the gayest apparel, bearing pictured banners and flags of all colors, whose silken luster would have been gorgeous in sunshine; these were followed by mounted heralds with trumpets, and after them were led the running horses entered for the race. The banners go up on the royal stand, and group themselves picturesquely; the heralds disappear at the other end of the list; and almost immediately the horses, ridden by young jockeys in stunning colors, come flying past in a general scramble. There are a dozen or more horses; but, after the first round, the race lies between two. The course is considerably over an English mile, and they make four circuits; so that the race is fully six-miles,--a very hard one. It was a run in a rain, however, which began when it did, and soon forced up the umbrellas. The vast crowd disappeared under a shed of umbrellas, of all colors,--black, green, red, blue; and the effect was very singular, especially when it moved from the field: there was then a Niagara of umbrellas. The race was soon over: it is only a peasants' race, after all; the aristocratic races of the best horses take place in May. It was over. The king's carriage was brought round, the people again shouted, the cannon roared, the six black horses reared and plunged, and away he went.

After all, says the artist, "the King of Bavaria has not much power."

"You can see," returns a gentleman who speaks English, "just how much he has: it is a six-horse power."

On other days there was horse-trotting, music production, and for several days prize-shooting. The latter was admirably conducted: the targets were placed at the foot of the bank; and opposite, I should think not more than two hundred yards off, were shooting-houses, each with a room for the register of the shots, and on each side of him closets where the shooters stand. Signal-wires run from these houses to the targets, where there are attendants who telegraph the effect of every shot. Each competitor has a little book; and he shoots at any booth he pleases, or at all, and has his shots registered. There was a continual fusillade for a couple of days; but what it all came to, I cannot tell. I can only say, that, if they shoot as steadily as they drink beer, there is no other corps of shooters that can stand before them.

INDIAN SUMMER

We are all quiet along the Isar since the October Fest; since the young king has come back from his summer castle on the Starnberg See to live in his dingy palace; since the opera has got into good working order, and the regular indoor concerts at the cafes have begun. There is no lack of amusements, with balls, theaters, and the cheap concerts, vocal and instrumental. I stepped into the West Ende Halle the other night, having first surrendered twelve kreuzers to the money-changer at the entrance,--double the usual fee, by the way. It was large and well lighted, with a gallery all round it and an orchestral platform at one end. The floor and gallery were filled with people of the most respectable class, who sat about little round tables, and drank beer. Every man was smoking a cigar; and the atmosphere was of that degree of haziness that we associate with Indian summer at home; so that through it the people in the gallery appeared like glorified objects in a heathen Pantheon, and the orchestra like men playing in a dream. Yet nobody seemed to mind it; and there was, indeed, a general air of social enjoyment and good feeling. Whether this good feeling was in process of being produced by the twelve or twenty glasses of beer which it is not unusual for a German to drink of an evening, I do not know. "I do not drink much beer now," said a German acquaintance,--"not more than four or five glasses in an evening." This is indeed moderation, when we remember that sixteen glasses of beer is only two gallons. The orchestra playing that night was Gungl's; and it performed, among other things, the whole of the celebrated Third (or Scotch) Symphony of Mendelssohn in a manner that would be greatly to the credit of orchestras that play without the aid of either smoke or beer. Concerts of this sort, generally with more popular music and a considerable dash of Wagner, in whom the Munichers believe, take place every night in several cafes; while comic singing, some of it exceedingly well done, can be heard in others. Such amusements--and nothing can be more harmless--are very cheap.

Speaking of Indian summer, the only approach to it I have seen was in the hazy atmosphere at the West Ende Halle. October outdoors has been an almost totally disagreeable month, with the exception of some days, or rather parts of days, when we have seen the sun, and experienced a mild atmosphere. At such times, I have liked to sit down on one of the empty benches in the Hof Garden, where the leaves already half cover the ground, and the dropping horse-chestnuts keep up a pattering on them. Soon the fat woman who has a fruit-stand at the gate is sure to come waddling along, her beaming face making a sort of illumination in the autumn scenery, and sit down near me. As soon as she comes, the little brown birds and the doves all fly that way, and look up expectant at her. They all know her, and expect the usual supply of bread-crumbs. Indeed, I have seen her on a still Sunday morning, when I have been sitting there waiting for the English ceremony of praying for Queen Victoria and Albert Edward to begin in the Odeon, sit for an hour, and cut up bread for her little brown flock. She sits now knitting a red stocking, the picture of content; one after another her old gossips pass that way, and stop a moment to exchange the chat of the day; or the policeman has his joke with her, and when there is nobody else to converse with, she talks to the birds. A benevolent old soul, I am sure, who in a New England village would be universally called "Aunty," and would lay all the rising generation under obligation to her for doughnuts and sweet-cake. As she rises to go away, she scrapes together a half-dozen shining chestnuts with her feet; and as she cannot possibly stoop to pick them up, she motions to a boy playing near, and smiles so happily as the urchin gathers them and runs away without even a "thank ye."

A TASTE OF ULTRAMONTANISM

If that of which every German dreams, and so few are ready to take any practical steps to attain,--German unity,--ever comes, it must ride roughshod over the Romish clergy, for one thing. Of course there are other obstacles. So long as beer is cheap, and songs of the Fatherland are set to lilting strains, will these excellent people "Ho, ho, my brothers," and "Hi, hi, my brothers," and wait for fate, in the shape of some compelling Bismarck, to drive them into anything more than the brotherhood of brown mugs of beer and Wagner's mysterious music of the future. I am not sure, by the way, that the music of Richard Wagner is not highly typical of the present (1868) state of German unity,--an undefined longing which nobody exactly understands. There are those who think they can discern in his music the same revolutionary tendency which placed the composer on the right side of a Dresden barricade in 1848, and who go so far as to believe that the liberalism of the young King of Bavaria is not a little due to his passion for the disorganizing operas of this transcendental writer. Indeed, I am not sure that any other people than Germans would not find in the repetition of the five hours of the "Meister-Singer von Nurnberg," which was given the other night at the Hof Theater, sufficient reason for revolution.

Well, what I set out to say was, that most Germans would like unity if they could be the unit. Each State would like to be the center of the consolidated system, and thus it happens that every practical step toward political unity meets a host of opponents at once. When Austria, or rather the house of Hapsburg, had a preponderance in the Diet, and it seemed, under it, possible to revive the past reality, or to realize the dream of a great German empire, it was clearly seen that Austria was a tyranny that would crush out all liberties. And now that Prussia, with its vital Protestantism and free schools, proposes to undertake the reconstruction of Germany, and make a nation where there are now only the fragmentary possibilities of a great power, why, Prussia is a military despot, whose subjects must be either soldiers or slaves, and the young emperor at Vienna is indeed another Joseph, filled with the most tender solicitude for the welfare of the chosen German people.

But to return to the clergy. While the monasteries and nunneries are going to the ground in superstition-saturated Spain; while eager workmen are demolishing the last hiding-places of monkery, and letting the daylight into places that have well kept the frightful secrets of three hundred years, and turning the ancient cloister demesne into public parks and pleasure-grounds,--the Romish priesthood here, in free Bavaria, seem to imagine that they cannot only resist the progress of events, but that they can actually bring back the owlish twilight of the Middle Ages. The reactionary party in Bavaria has, in some of the provinces, a strong majority; and its supporters and newspapers are belligerent and aggressive. A few words about the politics of Bavaria will give you a clew to the general politics of the country.

The reader of the little newspapers here in Munich finds evidence of at least three parties. There is first the radical. Its members sincerely desire a united Germany, and, of course, are friendly to Prussia, hate Napoleon, have little confidence in the Hapsburgs, like to read of uneasiness in Paris, and hail any movement that overthrows tradition and the prescriptive right of classes. If its members are Catholic, they are very mildly so; if they are Protestant, they are not enough so to harm them; and, in short, if their religious opinions are not as deep as a well, they are certainly broader than a church door. They are the party of free inquiry, liberal thought, and progress. Akin to them are what may be called the conservative liberals, the majority of whom may be Catholics in profession, but are most likely rationalists in fact; and with this party the king naturally affiliates, taking his music devoutly every Sunday morning in the Allerheiligenkirche, attached to the Residenz, and getting his religion out of Wagner; for, progressive as the youthful king is, he cannot be supposed to long for a unity which would wheel his throne off into the limbo of phantoms. The conservative liberals, therefore, while laboring for thorough internal reforms, look with little delight on the increasing strength of Prussia, and sympathize with the present liberal tendencies of Austria. Opposed to both these parties is the ultramontane, the head of which is the Romish hierarchy, and the body of which is the inert mass of ignorant peasantry, over whom the influence of the clergy seems little shaken by any of the modern moral earthquakes. Indeed I doubt if any new ideas will ever penetrate a class of peasants who still adhere to styles of costume that must have been ancient when the Turks threatened Vienna, which would be highly picturesque if they were not painfully ugly, and arrayed in which their possessors walk about in the broad light of these latter days, with entire unconsciousness that they do not belong to this age, and that their appearance is as much of an anachronism as if the figures should step out of Holbein's pictures (which Heaven forbid), or the stone images come down from the portals of the cathedral and walk about. The ultramontane party, which, so far as it is an intelligent force in modern affairs, is the Romish clergy, and nothing more, hears with aversion any hint of German unity, listens with dread to the needle-guns at Sadowa, hates Prussia in proportion as it fears her, and just now does not draw either with the Austrian Government, whose liberal tendencies are exceedingly distasteful. It relies upon that great unenlightened mass of Catholic people in Southern Germany and in Austria proper, one of whose sins is certainly not skepticism. The practical fight now in Bavaria is on the question of education; the priests being resolved to keep the schools of the people in their own control, and the liberal parties seeking to widen educational facilities and admit laymen to a share in the management of institutions of learning. Now the school visitors must all be ecclesiastics; and although their power is not to be dreaded in the cities, where teachers, like other citizens, are apt to be liberal, it gives them immense power in the rural districts. The election of the Lower House of the Bavarian parliament, whose members have a six years' tenure of office, which takes place next spring, excites uncommon interest; for the leading issue will be that of education. The little local newspapers--and every city has a small swarm of them, which are remarkable for the absence of news and an abundance of advertisements--have broken out into a style of personal controversy, which, to put it mildly, makes me, an American, feel quite at home. Both parties are very much in earnest, and both speak with a freedom that is, in itself, a very hopeful sign.

The pretensions of the ultramontane clergy are, indeed, remarkable enough to attract the attention of others besides the liberals of Bavaria. They assume an influence and an importance in the ecclesiastical profession, or rather an authority, equal to that ever asserted by the Church in its strongest days. Perhaps you will get an idea of the height of this pretension if I translate a passage which the liberal jour-

nal here takes from a sermon preached in the parish church of Ebersburg, in Ober-
Dorfen, by a priest, Herr Kooperator Anton Hiring, no longer ago than August 16,
1868. It reads: "With the power of absolution, Christ has endued the priesthood
with a might which is terrible to hell, and against which Lucifer himself cannot
stand,-a might which, indeed, reaches over into eternity, where all other earthly
powers find their limit and end,--a might, I say, which is able to break the fetters
which, for an eternity, were forged through the commission of heavy sin. Yes, further, this Power of the forgiveness of sins makes the priest, in a certain measure, a
second God; for God alone naturally can forgive sins. And yet this is not the highest
reach of the priestly might: his power reaches still higher; he compels God himself
to serve him. How so? When the priest approaches the altar, in order to bring there
the holy mass-offering, there, at that moment, lifts himself up Jesus Christ, who sits
at the right hand of the Father, upon his throne, in order to be ready for the beck of
his priests upon earth. And scarcely does the priest begin the words of consecration,
than there Christ already hovers, surrounded by the heavenly host, come down
from heaven to earth, and to the altar of sacrifice, and changes, upon the words of
the priest, the bread and wine into his holy flesh and blood, and permits himself
then to be taken up and to lie in the hands of the priest, even though the priest is the
most sinful and the most unworthy. Further, his power surpasses that of the highest archangels, and of the Queen of Heaven. Right did the holy Franciscus say, 'If I
should meet a priest and an angel at the same time, I should salute the priest first,
and then the angel; because the priest is possessed of far higher might and holiness
than the angel.'"

The radical journal calls this "ultramontane blasphemy," and, the day after
quoting it, adds a charge that must be still more annoying to the Herr Kooperator
Hiring than that of blasphemy: it accuses him of plagiarism; and, to substantiate the
charge, quotes almost the very same language from a sermon preached in 1785--In
this it is boldly claimed that "in heaven, on earth, or under the earth, there is nothing mightier than a priest, except God; and, to be exact, God himself must obey the
priest in the mass." And then, in words which I do not care to translate, the priest
is made greater than the Virgin Mary, because Christ was only born of the Virgin
once, while the priest "with five words, as often and wherever he will," can "bring
forth the Saviour of the world." So to-day keeps firm hold of the traditions of a

hundred years ago, and ultramontanism wisely defends the last citadel where the Middle Age superstition makes a stand,--the popular veneration for the clergy.

And the clergy take good care to keep up the pomps and shows even here in skeptical Munich. It was my inestimable privilege the other morning--it was All-Saints' Day--to see the archbishop in the old Frauenkirche, the ancient cathedral, where hang tattered banners that were captured from the Turks three centuries ago,--to see him seated in the choir, overlooked by saints and apostles carved in wood by some forgotten artist of the fifteenth century. I supposed he was at least an archbishop, from the retinue of priests who attended and served him, and also from his great size. When he sat down, it required a dignitary of considerable rank to put on his hat; and when he arose to speak a few precious words, the effect was visible a good many yards from where he stood. At the close of the service he went in great state down the center aisle, preceded by the gorgeous beadle--a character that is always awe-inspiring to me in these churches, being a cross between a magnificent drum-major and a verger and two persons in livery, and followed by a train of splendidly attired priests, six of whom bore up his long train of purple silk. The whole cortege was resplendent in embroidery and ermine; and as the great man swept out of my sight, and was carried on a priestly wave into his shining carriage, and the noble footman jumped up behind, and he rolled away to his dinner, I stood leaning against a pillar, and reflected if it could be possible that that religion could be anything but genuine which had so much genuine ermine. And the organ-notes, rolling down the arches, seemed to me to have a very ultramontane sound.

CHANGING QUARTERS

Perhaps it may not interest you to know how we moved, that is, changed our apartments. I did not see it mentioned in the cable dispatches, and it may not be generally known, even in Germany; but then, the cable is so occupied with relating how his Serenity this, and his Highness that, and her Loftiness the other one, went outdoors and came in again, owing to a slight superfluity of the liquid element in the atmosphere, that it has no time to notice the real movements of the people. And yet, so dry are some of these little German newspapers of news, that it is refreshing to read, now and then, that the king, on Sunday, walked out with the Duke of Hesse after dinner (one would like to know if they also had sauerkraut and sausage), and that his prospective mother-in-law, the Empress of Russia, who was here the other day, on her way home from Como, where she was nearly drowned out by the inundation, sat for an hour on Sunday night, after the opera, in the winter garden of the palace, enjoying the most easy family intercourse.

But about moving. Let me tell you that to change quarters in the face of a Munich winter, which arrives here the 1st of November, is like changing front to the enemy just before a battle; and if we had perished in the attempt, it might have been put upon our monuments, as it is upon the out-of-cannon-cast obelisk in the Karolina Platz, erected to the memory of the thirty thousand Bavarian soldiers who fell in the disastrous Russian winter campaign of Napoleon, fighting against all the interests of Germany,--"they, too, died for their Fatherland." Bavaria happened also to fight on the wrong side at Sadowa and I suppose that those who fell there also died for Fatherland: it is a way the Germans have of doing, and they mean nothing serious by it. But, as I was saying, to change quarters here as late as November is a little difficult, for the wise ones seek to get housed for the winter by October: they select the sunny apartments, get on the double windows, and store up wood. The plants are tied up in the gardens, the fountains are covered over, and the inhabitants go about in furs and the heaviest winter clothing long before we should think of doing so at home. And they are wise: the snow comes early, and, besides, a cruel fog, cold as the grave and penetrating as remorse, comes down out of the near Tyrol. One morning early in November, I looked out of the window to find snow falling, and the ground covered with it. There was dampness and frost enough in the air to make it cling to all the tree-twigs, and to take fantastic shapes on all the queer roofs and the slenderest pinnacles and most delicate architectural ornamentations. The city spires had a mysterious appearance in the gray haze; and above all, the round-topped towers of the old Frauenkirche, frosted with a little snow, loomed up more grandly than ever. When I went around to the Hof Garden, where I late had sat in the sun, and heard the brown horse-chestnuts drop on the leaves, the benches were now full of snow, and the fat and friendly fruit-woman at the gate had retired behind glass windows into a little shop, which she might well warm by her own person, if she radiated heat as readily as she used to absorb it on the warm autumn days, when I have marked her knitting in the sunshine.

But we are not moving. The first step we took was to advertise our wants in the "Neueste Nachrichten" ("Latest News ") newspaper. We desired, if possible, admission into some respectable German family, where we should be forced to speak German, and in which our society, if I may so express it, would be some compensation for our bad grammar. We wished also to live in the central part of the city,--in short, in the immediate neighborhood of all the objects of interest (which are here very much scattered), and to have pleasant rooms. In Dresden, where the people are not so rich as in Munich, and where different customs prevail, it is customary for the best people, I mean the families of university professors, for instance, to take in foreigners, and give them tolerable food and a liberal education. Here it is otherwise. Nearly all families occupy one floor of a building, renting just rooms enough for the family, so that their apartments are not elastic enough to take in strangers, even if they desire to do so. And generally they do not. Munich society is perhaps chargeable with being a little stiff and exclusive. Well, we advertised in the "Neueste Nachrichten." This is the liberal paper of Munich. It is a poorly printed, black-looking daily sheet, folded in octavo size, and containing anywhere from sixteen to thirty-four pages, more or less, as it happens to have advertisements. It sometimes will not have more than two or three pages of reading matter. There will be a scrap or two of local news, the brief telegrams taken from the official paper of the day before, a bit or two of other news, and perhaps a short and slashing editorial on the ultramontane party. The advantage of printing and folding it in such small leaves is, that the size can be varied according to the demands of advertisements or news (if the German papers ever find out what that is); so that the publisher is always giving, every day, just what it pays to give that day; and the reader has his regular quantity of reading matter, and does not have to pay for advertising space, which in journals of unchangeable form cannot always be used profitably. This little journal was started something like twenty years ago. It probably spends little for news, has only one or, at most, two editors, is crowded with advertisements, which are inserted cheap, and costs, delivered, a little over six francs a year. It circulates in the city some thirty-five thousand. There is another little paper here of the same size, but not so many leaves, called "The Daily Advertiser," with nothing but advertisements, principally of theaters, concerts, and the daily sights, and one page devoted to some prodigious yarn, generally concerning America, of which country its readers must get the most extraordinary and frightful impression. The "Nachrichten" made the fortune of its first owner, who built himself a fine house out of it, and retired to enjoy his wealth. It was recently sold for one hundred thousand guldens; and I can see that it is piling up another fortune for its present owner. The Germans, who herein show their good sense and the high state of civilization to which they have reached, are very free advertisers, going to the newspapers with all their wants, and finding in them that aid which all interests and all sorts of people, from kaiser to kerl, are compelled, in these days, to seek in the daily journal. Every German town of any size has three or four of these little journals of flying leaves, which are excellent papers in every respect, except that they look like badly printed handbills, and have very little news and no editorials worth speaking of. An exception to these in Bavaria is the "Allgerneine Zeitung" of Augsburg, which is old and immensely respectable, and is perhaps, for extent of correspondence and splendidly written editorials on a great variety of topics, excelled by no journal in Europe except the London "Times." It gives out two editions daily, the evening one about the size of the New York "Nation;" and it has all the telegraphic news. It is absurdly old-grannyish, and is malevolent in its pretended conservatism and impartiality. Yet it circulates over forty thousand copies, and goes all over Germany.

But were we not saying something about moving? The truth is, that the best German families did not respond to our appeal with that alacrity which we had no right to expect, and did not exhibit that anxiety for our society which would have been such a pleasant evidence of their appreciation of the honor done to the royal city of Munich by the selection of it as a residence during the most disagreeable months of the year by the advertising undersigned. Even the young king, whose approaching marriage to the Russian princess, one would think, might soften his heart, did nothing to win our regard, or to show that he appreciated our residence "near" his court, and, so far as I know, never read with any sort of attention our advertisement, which was composed with as much care as Goethe's "Faust," and probably with the use of more dictionaries. And this, when he has an extraordinary large Residenz, to say nothing about other outlying palaces and comfortable places to live in, in which I know there are scores of elegantly furnished apartments, which stand idle almost the year round, and might as well be let to appreciative strangers, who would accustom the rather washy and fierce frescoes on the walls to be stared at. I might have selected rooms, say on the court which looks on the exquisite bronze fountain, Perseus with the head of Medusa, a copy of the one in Florence by Benvenuto Cellini, where we could have a southern exposure. Or we might, so it would seem, have had rooms by the winter garden, where tropical plants rejoice in perennial summer, and blossom and bear fruit, while a northern winter rages without. Yet the king did not see it "by those lamps;" and I looked in vain on the gates of the Residenz for the notice so frequently seen on other houses, of apartments to let. And yet we had responses. The day after the announcement appeared, our bell ran perpetually; and we had as many letters as if we had advertised for wives innumerable. The German notes poured in upon us in a flood; each one of them containing an offer tempting enough to beguile an angel out of paradise, at least, according to our translation: they proffered us chambers that were positively overheated by the flaming sun (which, I can take my oath, only ventures a few feet above the horizon at this season), which were friendly in appearance, splendidly furnished and near to every desirable thing, and in which, usually, some American family had long resided, and experienced a content and happiness not to be felt out of Germany.

I spent some days in calling upon the worthy frauen who made these alluring offers. The visits were full of profit to the student of human nature, but profitless otherwise. I was ushered into low, dark chambers, small and dreary, looking towards the sunless north, which I was assured were delightful and even elegant. I was taken up to the top of tall houses, through a smell of cabbage that was appalling, to find empty and dreary rooms, from which I fled in fright. We were visited by so many people who had chambers to rent, that we were impressed with the idea that all Munich was to let; and yet, when we visited the places offered, we found they were only to be let alone. One of the frauen who did us the honor to call, also wrote a note, and inclosed a letter that she had just received from an American gentleman (I make no secret of it that he came from Hartford), in which were many kindly expressions for her welfare, and thanks for the aid he had received in his study of German; and yet I think her chambers are the most uninviting in the entire city. There were people who were willing to teach us German, without rooms or board; or to lodge us without giving us German or food; or to feed us, and let us starve intellectually, and lodge where we could.

But all things have an end, and so did our hunt for lodgings. I chanced one day in my walk to find, with no help from the advertisement, very nearly what we desired,--cheerful rooms in a pleasant neighborhood, where the sun comes when it comes out at all, and opposite the Glass Palace, through which the sun streams in the afternoon with a certain splendor, and almost next door to the residence and laboratory of the famous chemist, Professor Liebig; so that we can have our feelings analyzed whenever it is desirable. When we had set up our household gods, and a fire was kindled in the tall white porcelain family monument, which is called here a stove,--and which, by the way, is much more agreeable than your hideous black and air-scorching cast-iron stoves,--and seen that the feather-beds under which we were expected to lie were thick enough to roast the half of the body, and short enough to let the other half freeze, we determined to try for a season the regular German cookery, our table heretofore having been served with food cooked in the English style with only a slight German flavor. A week of the experiment was quite enough. I do not mean to say that the viands served us were not good, only that we could not make up our minds to eat them. The Germans eat a great deal of meat; and we were obliged to take meat when we preferred vegetables. Now, when a deep dish is set before you wherein are chunks of pork reposing on stewed potatoes, and another wherein a fathomless depth of sauerkraut supports coils of boiled sausage, which, considering that you are a mortal and responsible being, and have a stomach, will you choose? Herein Munich, nearly all the bread is filled with anise or caraway seed; it is possible to get, however, the best wheat bread we have eaten in Europe, and we usually have it; but one must maintain a constant vigilance against the in-roads of the fragrant seeds. Imagine, then, our despair, when one day the potato, the one vegetable we had always eaten with perfect confidence, appeared stewed with caraway seeds. This was too much for American human nature, constituted as it is. Yet the dish that finally sent us back to our ordinary and excellent way of living is one for which I have no name. It may have been compounded at different times, have been the result of many tastes or distastes: but there was, after all, a unity in it that marked it as the composition of one master artist; there was an unspeakable harmony in all its flavors and apparently ununitable substances. It looked like a ter-rapin soup, but it was not. Every dive of the spoon into its dark liquid brought up a different object,--a junk of unmistakable pork, meat of the color of roast hare, what seemed to be the neck of a goose, something in strings that resembled the rags of a silk dress, shreds of cabbage, and what I am quite willing to take my oath was a bit of Astrachan fur. If Professor Liebig wishes to add to his reputation, he could do so by analyzing this dish, and publishing the result to the world.

And, while we are speaking of eating, it may be inferred that the Germans are good eaters; and although they do not begin early, seldom taking much more than a cup of coffee before noon, they make it up by very substantial dinners and suppers. To say nothing of the extraordinary dishes of meats which the restaurants serve at night, the black bread and odorous cheese and beer which the men take on board in the course of an evening would soon wear out a cast-iron stomach in America; and yet I ought to remember the deadly pie and the corroding whisky of my native land. The restaurant life of the people is, of course, different from their home life, and perhaps an evening entertainment here is no more formidable than one in America, but it is different. Let me give you the outlines of a supper to which we were invited the other night: it certainly cannot hurt you to read about it. We sat down at eight. There were first courses of three sorts of cold meat, accompanied with two sorts of salad; the one, a composite, with a potato basis, of all imaginable things that are eaten. Beer and bread were unlimited. There was then roast hare, with some supporting dish, followed by jellies of various sorts, and ornamented plates of something that seemed unable to decide whether it would be jelly or cream; and then came assorted cake and the white wine of the Rhine and the red of Hungary. We were then surprised with a dish of fried eels, with a sauce. Then came cheese; and, to crown all, enormous, triumphal-looking loaves of cake, works of art in appearance, and delicious to the taste. We sat at the table till twelve o'clock; but you must not imagine that everybody sat still all the time, or that, appearances to the contrary notwithstanding, the principal object of the entertainment was eating. The songs that were sung in Hungarian as well as German, the poems that were recited, the burlesques of actors and acting, the imitations that were inimitable, the take-off of table-tipping and of prominent musicians, the wit and constant flow of fun, as constant as the good-humor and free hospitality, the unconstrained ease of the whole evening, these things made the real supper which one remembers when the grosser meal has vanished, as all substantial things do vanish.

CHRISTMAS TIME-MUSIC

For a month Munich has been preparing for Christmas. The shop windows have had a holiday look all December. I see one every day in which are displayed all the varieties of fruits, vegetables, and confectionery possible to be desired for a feast, done in wax,--a most dismal exhibition, and calculated to make the adjoining window, which has a little fountain and some green plants waving amidst enormous pendent sausages and pigs' heads and various disagreeable hashes of pressed meat, positively enticing. And yet there are some vegetables here that I should prefer to have in wax,--for instance, sauerkraut. The toy windows are worthy of study, and next to them the bakers'. A favorite toy of the season is a little crib, with the Holy Child, in sugar or wax, lying in it in the most uncomfortable attitude. Babies here are strapped upon pillows, or between pillows, and so tied up and wound up that they cannot move a muscle, except, perhaps, the tongue; and so, exactly like little mummies, they are carried about the street by the nurses,--poor little things, packed away so, even in the heat of summer, their little faces looking out of the down in a most pitiful fashion. The popular toy is a representation, in sugar or wax, of this period of life. Generally the toy represents twins, so swathed and bound; and, not infrequently, the bold conception of the artist carries the point of the humor so far as to introduce triplets, thus sporting with the most dreadful possibilities of life.

The German bakers are very ingenious; and if they could be convinced of this great error, that because things are good separately, they must be good in combination, the produce of their ovens would be much more eatable. As it is, they make delicious cake, and of endless variety; but they also offer us conglomerate formations that may have a scientific value, but are utterly useless to a stomach not trained in Germany. Of this sort, for the most part, is the famous Lebkuchen, a sort of gingerbread manufactured in Nurnberg, and sent all over Germany. "age does not [seem to] impair, nor custom stale its infinite variety." It is very different from our simple cake of that name, although it is usually baked in flat cards. It may contain nuts or fruit, and is spoiled by a flavor of conflicting spices. I should think it might be sold by the cord, it is piled up in such quantities; and as it grows old and is much handled, it acquires that brown, not to say dirty, familiar look, which may, for aught I know, be one of its chief recommendations. The cake, however, which prevails at this season of the year comes from the Tyrol; and as the holidays approach, it is literally piled up on the fruit-stands. It is called Klatzenbrod, and is not a bread at all, but and amalgamation of fruits and spices. It is made up into small round or oblong forms; and the top is ornamented in various patterns, with split almond meats. The color is a faded black, as if it had been left for some time in a country store; and the weight is just about that of pig-iron. I had formed a strong desire, mingled with dread, to taste it, which I was not likely to gratify,--one gets so tired of such experiments after a time--when a friend sent us a ball of it. There was no occasion to call in Professor Liebig to analyze the substance: it is a plain case. The black mass contains, cut up and pressed together, figs, citron, oranges, raisins, dates, various kinds of nuts, cinnamon, nutmeg, cloves, and I know not what other spices, together with the inevitable anise and caraway seeds. It would make an excellent cannon-ball, and would be specially fatal if it hit an enemy in the stomach. These seeds invade all dishes. The cooks seem possessed of one of the rules of whist,--in case of doubt, play a trump: in case of doubt, they always put in anise seed. It is sprinkled profusely in the blackest rye bread, it gets into all the vegetables, and even into the holiday cakes.

The extensive Maximilian Platz has suddenly grown up into booths and shanties, and looks very much like a temporary Western village. There are shops for the sale of Christmas articles, toys, cakes, and gimcracks; and there are, besides, places of amusement, if one of the sorry menageries of sick beasts with their hair half worn off can be so classed. One portion of the platz is now a lively and picturesque forest of evergreens, an extensive thicket of large and small trees, many of them trimmed with colored and gilt strips of paper. I meet in every street persons lugging home their little trees; for it must be a very poor household that cannot have its Christmas tree, on which are hung the scanty store of candy, nuts, and fruit, and the simple toys that the needy people will pinch themselves otherwise to obtain.

At this season, usually, the churches get up some representations for the children, the stable at Bethlehem, with the figures of the Virgin and Child, the wise men, and the oxen standing by. At least, the churches must be put in spick-and-span order. I confess that I like to stray into these edifices, some of them gaudy enough when they are, so to speak, off duty, when the choir is deserted, and there is only here and there a solitary worshiper at his prayers; unless, indeed, as it sometimes happens, when I fancy myself quite alone, I come by chance upon a hundred people, in some remote corner before a side chapel, where mass is going on, but so quietly that the sense of solitude in the church is not disturbed. Sometimes, when the place is left entirely to myself, and the servants who are putting it to rights and, as it were, shifting the scenes, I get a glimpse of the reality of all the pomp and parade of the services. At first I may be a little shocked with the familiar manner in which the images and statues and the gilded paraphernalia are treated, very different from the stately ceremony of the morning, when the priests are at the altar, the choir is in the organ-loft, and the people crowd nave and aisles. Then everything is sanctified and inviolate. Now, as I loiter here, the old woman sweeps and dusts about as if she were in an ordinary crockery store: the sacred things are handled without gloves. And, lo! an unclerical servant, in his shirt-sleeves, climbs up to the altar, and, taking down the silver-gilded cherubs, holds them, head down, by one fat foot, while he wipes them off with a damp cloth. To think of submitting a holy cherub to the indignity of a damp cloth!

One could never say too much about the music here. I do not mean that of the regimental bands, or the orchestras in every hall and beer-garden, or that in the churches on Sundays, both orchestral and vocal. Nearly every day, at half-past eleven, there is a parade by the Residenz, and another on the Marian Platz; and at each the bands play for half an hour. In the Loggie by the palace the music-stands can always be set out, and they are used in the platz when it does not storm; and the bands play choice overtures and selections from the operas in fine style. The bands are always preceded and followed by a great crowd as they march through the streets, people who seem to live only for this half hour in the day, and whom no mud or snow can deter from keeping up with the music. It is a little gleam of comfort in the day for the most wearied portion of the community: I mean those who have nothing to do.

But the music of which I speak is that of the conservatoire and opera. The Hof Theater, opera, and conservatoire are all under one royal direction. The latter has been recently reorganized with a new director, in accordance with the Wagner notions somewhat. The young king is cracked about Wagner, and appears to care little for other music: he brings out his operas at great expense, and it is the fashion here to like Wagner whether he is understood or not. The opera of the "Meister-Singer von Nurnberg," which was brought out last summer, occupied over five hours in the representation, which is unbearable to the Germans, who go to the opera at six o'clock or half-past, and expect to be at home before ten. His latest opera, which has not yet been produced, is founded on the Niebelungen Lied, and will take three evenings in the representation, which is almost as bad as a Chinese play. The present director of the conservatoire and opera, a Prussian, Herr von Bulow, is a friend of Wagner. There are formed here in town two parties: the Wagner and the conservative, the new and the old, the modern and classical; only the Wagnerites do not admit that their admiration of Beethoven and the older composers is less than that of the others, and so for this reason Bulow has given us more music of Beethoven than of any other composer. One thing is certain, that the royal orchestra is trained to a high state of perfection: its rendition of the grand operas and its weekly concerts in the Odeon cannot easily be surpassed. The singers are not equal to the orchestra, for Berlin and Vienna offer greater inducements; but there are people here who regard this orchestra as superlative. They say that the best orchestras in the world are in Germany; that the best in Germany is in Munich; and, therefore, you can see the inevitable deduction. We have another parallel syllogism. The greatest pianist in the world is Liszt; but then Herr Bulow is actually a better performer than Liszt; therefore you see again to what you must come. At any rate, we are quite satisfied in this provincial capital; and, if there is anywhere better music, we don't know it. Bulow's orchestra is not very large,--there are less than eighty pieces, but it is so handled and drilled, that when we hear it give one of the symphonies of Beethoven or Mendelssohn, there is little left to be desired. Bulow is a wonderful conductor, a little man, all nerve and fire, and he seems to inspire every instrument. It is worth something to see him lead an orchestra: his baton is magical; head, arms, and the whole body are in motion; he knows every note of the compositions; and the precision with which he evokes a solitary note out of a distant instrument with a jerk of his rod, or brings a wail from the concurring violins, like the moaning of a pine forest in winter, with a sweep of his arm, is most masterly. About the platform of the Odeon are the marble busts of the great composers; and while the orchestra is giving some of Beethoven's masterpieces, I like to fix my eyes on his serious and genius-full face, which seems cognizant of all that is passing, and believe that he has a posthumous satisfaction in the interpretation of his great thoughts.

The managers of the conservatoire also give vocal concerts, and there are, besides, quartette soirees; so that there are few evenings without some attraction. The opera alternates with the theater two or three times a week. The singers are, perhaps, not known in Paris and London, but some of them are not unworthy to be. There is the baritone, Herr Kindermann, who now, at the age of sixty-five, has a superb voice and manner, and has had few superiors in his time on the German stage. There is Frau Dietz, at forty-five, the best of actresses, and with a still fresh and lovely voice. There is Herr Nachbar, a tenor, who has a future; Fraulein Stehle, a soprano, young and with an uncommon voice, who enjoys a large salary, and was the favorite until another soprano, the Malinger, came and turned the heads of king and opera habitues. The resources of the Academy are, however, tolerably large; and the practice of pensioning for life the singers enables them to keep always a tolerable company. This habit of pensioning officials, as well as musicians and poets, is very agreeable to the Germans. A gentleman the other day, who expressed great surprise at the smallness of the salary of our President, said, that, of course, Andrew Johnson would receive a pension when he retired from office. I could not explain to him how comical the idea was to me; but when I think of the American people pensioning Andrew Johnson,--well, like the fictitious Yankee in "Mugby Junction," "I laff, I du."

There is some fashion, in a fudgy, quaint way, here in Munich; but it is not exhibited in dress for the opera. People go--and it is presumed the music is the attraction in ordinary apparel. They save all their dress parade for the concerts; and the hall of the Odeon is as brilliant as provincial taste can make it in toilet. The ladies also go to operas and concerts unattended by gentlemen, and are brought, and fetched away, by their servants. There is a freedom and simplicity about this which I quite like; and, besides, it leaves their husbands and brothers at liberty to spend a congenial evening in the cafes, beer-gardens, and clubs. But there is always a heavy fringe of young officers and gallants both at opera and concert, standing in the outside passages. It is cheaper to stand, and one can hear quite as well, and see more.

LOOKING FOR WARM WEATHER FROM MUNICH TO NAPLES

At all events, saith the best authority, "pray that your flight be not in winter;" and it might have added, don't go south if you desire warm weather. In January, 1869, I had a little experience of hunting after genial skies; and I will give you the benefit of it in some free running notes on my journey from Munich to Naples.

It was the middle of January, at eleven o'clock at night, that we left Munich, on a mixed railway train, choosing that time, and the slowest of slow trains, that we might make the famous Brenner Pass by daylight. It was no easy matter, at last, to pull up from the dear old city in which we had become so firmly planted, and to leave the German friends who made the place like home to us. One gets to love Germany and the Germans as he does no other country and people in Europe. There has been something so simple, honest, genuine, in our Munich life, that we look back to it with longing eyes from this land of fancy, of hand-organ music, and squalid splendor. I presume the streets are yet half the day hid in a mountain fog; but I know the superb military bands are still playing at noon in the old Marian Platz and in the Loggie by the Residenz; that at half-past six in the evening our friends are quietly stepping in to hear the opera at the Hof Theater, where everybody goes to hear the music, and nobody for display, and that they will be at home before half-past nine, and have dispatched the servant for the mugs of foaming beer; I know that they still hear every week the choice conservatoire orchestral concerts in the Odeon; and, alas that experience should force me to think of it! I have no doubt that they sip, every morning, coffee which is as much superior to that of Paris as that of Paris is to that of London; and that they eat the delicious rolls, in comparison with which those of Paris are tasteless. I wonder, in this land of wine,--and yet it must be so,--if the beer-gardens are still filled nightly; and if it could be that I should sit at a little table there, a comely lass would, before I could ask for what everybody is presumed to want, place before me a tall glass full of amber liquid, crowned with creamy foam. Are the handsome officers still sipping their coffee in the Cafe Maximilian; and, on sunny days, is the crowd of fashion still streaming down to the Isar, and the high, sightly walks and gardens beyond?

As I said, it was eleven o'clock of a clear and not very severe night; for Munich had had no snow on the ground since November. A deputation of our friends were at the station to see us off, and the farewells between the gentlemen were in the hearty fashion of the country. I know there is a prejudice with us against kissing between men; but it is only a question of taste: and the experience of anybody will tell him that the theory that this sort of salutation must necessarily be desirable between opposite sexes is a delusion. But I suppose it cannot be denied that kissing between men was invented in Germany before they wore full beards. Well, our goodbyes said, we climbed into our bare cars. There is no way of heating the German cars, except by tubes filled with hot water, which are placed under the feet, and are called foot-warmers. As we slowly moved out over the plain, we found it was cold; in an hour the foot-warmers, not hot to start with, were stone cold. You are going to sunny Italy, our friends had said: as soon as you pass the Brenner you will have sunshine and delightful weather. This thought consoled us, but did not warm our feet. The Germans, when they travel by rail, wrap themselves in furs and carry foot-sacks.

We creaked along, with many stoppings. At two o'clock we were at Rosenheim. Rosenheim is a windy place, with clear starlight, with a multitude of cars on a multiplicity of tracks, and a large, lighted refreshment-room, which has a glowing, jolly stove. We stay there an hour, toasting by the fire and drinking excellent coffee. Groups of Germans are seated at tables playing cards, smoking, and taking coffee. Other trains arrive; and huge men stalk in, from Vienna or Russia, you would say, enveloped in enormous fur overcoats, reaching to the heels, and with big fur boots coming above the knees, in which they move like elephants. Another start, and a cold ride with cooling foot-warmers, droning on to Kurfstein. It is five o'clock when we reach Kurfstein, which is also a restaurant, with a hot stove, and more Germans going on as if it were daytime; but by this time in the morning the coffee had got to be wretched.

After an hour's waiting, we dream on again, and, before we know it, come out of our cold doze into the cold dawn. Through the thick frost on the windows we see the faint outlines of mountains. Scraping away the incrustation, we find that we are in the Tyrol, high hills on all sides, no snow in the valley, a bright morning, and the snow-peaks are soon rosy in the sunrise. It is just as we expected,--little villages under the hills, and slender church spires with brick-red tops. At nine o'clock we are in Innsbruck, at the foot of the Brenner. No snow yet. It must be charming here in the summer.

During the night we have got out of Bavaria. The waiter at the restaurant wants us to pay him ninety kreuzers for our coffee, which is only six kreuzers a cup in Munich. Remembering that it takes one hundred kreuzers to make a gulden in Austria, I launch out a Bavarian gulden, and expect ten kreuzers in change. I have heard that sixty Bavarian kreuzers are equal to one hundred Austrian; but this waiter explains to me that my gulden is only good for ninety kreuzers. I, in my turn, explain to the waiter that it is better than the coffee; but we come to no understanding, and I give up, before I begin, trying to understand the Austrian currency. During the day I get my pockets full of coppers, which are very convenient to take in change, but appear to have a very slight purchasing, power in Austria even, and none at all elsewhere, and the only use for which I have found is to give to Italian beggars. One of these pieces satisfies a beggar when it drops into his hat; and then it detains him long enough in the examination of it, so that your carriage has time to get so far away that his renewed pursuit is usually unavailing.

The Brenner Pass repaid us for the pains we had taken to see it, especially as the sun shone and took the frost from our windows, and we encountered no snow on the track; and, indeed, the fall was not deep, except on the high peaks about us. Even if the engineering of the road were not so interesting, it was something to be again amidst mountains that can boast a height of ten thousand feet. After we passed the summit, and began the zigzag descent, we were on a sharp lookout for sunny Italy. I expected to lay aside my heavy overcoat, and sun myself at the first station among the vineyards. Instead of that, we bade good-by to bright sky, and plunged into a snowstorm, and, so greeted, drove down into the narrow gorges, whose steep slopes we could see were terraced to the top, and planted with vines. We could distinguish enough to know that, with the old Roman ruins, the churches and convent towers perched on the crags, and all, the scenery in summer must be finer than that of the Rhine, especially as the vineyards here are picturesque,--the vines being trained so as to hide and clothe the ground with verdure.

It was four o'clock when we reached Trent, and colder than on top of the

Brenner. As the Council, owing to the dead state of its members for now three centuries, was not in session, we made no long tarry. We went into the magnificent large refreshment-room to get warm; but it was as cold as a New England barn. I asked the proprietor if we could not get at a fire; but he insisted that the room was warm, that it was heated with a furnace, and that he burned good stove-coal, and pointed to a register high up in the wall. Seeing that I looked incredulous, he insisted that I should test it. Accordingly, I climbed upon a table, and reached up my hand. A faint warmth came out; and I gave it up, and congratulated the landlord on his furnace. But the register had no effect on the great hall. You might as well try to heat the dome of St. Peter's with a lucifer-match. At dark, Allah be praised! we reached Ala, where we went through the humbug of an Italian custom-house, and had our first glimpse of Italy in the picturesque-looking idlers in red-tasseled caps, and the jabber of a strange tongue. The snow turned into a cold rain: the foot-warmers, we having reached the sunny lands, could no longer be afforded; and we shivered along till nine o'clock, dark and rainy, brought us to Verona. We emerged from the station to find a crowd of omnibuses, carriages, drivers, runners, and people anxious to help us, all vociferating in the highest key. Amidst the usual Italian clamor about nothing, we gained our hotel omnibus, and sat there for ten minutes watching the dispute over our luggage, and serenely listening to the angry vituperations of policemen and drivers. It sounded like a revolution, but it was only the ordinary Italian way of doing things; and we were at last rattling away over the broad pavements.

Of course, we stopped at a palace turned hotel, drove into a court with double flights of high stone and marble stairways, and were hurried up to the marble-mosaic landing by an active boy, and, almost before we could ask for rooms, were shown into a suite of magnificent apartments. I had a glimpse of a garden in the rear,--flowers and plants, and a balcony up which I suppose Romeo climbed to hold that immortal love-prattle with the lovesick Juliet. Boy began to light the candles. Asked in English the price of such fine rooms. Reply in Italian. Asked in German. Reply in Italian. Asked in French, with the same result. Other servants appeared, each with a piece of baggage. Other candles were lighted. Everybody talked in chorus. The landlady--a woman of elegant manners and great command of her native tongue--appeared with a candle, and joined in the melodious confusion. What is the price of these rooms? More jabber, more servants bearing lights. We seemed suddenly to have come into an illumination and a private lunatic asylum. The land-lady and her troop grew more and more voluble and excited. Ah, then, if these rooms do not suit the signor and signoras, there are others; and we were whisked off to apartments yet grander, great suites with high, canopied beds, mirrors, and furniture that was luxurious a hundred years ago. The price? Again a torrent of Ital-ian; servants pouring in, lights flashing, our baggage arriving, until, in the tumult, hopeless of any response to our inquiry for a servant who could speak anything but Italian, and when we had decided, in despair, to hire the entire establishment, a waiter appeared who was accomplished in all languages, the row subsided, and we were left alone in our glory, and soon in welcome sleep forgot our desperate search for a warm climate.

The next day it was rainy and not warm; but the sun came out occasionally, and we drove about to see some of the sights. The first Italian town which the stranger sees he is sure to remember, the outdoor life of the people is so different from that at the North. It is the fiction in Italy that it is always summer; and the people sit in the open market-place, shiver in the open doorways, crowd into corners where the sun comes, and try to keep up the beautiful pretense. The picturesque groups of idlers and traffickers were more interesting to us than the palaces with sculptured fronts and old Roman busts, or tombs of the Scaligers, and old gates. Perhaps I ought to except the wonderful and perfect Roman amphitheater, over every foot of which a handsome boy in rags followed us, looking over every wall that we looked over, peering into every hole that we peered into, thus showing his fellowship with us, and at every pause planting himself before us, and throwing a somerset, and then extending his greasy cap for coppers, as if he knew that the modern mind ought not to dwell too exclusively on hoary antiquity without some relief.

Anxious, as I have said, to find the sunny South, we left Verona that afternoon for Florence, by way of Padua and Bologna. The ride to Padua was through a plain, at this season dreary enough, were it not, here and there, for the abrupt little hills and the snowy Alps, which were always in sight, and towards sundown and be-tween showers transcendently lovely in a purple and rosy light. But nothing now could be more desolate than the rows of unending mulberry-trees, pruned down to the stumps, through which we rode all the afternoon. I suppose they look better when the branches grow out with the tender leaves for the silk-worms, and when they are clothed with grapevines. Padua was only to us a name. There we turned south, lost mountains and the near hills, and had nothing but the mulberry flats and ditches of water, and chilly rain and mist. It grew unpleasant as we went south. At dark we were riding slowly, very slowly, for miles through a country overflowed with water, out of which trees and houses loomed up in a ghastly show. At all the stations soldiers were getting on board, shouting and singing discordantly choruses from the operas; for there was a rising at Padua, and one feared at Bologna the populace getting up insurrections against the enforcement of the grist-tax,--a tax which has made the government very unpopular, as it falls principally upon the poor.

Creeping along at such a slow rate, we reached Bologna too late for the Florence train, It was eight o'clock, and still raining. The next train went at two o'clock in the morning, and was the best one for us to take. We had supper in an inn near by, and a fair attempt at a fire in our parlor. I sat before it, and kept it as lively as possible, as the hours wore away, and tried to make believe that I was ruminating on the ancient greatness of Bologna and its famous university, some of whose chairs had been occupied by women, and upon the fact that it was on a little island in the Reno, just below here, that Octavius and Lepidus and Mark Antony formed the second Triumvirate, which put an end to what little liberty Rome had left; but in reality I was thinking of the draught on my back, and the comforts of a sunny clime. But the time came at length for starting; and in luxurious cars we finished the night very comfortably, and rode into Florence at eight in the morning to find, as we had hoped, on the other side of the Apennines, a sunny sky and balmy air.

As this is strictly a chapter of travel and weather, I may not stop to say how impressive and beautiful Florence seemed to us; how bewildering in art treasures, which one sees at a glance in the streets; or scarcely to hint how lovely were the Boboli Gardens behind the Pitti Palace, the roses, geraniums etc, in bloom, the birds singing, and all in a soft, dreamy air. The next day was not so genial; and we sped on, following our original intention of seeking the summer in winter. In order to avoid trouble with baggage and passports in Rome, we determined to book through for Naples, making the trip in about twenty hours. We started at nine o'clock in the evening, and I do not recall a more thoroughly uncomfortable journey. It grew colder as the night wore on, and we went farther south. Late in the morning we were landed at the station outside of Rome. There was a general appearance of ruin and desolation. The wind blew fiercely from the hills, and the snowflakes from the flying clouds added to the general chilliness. There was no chance to get even a cup of coffee, and we waited an hour in the cold car. If I had not been so half frozen, the consciousness that I was actually on the outskirts of the Eternal City, that I saw the Campagna and the aqueducts, that yonder were the Alban Hills, and that every foot of soil on which I looked was saturated with history, would have excited me. The sun came out here and there as we went south, and we caught some exquisite lights on the near and snowy hills; and there was something almost homelike in the miles and miles of olive orchards, that recalled the apple-trees, but for their shining silvered leaves. And yet nothing could be more desolate than the brown marshy ground, the brown hillocks, with now and then a shabby stone hut or a bit of ruin, and the flocks of sheep shivering near their corrals, and their shepherd, clad in sheepskin, as his ancestor was in the time of Romulus, leaning on his staff, with his back to the wind. Now and then a white town perched on a hillside, its houses piled above each other, relieved the eye; and I could imagine that it might be all the poets have sung of it, in the spring, though the Latin poets, I am convinced, have wonderfully imposed upon us.

To make my long story short, it happened to be colder next morning at Naples than it was in Germany. The sun shone; but the northeast wind, which the natives poetically call the Tramontane, was blowing, and the white smoke of Vesuvius rolled towards the sea. It would only last three days, it was very unusual, and all that. The next day it was colder, and the next colder yet. Snow fell, and blew about unmelted: I saw it in the streets of Pompeii.

The fountains were frozen, icicles hung from the locks of the marble statues in the Chiaia. And yet the oranges glowed like gold among their green leaves; the roses, the heliotrope, the geraniums, bloomed in all the gardens. It is the most contradictory climate. We lunched one day, sitting in our open carriage in a lemon grove, and near at hand the Lucrine Lake was half frozen over. We feasted our eyes on the brilliant light and color on the sea, and the lovely outlined mountains round the shore, and waited for a change of wind. The Neapolitans declare that they have not had such weather in twenty years. It is scarcely one's ideal of balmy Italy.

Before the weather changed, I began to feel in this great Naples, with its roaring population of over half a million, very much like the sailor I saw at the American consul's, who applied for help to be sent home, claiming to be an American. He was an oratorical bummer, and told his story with all the dignity and elevated language of an old Roman. He had been cast away in London. How cast away? Oh! it was all along of a boarding-house. And then he found himself shipped on an English vessel, and he had lost his discharge-papers; and "Listen, your honor," said he, calmly extending his right hand, "here I am cast away on this desolate island with nothing before me but wind and weather."

RAVENNA
A DEAD CITY

Ravenna is so remote from the route of general travel in Italy, that I am certain you can have no late news from there, nor can I bring you anything much later than the sixth century. Yet, if you were to see Ravenna, you would say that that is late enough. I am surprised that a city which contains the most interesting early Christian churches and mosaics, is the richest in undisturbed specimens of early Christian art, and contains the only monuments of Roman emperors still in their original positions, should be so seldom visited. Ravenna has been dead for some centuries; and because nobody has cared to bury it, its ancient monuments are yet above ground. Grass grows in its wide streets, and its houses stand in a sleepy, vacant contemplation of each other: the wind must like to mourn about its silent squares. The waves of the Adriatic once brought the commerce of the East to its wharves; but the deposits of the Po and the tides have, in process of time, made it an inland town, and the sea is four miles away.

In the time of Augustus, Ravenna was a favorite Roman port and harbor for fleets of war and merchandise. There Theodoric, the great king of the Goths, set up his palace, and there is his enormous mausoleum. As early as A. D. 44 it became an episcopal see, with St. Apollinaris, a disciple of St. Peter, for its bishop. There some of the later Roman emperors fixed their residences, and there they repose. In and about it revolved the adventurous life of Galla Placidia, a woman of considerable talent and no principle, the daughter of Theodosius (the great Theodosius, who subdued the Arian heresy, the first emperor baptized in the true faith of the Trinity, the last who had a spark of genius), the sister of one emperor, and the mother of another,--twice a slave, once a queen, and once an empress; and she, too, rests there in the great mausoleum builded for her. There, also, lies Dante, in his tomb "by the upbraiding shore;" rejected once of ungrateful Florence, and forever after passionately longed for. There, in one of the earliest Christian churches in existence, are the fine mosaics of the Emperor Justinian and Theodora, the handsome courtesan whom he raised to the dignity and luxury of an empress on his throne in Constantinople. There is the famous forest of pines, stretching--unbroken twenty miles down the coast to Rimini, in whose cool and breezy glades Dante and Boccaccio walked and meditated, which Dryden has commemorated, and Byron has invested with the fascination of his genius; and under the whispering boughs of which moved the glittering cavalcade which fetched the bride to Rimini,--the fair Francesca, whose sinful confession Dante heard in hell.

We went down to Ravenna from Bologna one afternoon, through a country level and rich, riding along toward hazy evening, the land getting flatter as we proceeded (you know, there is a difference between level and flat), through interminable mulberry-trees and vines, and fields with the tender green of spring, with church spires in the rosy horizon; on till the meadows became marshes, in which millions of frogs sang the overture of the opening year. Our arrival, I have reason to believe, was an event in the old town. We had a crowd of moldy loafers to witness it at the station, not one of whom had ambition enough to work to earn a sou by lifting our traveling-bags. We had our hotel to ourselves, and wished that anybody else had it. The rival house was quite aware of our advent, and watched us with jealous eyes; and we, in turn, looked wistfully at it, for our own food was so scarce that, as an old traveler says, we feared that we shouldn't have enough, until we saw it on the table, when its quality made it appear too much. The next morning, when I sallied out to hire a conveyance, I was an object of interest to the entire population, who seemed to think it very odd that any one should walk about and explore the quiet streets. If I were to describe Ravenna, I should say that it is as flat as Holland and as lively as New London. There are broad streets, with high houses, that once were handsome, palaces that were once the abode of luxury, gardens that still bloom, and churches by the score. It is an open gate through which one walks unchallenged into the past, with little to break the association with the early Christian ages, their monuments undimmed by time, untouched by restoration and innovation, the whole struck with ecclesiastical death. With all that we saw that day,--churches, basilicas, mosaics, statues, mausoleums,--I will not burden these pages; but I will set down is enough to give you the local color, and to recall some of the most interesting passages in Christian history in this out-of-the-way city on the Adriatic.

Our first pilgrimage was to the Church of St. Apollinare Nuova; but why it is called new I do not know, as Theodoric built it for an Arian cathedral in about the year 500. It is a noble interior, having twenty-four marble columns of gray Cippolino, brought from Constantinople, with composite capitals, on each of which is an impost with Latin crosses sculptured on it. These columns support round arches, which divide the nave from the aisles, and on the whole length of the wall of the nave so supported are superb mosaics, full-length figures, in colors as fresh as if done yesterday, though they were executed thirteen hundred years ago. The mosaic on the left side--which is, perhaps, the finest one of the period in existence--is interesting on another account. It represents the city of Classis, with sea and ships, and a long procession of twenty-two virgins presenting offerings to the Virgin and Child, seated on a throne. The Virgin is surrounded by angels, and has a glory round her head, which shows that homage is being paid to her. It has been supposed, from the early monuments of Christian art, that the worship of the Virgin is of comparatively recent origin; but this mosaic would go to show that Mariolatry was established before the end of the sixth century. Near this church is part of the front of the palace of Theodoric, in which the Exarchs and Lombard kings subsequently resided. Its treasures and marbles Charlemagne carried off to Germany.

DOWN TO THE PINETA

We drove three miles beyond the city, to the Church of St. Apollinare in Classe, a lonely edifice in a waste of marsh, a grand old basilica, a purer specimen of Christian art than Rome or any other Italian town can boast. Just outside the city gate stands a Greek cross on a small fluted column, which marks the site of the once magnificent Basilica of St. Laurentius, which was demolished in the sixteenth century, its stone built into a new church in town, and its rich marbles carried to all-absorbing Rome. It was the last relic of the old port of Caesarea, famous since the time of Augustus. A marble column on a green meadow is all that remains of a once prosperous city. Our road lay through the marshy plain, across an elevated bridge over the sluggish united stream of the Ronco and Montone, from which there is a wide view, including the Pineta (or Pine Forest), the Church of St. Apollinare in the midst of rice-fields and marshes, and on a clear day the Alps and Apennines.

I can imagine nothing more desolate than this solitary church, or the approach to it. Laborers were busy spading up the heavy, wet ground, or digging trenches, which instantly filled with water, for the whole country was afloat. The frogs greeted us with clamorous chorus out of their slimy pools, and the mosquitoes attacked us as we rode along. I noticed about on the bogs, wherever they could find standing-room, half-naked wretches, with long spears, having several prongs like tridents, which they thrust into the grass and shallow water. Calling one of them to us, we found that his business was fishing, and that he forked out very fat and edible-looking fish with his trident. Shaggy, undersized horses were wading in the water, nipping off the thin spears of grass. Close to the church is a rickety farmhouse. If I lived there, I would as lief be a fish as a horse.

The interior of this primitive old basilica is lofty and imposing, with twenty-four handsome columns of the gray Cippolino marble, and an elevated high altar and tribune, decorated with splendid mosaics of the sixth century,--biblical subjects, in all the stiff faithfulness of the holy old times. The marble floor is green and damp and slippery. Under the tribune is the crypt, where the body of St. Apollinaris used to lie (it is now under the high altar above); and as I desired to see where he used to rest, I walked in. I also walked into about six inches of water, in the dim, irreligious light; and so made a cold-water Baptist devotee of myself. In the side aisles are wonderful old sarcophagi, containing the ashes of archbishops of Ravenna, so old that the owners' names are forgotten of two of them, which shows that a man may build a tomb more enduring than his memory. The sculptured bas-reliefs are very interesting, being early Christian emblems and curious devices,--symbols of sheep, palms, peacocks, crosses, and the four rivers of Paradise flowing down in stony streams from stony sources, and monograms, and pious rebuses. At the entrance of the crypt is an open stone book, called the Breviary of Gregory the Great. Detached from the church is the Bell Tower, a circular campanile of a sort peculiar to Ravenna, which adds to the picturesqueness of the pile, and suggests the notion that it is a mast unshipped from its vessel, the church, which consequently stands there water-logged, with no power to catch any wind, of doctrine or other, and move. I forgot to say that the basilica was launched in the year 534.

A little weary with the good but damp old Christians, we ordered our driver to continue across the marsh to the Pineta, whose dark fringe bounded all our horizon toward the Adriatic. It is the largest unbroken forest in Italy, and by all odds the most poetic in itself and its associations. It is twenty-five miles long, and from one to three in breadth, a free growth of stately pines, whose boughs are full of music and sweet odors,--a succession of lovely glades and avenues, with miles and miles of drives over the springy turf. At the point where we entered is a farmhouse. Laborers had been gathering the cones, which were heaped up in immense windrows, hundreds of feet in length. Boys and men were busy pounding out the seeds from the cones. The latter are used for fuel, and the former are pressed for their oil. They are also eaten: we have often had them served at hotel tables, and found them rather tasteless, but not unpleasant. The turf, as we drove into the recesses of the forest, was thickly covered with wild flowers, of many colors and delicate forms; but we liked best the violets, for they reminded us of home, though the driver seemed to think them less valuable than the seeds of the pine-cones. A lovely day and history and romance united to fascinate us with the place. We were driving over the spot where, eighteen centuries ago, the Roman fleet used to ride at anchor. Here, it is certain, the gloomy spirit of Dante found congenial place for meditation, and the gay Boccaccio material for fiction. Here for hours, day after day, Byron used to gallop his horse, giving vent to that restless impatience which could not all escape from his fiery pen, hearing those voices of a past and dead Italy which he, more truthfully and pathetically than any other poet, has put into living verse. The driver pointed out what is called Byron's Path, where he was wont to ride. Everybody here, indeed, knows of Byron; and I think his memory is more secure than any saint of them all in their stone boxes, partly because his poetry has celebrated the region, perhaps rather from the perpetuated tradition of his generosity. No foreigner was ever so popular as he while he lived at Ravenna. At least, the people say so now, since they find it so profitable to keep his memory alive and to point out his haunts. The Italians, to be sure, know how to make capital out of poets and heroes, and are quick to learn the curiosity of foreigners, and to gratify it for a compensation. But the evident esteem in which Byron's memory is held in the Armenian monastery of St. Lazzaro, at Venice, must be otherwise accounted for. The monks keep his library-room and table as they were when he wrote there, and like to show his portrait, and tell of his quick mastery of the difficult Armenian tongue. We have a notable example of a Person who became a monk when he was sick; but Byron accomplished too much work during the few months he was on the Island of St. Lazzaro, both in original composition and in translating English into Armenian, for one physically ruined and broken.

DANTE AND BYRON

The pilgrim to Ravenna, who has any idea of what is due to the genius of Dante, will be disappointed when he approaches his tomb. Its situation is in a not very conspicuous corner, at the foot of a narrow street, bearing the poet's name, and beside the Church of San Francisco, which is interesting as containing the tombs of the Polenta family, whose hospitality to the wandering exile has rescued their names from oblivion. Opposite the tomb is the shabby old brick house of the Po-lentas, where Dante passed many years of his life. It is tenanted now by all sorts of people, and a dirty carriage-shop in the courtyard kills the poetry of it. Dante died in 1321, and was at first buried in the neighboring church; but this tomb, since twice renewed, was erected, and his body removed here, in 1482. It is a square stuccoed structure, stained light green, and covered by a dome,--a tasteless monument, embellished with stucco medallions, inside, of the poet, of Virgil, of Brunetto Latini, the poet's master, and of his patron, Guido da Polenta. On the sarcophagus is the epitaph, composed in Latin by Dante himself, who seems to have thought, with Shakespeare, that for a poet to make his own epitaph was the safest thing to do. Notwithstanding the mean appearance of this sepulcher, there is none in all the soil of Italy that the traveler from America will visit with deeper interest. Near by is the house where Byron first resided in Ravenna, as a tablet records.

The people here preserve all the memorials of Byron; and, I should judge, hold his memory in something like affection. The Palace Guiccioli, in which he subsequently resided, is in another part of the town. He spent over two years in Ravenna, and said he preferred it to any place in Italy. Why I cannot see, unless it was remote from the route of travel, and the desolation of it was congenial to him. Doubtless he loved these wide, marshy expanses on the Adriatic, and especially the great forest of pines on its shore; but Byron was apt to be governed in his choice of a residence by the woman with whom he was intimate. The palace was certainly pleasanter than his gloomy house in the Strada di Porta Sisi, and the society of the Countess Guiccioli was rather a stimulus than otherwise to his literary activity. At her suggestion he wrote the "Prophecy of Dante;" and the translation of "Francesca da Rimini" was "executed at Ravenna, where, five centuries before, and in the very house in which the unfortunate lady was born, Dante's poem had been composed." Some of his finest poems were also produced here, poems for which Venice is as grateful as Ravenna. Here he wrote "Marino Faliero," "The Two Foscari," "Morganti Maggiore," "Sardanapalus," "The Blues," "The fifth canto of Don Juan," "Cain," "Heaven and Earth," and "The Vision of Judgment." I looked in at the court of the palace,--a pleasant, quiet place,--where he used to work, and tried to guess which were the windows of his apartments. The sun was shining brightly, and a bird was singing in the court; but there was no other sign of life, nor anything to remind one of the profligate genius who was so long a guest here.

RESTING-PLACE OF CAESARS--PICTURE OF A BEAUTIFUL HERETIC

Very different from the tomb of Dante, and different in the associations it awakes, is the Rotunda or Mausoleum of Theodoric the Goth, outside the Porta Serrata, whose daughter, Amalasuntha, as it is supposed, about the year 530, erected this imposing structure as a certain place "to keep his memory whole and mummy hid" for ever. But the Goth had not lain in it long before Arianism went out of fashion quite, and the zealous Roman Catholics despoiled his costly sleeping-place, and scattered his ashes abroad. I do not know that any dead person has lived in it since.

The tomb is still a very solid affair,--a rotunda built of solid blocks of limestone, and resting on a ten-sided base, each side having a recess surmounted by an arch. The upper story is also decagonal, and is reached by a flight of modern stone steps. The roof is composed of a single block of Istrian limestone, scooped out like a shallow bowl inside; and, being the biggest roof-stone I ever saw, I will give you the dimensions. It is thirty-six feet in diameter, hollowed out to the depth of ten feet, four feet thick at the center, and two feet nine inches at the edges, and is estimated to weigh two hundred tons. Amalasuntha must have had help in getting it up there. The lower story is partly under water. The green grass of the inclosure in which it stands is damp enough for frogs. An old woman opened the iron gate to let us in. Whether she was any relation of the ancient proprietor, I did not inquire; but she had so much trouble in, turning the key in the rusty lock, and letting us in, that I presume we were the only visitors she has had for some centuries.

Old women abound in Ravenna; at least, she was not young who showed us the mausoleum of Galla Placidia. Placidia was also prudent and foreseeing, and built this once magnificent sepulcher for her own occupation. It is in the form of a Latin cross, forty-six feet in length by about forty in width. The floor is paved with rich marbles; the cupola is covered with mosaics of the time of the empress; and in the arch over the door is a fine representation of the Good Shepherd. Behind the altar is the massive sarcophagus of marble (its cover of silver plates was long ago torn off) in which are literally the ashes of the empress. She was immured in it as a mummy, in a sitting position, clothed in imperial robes; and there the ghastly corpse sat in a cypress-wood chair, to be looked at by anybody who chose to peep through the aperture, for more than eleven hundred years, till one day, in 1577, some children introduced a lighted candle, perhaps out of compassion for her who sat so long in darkness, when her clothes caught fire, and she was burned up,--a warning to all children not to play with a dead and dry empress. In this resting-place are also the tombs of Honorius II., her brother, of Constantius III., her second husband, and of Honoria, her daughter.

There are no other undisturbed tombs of the Caesars in existence. Hers is almost the last, and the very small last, of a great succession. What thoughts of a great empire in ruins do not force themselves on one in the confined walls of this little chamber! What a woman was she whose ashes lie there! She saw and aided the ruin of the empire; but it may be said of her, that her vices were greater than her misfortunes. And what a story is her life! Born to the purple, educated in the palace at Constantinople, accomplished but not handsome, at the age of twenty she was in Rome when Alaric besieged it. Carried off captive by the Goths, she became the not unwilling object of the passion of King Adolphus, who at length married her at Narbonne. At the nuptials the king, in a Roman habit, occupied a seat lower than hers, while she sat on a throne habited as a Roman empress, and received homage. Fifty handsome youths bore to her in each hand a dish of gold, one filled with coin, and the other with precious stones,--a small part only, these hundred vessels of treasure, of the spoils the Goths brought from her country. When Adolphus, who never abated his fondness for his Roman bride, was assassinated at Barcelona, she was treated like a slave by his assassins, and driven twelve miles on foot before the horse of his murderer. Ransomed at length for six hundred thousand measures of wheat by her brother Honorius, who handed her over struggling to Constantius, one of his generals. But, once married, her reluctance ceased; and she set herself to advance the interests of herself and husband, ruling him as she had done the first one. Her purpose was accomplished when he was declared joint emperor with Honorius. He died shortly after; and scandalous stories of her intimacy with her brother caused her removal to Constantinople; but she came back again, and reigned long as the regent of her son, Valentinian III.,--a feeble youth, who never grew to have either passions or talents, and was very likely, as was said, enervated by his mother in dissolute indulgence, so that she might be supreme. But she died at Rome in 450, much praised for her orthodoxy and her devotion to the Trinity. And there was her daughter, Honoria, who ran off with a chamberlain, and afterward offered to throw herself into the arms of Attila who wouldn't take her as a gift at first, but afterward demanded her, and fought to win her and her supposed inheritance. But they were a bad lot altogether; and it is no credit to a Christian of the nineteenth century to stay in this tomb so long.

Near this mausoleum is the magnificent Basilica of St. Vitale, built in the reign of Justinian, and consecrated in 547, I was interested to see it because it was erected in confessed imitation of St. Sophia at Constantinople, is in the octagonal form, and has all the accessories of Eastern splendor, according to the architectural authorities. Its effect is really rich and splendid; and it rather dazzled us with its maze of pillars, its upper and lower columns, its galleries, complicated capitals, arches on arches, and Byzantine intricacies. To the student of the very early ecclesiastical art, it must be an object of more interest than even of wonder. But what I cared most to see were the mosaics in the choir, executed in the time of Justinian, and as fresh and beautiful as on the day they were made. The mosaics and the exquisite arabesques on the roof of the choir, taken together, are certainly unequaled by any other early church decoration I have seen; and they are as interesting as they are beautiful. Any description of them is impossible; but mention may be made of two characteristic groups, remarkable for execution, and having yet a deeper interest.

In one compartment of the tribune is the figure of the Emperor Justinian, holding a vase with consecrated offerings, and surrounded by courtiers and soldiers. Opposite is the figure of the Empress Theodora, holding a similar vase, and attended by ladies of her court. There is a refinement and an elegance about the empress, a grace and sweet dignity, that is fascinating. This is royalty,--stately and cold perhaps: even the mouth may be a little cruel, I begin to perceive, as I think of her; but she wears the purple by divine right. I have not seen on any walls any figure walking out of history so captivating as this lady, who would seem to have been worthy of apotheosis in a Christian edifice. Can there be any doubt that this lovely woman was orthodox? She, also, has a story, which you doubtless have been recalling as you read. Is it worth while to repeat even its outlines? This charming regal woman was the daughter of the keeper of the bears in the circus at Constantinople; and she early went upon the stage as a pantomimist and buffoon. She was beautiful, with regular features, a little pale, but with a tinge of natural color, vivacious eyes, and an easy motion that displayed to advantage the graces of her small but elegant figure. I can see all that in the mosaic. But she sold her charms to whoever cared to buy them in Constantinople; she led a life of dissipation that cannot be even hinted at in these days; she went off to Egypt as the concubine of a general; was deserted, and destitute even to misery in Cairo; wandered about a vagabond in many Eastern cities, and won the reputation everywhere of the most beautiful courtesan of her time; reappeared in Constantinople; and, having, it is said, a vision of her future, suddenly took to a pretension of virtue and plain sewing; contrived to gain the notice of Justinian, to inflame his passions as she did those of all the world besides, to captivate him into first an alliance, and at length a marriage. The emperor raised her to an equal seat with himself on his throne; and she was worshiped as empress in that city where she had been admired as harlot. And on the throne she was a wise woman, courageous and chaste; and had her palaces on the Bosphorus; and took good care of her beauty, and indulged in the pleasures of a good table; had ministers who kissed her feet; a crowd of women and eunuchs in her secret chambers, whose passions she indulged; was avaricious and sometimes cruel; and founded a convent for the irreclaimably bad of her own sex, some of whom liked it, and some of whom threw themselves into the sea in despair; and when she died was an irreparable loss to her emperor. So that it seems to me it is a pity that the historian should say that she was devout, but a little heretic.

A HIGH DAY IN ROME
PALM SUNDAY IN ST. PETER'S

The splendid and tiresome ceremonies of Holy Week set in; also the rain, which held up for two days. Rome without the sun, and with rain and the bone-penetrating damp cold of the season, is a wretched place. Squalor and ruins and cheap splendor need the sun; the galleries need it; the black old masters in the dark corners of the gaudy churches need it; I think scarcely anything of a cardinal's big, blazing footman, unless the sun shines on him, and radiates from his broad back and his splendid calves; the models, who get up in theatrical costumes, and get put into pictures, and pass the world over for Roman peasants (and beautiful many of them are), can't sit on the Spanish Stairs in indolent pose when it rains; the streets are slimy and horrible; the carriages try to run over you, and stand a very good chance of succeeding, where there are no sidewalks, and you are limping along on the slippery round cobble-stones; you can't get into the country, which is the best part of Rome: but when the sun shines all this is changed; the dear old dirty town exercises, its fascinations on you then, and you speedily forget your recent misery.

Holy Week is a vexation to most people. All the world crowds here to see its exhibitions and theatrical shows, and works hard to catch a glimpse of them, and is tired out, if not disgusted, at the end. The things to see and hear are Palm Sunday in St. Peter's; singing of the Miserere by the pope's choir on Wednesday, Thursday, and Friday in the Sistine Chapel; washing of the pilgrims' feet in a chapel of St. Peter's, and serving the apostles at table by the pope on Thursday, with a papal benediction from the balcony afterwards; Easter Sunday, with the illumination of St. Peter's in the evening; and fireworks (this year in front of St. Peter's in Montorio) Monday evening. Raised seats are built up about the high altar under the dome in St. Peter's, which will accommodate a thousand, and perhaps more, ladies; and for these tickets are issued without numbers, and for twice as many as they will seat. Gentlemen who are in evening dress are admitted to stand in the reserved places inside the lines of soldiers. For the Miserere in the Sistine Chapel tickets are also issued. As there is only room for about four hundred ladies, and a thousand and more tickets are given out, you may imagine the scramble. Ladies go for hours before the singing begins, and make a grand rush when the doors are open. I do not know any sight so unseemly and cruel as a crowd of women intent on getting in to such a ceremony: they are perfectly rude and unmerciful to each other. They push and trample one another under foot; veils and dresses are torn; ladies faint away in the scrimmage, and only the strongest and most unscrupulous get in. I have heard some say, who have been in the pellmell, that, not content with elbowing and pushing and pounding, some women even stick pins into those who are in the way. I hope this latter is not true; but it is certain that the conduct of most of the women is brutal. A weak or modest or timid woman stands no more chance than she would in a herd of infuriated Campagna cattle. The same scenes are enacted in the efforts to see the pope wash feet, and serve at the table. For the possession of the seats under the dome on Palm Sunday and Easter there is a like crush. The ceremonies do not begin until half-past nine; but ladies go between five and six o'clock in the morning, and when the passages are open they make a grand rush. The seats, except those saved for the nobility, are soon all taken, and the ladies who come after seven are lucky if they can get within the charmed circle, and find a spot to sit down on a campstool. They can then see only a part of the proceedings, and have a weary, exhausting time of it for hours. This year Rome is more crowded than ever before. There are American ladies enough to fill all the reserved places; and I fear they are energetic enough to get their share of them.

It rained Sunday; but there was a steady stream of people and carriages all the morning pouring over the Bridge of St. Angelo, and discharging into the piazza of

St. Peter's. It was after nine when I arrived on the ground. There was a crowd of carriages under the colonnades, and a heavy fringe in front of them; but the hundreds of people moving over the piazza, and up the steps to the entrances, made only the impression of dozens in the vast space. I do not know if there are people enough in Rome to fill St. Peter's; certainly there was no appearance of a crowd as we entered, although they had been pouring in all the morning, and still thronged the doors. I heard a traveler say that he followed ten thousand soldiers into the church, and then lost them from sight: they disappeared in the side chapels. He did not make his affidavit as to the number of soldiers. The interior area of the building is not much greater than the square of St. Mark in Venice. To go into the great edifice is almost like going outdoors. Lines of soldiers kept a wide passage clear from the front door away down to the high altar; and there was a good mass of spectators on the outside. The tribunes for the ladies, built up under the dome, were of course, filled with masses of ladies in solemn black; and there was more or less of a press of people surging about in that vicinity. Thousands of people were also roaming about in the great spaces of the edifice; but there was nowhere else anything like a crowd. It had very much the appearance of a large fair-ground, with little crowds about favorite booths. Gentlemen in dress-coats were admitted to the circle under the dome. The pope's choir was stationed in a gallery there opposite the high altar. Back of the altar was a wide space for the dignitaries; seats were there, also, for ambassadors and those born to the purple; and the pope's seat was on a raised dais at the end. Outsiders could see nothing of what went on within there; and the ladies under the dome could only partially see, in the seats they had fought so gallantly to obtain.

St. Peter's is a good place for grand processions and ceremonies; but it is a poor one for viewing them. A procession which moves down the nave is hidden by the soldiers who stand on either side, or is visible only by sections as it passes: there is no good place to get the grand effect of the masses of color, and the total of the gorgeous pageantry. I should like to see the display upon a grand stage, and enjoy it in a coup d'oeil. It is a fine study of color and effect, and the groupings are admirable; but the whole affair is nearly lost to the mass of spectators. It must be a sublime feeling to one in the procession to walk about in such monstrous fine clothes; but what would his emotions be if more people could see him! The grand altar stuck up under the dome not only breaks the effect of what would be the fine sweep of the nave back to the apse, but it cuts off all view of the celebration of the mass behind it, and, in effect, reduces what should be the great point of display in the church to a mere chapel. And when you add to that the temporary tribunes erected under the dome for seating the ladies, the entire nave is shut off from a view of the gorgeous ceremony of high mass. The effect would be incomparable if one could stand in the door, or anywhere in the nave, and, as in other churches, look down to the end upon a great platform, with the high altar and all the sublime spectacle in full view, with the blaze of candles and the clouds of incense rising in the distance.

At half-past nine the great doors opened, and the procession began, in slow and stately moving fashion, to enter. One saw a throng of ecclesiastics in robes and ermine; the white plumes of the Guard Noble; the pages and chamberlains in scarlet; other pages, or what not, in black short-clothes, short swords, gold chains, cloak hanging from the shoulder, and stiff white ruffs; thirty-six cardinals in violet robes, with high miter-shaped white silk hats, that looked not unlike the pasteboard "trainer-caps" that boys wear when they play soldier; crucifixes, and a blazoned banner here and there; and, at last, the pope, in his red chair, borne on the shoulders of red lackeys, heaving along in a sea-sicky motion, clad in scarlet and gold, with a silver miter on his head, feebly making the papal benediction with two upraised fingers, and moving his lips in blessing. As the pope came in, a supplementary choir of men and soprano hybrids, stationed near the door, set up a high, welcoming song, or chant, which echoed rather finely through the building. All the music of the day is vocal.

The procession having reached its destination, and disappeared behind the altar of the dome, the pope dismounted, and took his seat on his throne. The blessing of the palms began, the cardinals first approaching, and afterwards the members of the diplomatic corps, the archbishops and bishops, the heads of the religious orders, and such private persons as have had permission to do so. I had previously seen the palms carried in by servants in great baskets. It is, perhaps, not necessary to say that they are not the poetical green waving palms, but stiff sort of wands, woven out of dry, yellow, split palm-leaves, sometimes four or five feet in length, braided into the semblance of a crown on top,--a kind of rough basket-work. The palms having been blessed, a procession was again formed down the nave and out the door, all in it "carrying palms in their hands," the yellow color of which added a new element of picturesqueness to the splendid pageant. The pope was carried as before, and bore in his hand a short braided palm, with gold woven in, flowers added, and the monogram "I. H. S." worked in the top. It is the pope's custom to give this away when the ceremony is over. Last year he presented it to an American lady, whose devotion attracted him; this year I saw it go away in a gilded coach in the hands of an ecclesiastic. The procession disappeared through the great portal into the vestibule, and the door closed. In a moment somebody knocked three times on the door: it opened, and the procession returned, and moved again to the rear of the altar, the singers marching with it and chanting. The cardinals then changed their violet for scarlet robes; and high mass, for an hour, was celebrated by a cardinal priest: and I was told that it was the pope's voice that we heard, high and clear, singing the passion. The choir made the responses, and performed at intervals. The singing was not without a certain power; indeed, it was marvelous how some of the voices really filled the vast spaces of the edifice, and the choruses rolled in solemn waves of sound through the arches. The singing, with the male sopranos, is not to my taste; but it cannot be denied that it had a wild and strange effect.

While this was going on behind the altar, the people outside were wandering about, looking at each other, and on the watch not to miss any of the shows of the day. People were talking, chattering, and greeting each other as they might do in the street. Here and there somebody was kneeling on the pavement, unheeding the passing throng. At several of the chapels, services were being conducted; and there was a large congregation, an ordinary church full, about each of them. But the most of those present seemed to regard it as a spectacle only; and as a display of dress, costumes, and nationalities it was almost unsurpassed. There are few more wonderful sights in this world than an Englishwoman in what she considers full dress. An English dandy is also a pleasing object. For my part, as I have hinted, I like almost as well as anything the big footmen,--those in scarlet breeches and blue gold-embroidered coats. I stood in front of one of the fine creations for some time, and contemplated him as one does the Farnese Hercules. One likes to see to what a splendor his species can come, even if the brains have all run down into the calves of the legs. There were also the pages, the officers of the pope's household, in costumes of the Middle Ages; the pope's Swiss guard in the showy harlequin uniform designed by Michael Angelo; the foot-soldiers in white short-clothes, which threatened to burst, and let them fly into pieces; there were fine ladies and gentlemen, loafers and loungers, from every civilized country, jabbering in all the languages; there were beggars in rags, and boors in coats so patched that there was probably none of the original material left; there were groups of peasants from the Campagna, the men in short jackets and sheepskin breeches with the wool side out, the women with gay-colored folded cloths on their heads, and coarse woolen gowns; a squad of wild-looking Spanish gypsies, burning-eyed, olive-skinned, hair long, black, crinkled, and greasy, as wild in raiment as in face; priests and friars, Zouaves in jaunty light gray and scarlet; rags and velvets, silks and serge cloths,--a cosmopolitan gathering poured into the world's great place of meeting,--a fine religious Vanity Fair on Sunday.

There came an impressive moment in all this confusion, a point of august solemnity. Up to that instant, what with chanting and singing the many services, and the noise of talking and walking, there was a wild babel. But at the stroke of the bell and the elevation of the Host, down went the muskets of the guard with one clang on the marble; the soldiers kneeled; the multitude in the nave, in the aisles, at all the chapels, kneeled; and for a minute in that vast edifice there was perfect stillness: if the whole great concourse had been swept from the earth, the spot where it lately was could not have been more silent. And then the military order went down the line, the soldiers rose, the crowd rose, and the mass and the hum went on.

It was all over before one; and the pope was borne out again, and the vast crowd began to discharge itself. But it was a long time before the carriages were all filled and rolled off. I stood for a half hour watching the stream go by,--the pompous soldiers, the peasants and citizens, the dazzling equipages, and jaded, exhausted women in black, who had sat or stood half a day under the dome, and could get no carriage; and the great state coaches of the cardinals, swinging high in the air, painted and gilded, with three noble footmen hanging on behind each, and a cardinal's broad face in the window.

VESUVIUS
CLIMBING A VOLCANO

Everybody who comes to Naples,--that is, everybody except the lady who fell from her horse the other day at Resina and injured her shoulder, as she was mounting for the ascent,--everybody, I say, goes up Vesuvius, and nearly every one writes impressions and descriptions of the performance. If you believe the tales of travelers, it is an undertaking of great hazard, an experience of frightful emotions. How unsafe it is, especially for ladies, I heard twenty times in Naples before I had been there a day. Why, there was a lady thrown from her horse and nearly killed, only a week ago; and she still lay ill at the next hotel, a witness of the truth of the story. I imagined her plunged down a precipice of lava, or pitched over the lip of the crater, and only rescued by the devotion of a gallant guide, who threatened to let go of her if she didn't pay him twenty francs instantly. This story, which will live and grow for years in this region, a waxing and never-waning peril of the volcano, I found, subsequently, had the foundation I have mentioned above. The lady did go to Resina in order to make the ascent of Vesuvius, mounted a horse there, fell off, being utterly unhorsewomanly, and hurt herself; but her injury had no more to do with Vesuvius than it had with the entrance of Victor Emanuel into Naples, which took place a couple of weeks after. Well, as I was saying, it is the fashion to write descriptions of Vesuvius; and you might as well have mine, which I shall give to you in rough outline.

There came a day when the Tramontane ceased to blow down on us the cold air of the snowy Apennines, and the white cap of Vesuvius, which is, by the way, worn generally like the caps of the Neapolitans, drifted inland instead of toward the sea. Warmer weather had come to make the bright sunshine no longer a mockery. For some days I had been getting the gauge of the mountain. With its white plume it is a constant quantity in the landscape: one sees it from every point of view; and we had been scarcely anywhere that volcanic remains, or signs of such action,--a thin crust shaking under our feet, as at Solfatara, where blasts of sulphurous steam drove in our faces,--did not remind us that the whole ground is uncertain, and undermined by the subterranean fires that have Vesuvius for a chimney. All the coast of the bay, within recent historic periods, in different spots at different times, has risen and sunk and risen again, in simple obedience to the pulsations of the great fiery monster below. It puffs up or sinks, like the crust of a baking apple-pie. This region is evidently not done; and I think it not unlikely it may have to be turned over again before it is. We had seen where Herculaneum lies under the lava and under the town of Resina; we had walked those clean and narrow streets of Pompeii, and seen the workmen picking away at the imbedded gravel, sand, and ashes which still cover nearly two thirds of the nice little, tight little Roman city; we had looked at the black gashes on the mountain-sides, where the lava streams had gushed and rolled and twisted over vineyards and villas and villages; and we decided to take a nearer look at the immediate cause of all this abnormal state of things.

In the morning when I awoke the sun was just rising behind Vesuvius; and there was a mighty display of gold and crimson in that quarter, as if the curtain was about to be lifted on a grand performance, say a ballet at San Carlo, which is the only thing the Neapolitans think worth looking at. Straight up in the air, out of the mountain, rose a white pillar, spreading out at the top like a palm-tree, or, to compare it to something I have seen, to the Italian pines, that come so picturesquely into all these Naples pictures. If you will believe me, that pillar of steam was like a column of fire, from the sun shining on and through it, and perhaps from the reflection of the background of crimson clouds and blue and gold sky, spread out there and hung there in royal and extravagant profusion, to make a highway and a regal gateway, through which I could just then see coming the horses and the chariot of a southern perfect day. They said that the tree-shaped cloud was the sign of an eruption; but the hotel-keepers here are always predicting that. The eruption is usually about two or three weeks distant; and the hotel proprietors get this information from experienced guides, who observe the action of the water in the wells; so that there can be no mistake about it.

We took carriages at nine o'clock to Resina, a drive of four miles, and one of exceeding interest, if you wish to see Naples life. The way is round the curving bay by the sea; but so continuously built up is it, and so inclosed with high walls of villas, through the open gates of which the golden oranges gleam, that you seem never to leave the city. The streets and quays swarm with the most vociferous, dirty, multitudinous life. It is a drive through Rag Fair. The tall, whitey-yellow houses fronting the water, six, seven, eight stories high, are full as beehives; people are at all the open windows; garments hang from the balconies and from poles thrust out; up every narrow, gloomy, ascending street are crowds of struggling human shapes; and you see how like herrings in a box are packed the over half a million people of Naples. In front of the houses are the markets in the open air,--fish, vegetables, carts of oranges; in the sun sit women spinning from distaffs or weaving fishing-nets; and rows of children who were never washed and never clothed but once, and whose garments have nearly wasted away; beggars, fishermen in red caps, sailors, priests, donkeys, fruit-venders, street-musicians, carriages, carts, two-wheeled break-down vehicles,--the whole tangled in one wild roar and rush and babel,--a shifting, varied panorama of color, rags,--a pandemonium such as the world cannot show elsewhere, that is what one sees on the road to Resina. The drivers all drive in the streets here as if they held a commission from the devil, cracking their whips, shouting to their horses, and dashing into the thickest tangle with entire reckless-ness. They have one cry, used alike for getting more speed out of their horses or for checking them, or in warning to the endangered crowds on foot. It is an exclama-tory grunt, which may be partially expressed by the letters "a-e-ugh." Everybody shouts it, mule-driver, "coachee," or cattle-driver; and even I, a passenger, fancied I could do it to disagreeable perfection after a time. Out of this throng in the streets I like to select the meek, patient, diminutive little donkeys, with enormous panniers that almost hide them. One would have a woman seated on top, with a child in one pannier and cabbages in the other; another, with an immense stock of market-greens on his back, or big baskets of oranges, or with a row of wine-casks and a man seated behind, adhering, by some unknown law of adhesion, to the sloping tail. Then there was the cart drawn by one diminutive donkey, or by an ox, or by an ox and a donkey, or by a donkey and horse abreast, never by any possibility a matched team. And, funniest of all, was the high, two-wheeled caleche, with one scat, and top thrown back, with long thills and poor horse. Upon this vehicle were piled, Heaven knows how, behind, before, on the thills, and underneath the high seat, sometimes ten, and not seldom as many as eighteen people, men, women, and children,--all in flaunting rags, with a colored scarf here and there, or a gay petti-coat, or a scarlet cap,--perhaps a priest, with broad black hat, in the center,--driving along like a comet, the poor horse in a gallop, the bells on his ornamented saddle merrily jingling, and the whole load in a roar of merriment.

But we shall never get to Vesuvius at this rate. I will not even stop to examine the macaroni manufactories on the road. The long strips of it were hung out on poles to dry in the streets, and to get a rich color from the dirt and dust, to say nothing of its contact with the filthy people who were making it. I am very fond of macaroni. At Resina we take horses for the ascent. We had sent ahead for a guide and horses for our party of ten; but we found besides, I should think, pretty nearly the entire population of the locality awaiting us, not to count the importunate beggars, the hags, male and female, and the ordinary loafers of the place. We were besieged to take this and that horse or mule, to buy walking-sticks for the climb, to purchase lava cut into charms, and veritable ancient coins, and dug-up cameos, all manufactured for the demand. One wanted to hold the horse, or to lead it, to carry a shawl, or to show the way. In the midst of infinite clamor and noise, we at last got mounted, and, turning into a narrow lane between high walls, began the ascent, our cavalcade attended by a procession of rags and wretchedness up through the village. Some of them fell off as we rose among the vineyards, and they found us proof against begging; but several accompanied us all day, hoping that, in some unguarded moment, they could do us some slight service, and so establish a claim on us. Among these I noticed some stout fellows with short ropes, with which they intended to assist us up the steeps. If I looked away an instant, some urchin would seize my horse's bridle; and when I carelessly let my stick fall on his hand, in token for him to let go, he would fall back with an injured look, and grasp the tail, from which I could only loosen him by swinging my staff and preparing to break his head.

The ascent is easy at first between walls and the vineyards which produce the celebrated Lachryma Christi. After a half hour we reached and began to cross the lava of 1858, and the wild desolation and gloom of the mountain began to strike us. One is here conscious of the titanic forces at work. Sometimes it is as if a giant had ploughed the ground, and left the furrows without harrowing them to harden into black and brown stone. We could see again how the broad stream, flowing down, squeezed and squashed like mud, had taken all fantastic shapes,--now like gnarled tree roots; now like serpents in a coil; here the human form, or a part of it,-

-a torso or a limb,--in agony; now in other nameless convolutions and contortions, as if heaved up and twisted in fiery pain and suffering,--for there was almost a human feeling in it; and again not unlike stone billows. We could see how the cooling crust had been lifted and split and turned over by the hot stream underneath, which, continually oozing from the rent of the eruption, bore it down and pressed it upward. Even so low as the point where we crossed the lava of 1858 were fissures whence came hot air.

An hour brought us to the resting-place called the Hermitage, an osteria and observatory established by the government. Standing upon the end of a spur, it seems to be safe from the lava, whose course has always been on either side; but it must be an uncomfortable place in a shower of stones and ashes. We rode half an hour longer on horseback, on a nearly level path, to the foot of the steep ascent, the base of the great crater. This ride gave us completely the wide and ghastly desolation of the mountain, the ruin that the lava has wrought upon slopes that were once green with vine and olive, and busy with the hum of life. This black, contorted desert waste is more sterile and hopeless than any mountain of stone, because the idea of relentless destruction is involved here. This great hummocked, sloping plain, ridged and seamed, was all about us, without cheer or relaxation of grim solitude. Before us rose, as black and bare, what the guides call the mountain, and which used to be the crater. Up one side is worked in the lava a zigzag path, steep, but not very fatiguing, if you take it slowly. Two thirds of the way up, I saw specks of people climbing. Beyond it rose the cone of ashes, out of which the great cloud of sulphurous smoke rises and rolls night and day now. On the very edge of that, on the lip of it, where the smoke rose, I also saw human shapes; and it seemed as if they stood on the brink of Tartarus and in momently imminent peril.

We left our horses in a wild spot, where scorched boulders had fallen upon the lava bed; and guides and boys gathered about us like cormorants: but, declining their offers to pull us up, we began the ascent, which took about three quarters of an hour. We were then on the summit, which is, after all, not a summit at all, but an uneven waste, sloping away from the Cone in the center. This sloping lava waste was full of little cracks,--not fissures with hot lava in them, or anything of the sort,--out of which white steam issued, not unlike the smoke from a great patch of burned timber; and the wind blew it along the ground towards us. It was cool, for the sun was hidden by light clouds, but not cold. The ground under foot was slightly warm. I had expected to feel some dread, or shrinking, or at least some sense of insecurity, but I did not the slightest, then or afterwards; and I think mine is the usual experience. I had no more sense of danger on the edge of the crater than I had in the streets of Naples.

We next addressed ourselves to the Cone, which is a loose hill of ashes and sand,--a natural slope, I should say, of about one and a half to one, offering no foot-hold. The climb is very fatiguing, because you sink in to the ankles, and slide back at every step; but it is short,--we were up in six to eight minutes,--though the ladies, who had been helped a little by the guides, were nearly exhausted, and sank down on the very edge of the crater, with their backs to the smoke. What did we see? What would you see if you looked into a steam boiler? We stood on the ashy edge of the crater, the sharp edge sloping one way down the mountain, and the other into the bowels, whence the thick, stifling smoke rose. We rolled stones down, and heard them rumbling for half a minute. The diameter of the crater on the brink of which we stood was said to be an eighth of a mile; but the whole was completely filled with vapor. The edge where we stood was quite warm.

We ate some rolls we had brought in our pockets, and some of the party tried a bottle of the wine that one of the cormorants had brought up, but found it any-thing but the Lachryma Christi it was named. We looked with longing eyes down into the vapor-boiling caldron; we looked at the wide and lovely view of land and sea; we tried to realize our awful situation, munched our dry bread, and laughed at the monstrous demands of the vagabonds about us for money, and then turned and went down quicker than we came up.

We had chosen to ascend to the old crater rather than to the new one of the re-cent eruption on the side of the mountain, where there is nothing to be seen. When we reached the bottom of the Cone, our guide led us to the north side, and into a re-gion that did begin to look like business. The wind drove all the smoke round there, and we were half stifled with sulphur fumes to begin with. Then the whole ground was discolored red and yellow, and with many more gay and sulphur-suggesting colors. And it actually had deep fissures in it, over which we stepped and among which we went, out of which came blasts of hot, horrid vapor, with a roaring as if we were in the midst of furnaces. And if we came near the cracks the heat was powerful in our faces, and if we thrust our sticks down them they were instantly burned; and the guides cooked eggs; and the crust was thin, and very hot to our boots; and half the time we couldn't see anything; and we would rush away where the vapor was not so thick, and, with handkerchiefs to our mouths, rush in again to get the full effect. After we came out again into better air, it was as if we had been through the burning, fiery furnace, and had the smell of it on our garments. And, indeed, the sulphur had changed to red certain of our clothes, and noticeably my pantaloons and the black velvet cap of one of the ladies; and it was some days before they recovered their color. But, as I say, there was no sense of danger in the adventure.

We descended by a different route, on the south side of the mountain, to our horses, and made a lark of it. We went down an ash slope, very steep, where we sank in a foot or little less at every step, and there was nothing to do for it, but to run and jump. We took steps as long as if we had worn seven-league boots. When the whole party got in motion, the entire slope seemed to slide a little with us, and there appeared some danger of an avalanche. But we did n't stop for it. It was exactly like plunging down a steep hillside that is covered thickly with light, soft snow. There was a gray-haired gentleman with us, with a good deal of the boy in him, who thought it great fun.

I have said little about the view; but I might have written about nothing else, both in the ascent and descent. Naples, and all the villages which rim the bay with white, the gracefully curving arms that go out to sea, and do not quite clasp rocky Capri, which lies at the entrance, made the outline of a picture of surpassing loveliness. But as we came down, there was a sight that I am sure was unique. As one in a balloon sees the earth concave beneath, so now, from where we stood, it seemed to rise, not fall, to the sea, and all the white villages were raised to the clouds; and by the peculiar light, the sea looked exactly like sky, and the little boats on it seemed to float, like balloons in the air. The illusion was perfect. As the day waned, a heavy cloud hid the sun, and so let down the light that the waters were a dark purple. Then the sun went behind Posilipo in a perfect blaze of scarlet, and all the sea was violet. Only it still was not the sea at all; but the little chopping waves looked like flecked clouds; and it was exactly as if one of the violet, cloud-beautified skies that we see at home over some sunsets had fallen to the ground. And the slant white sails and the black specks of boats on it hung in the sky, and were as unsubstantial as the whole pageant. Capri alone was dark and solid. And as we descended and a high wall hid it, a little handsome rascal, who had attended me for an hour, now at the head and now at the tail of my pony, recalled me to the realities by the request that I should give him a franc. For what? For carrying signor's coat up the mountain. I rewarded the little liar with a German copper. I had carried my own overcoat all day.

SORRENTO DAYS
OUTLINES

The day came when we tired of the brilliancy and din of Naples, most noisy of cities. Neapolis, or Parthenope, as is well known, was founded by Parthenope, a siren who was cast ashore there. Her descendants still live here; and we have become a little weary of their inherited musical ability: they have learned to play upon many new instruments, with which they keep us awake late at night, and arouse us early in the morning. One of them is always there under the window, where the moonlight will strike him, or the early dawn will light up his love-worn visage, strumming the guitar with his horny thumb, and wailing through his nose as if his throat was full of seaweed. He is as inexhaustible as Vesuvius. We shall have to flee, or stop our ears with wax, like the sailors of Ulysses.

The day came when we had checked off the Posilipo, and the Grotto, Pozzuoli, Baiae, Cape Misenum, the Museum, Vesuvius, Pompeii, Herculaneum, the moderns buried at the Campo Santo; and we said, Let us go and lie in the sun at Sorrento. But first let us settle our geography.

The Bay of Naples, painted and sung forever, but never adequately, must consent to be here described as essentially a parallelogram, with an opening towards the southwest. The northeast side of this, with Naples in the right-hand corner, looking seaward and Castellamare in the left-hand corner, at a distance of some fourteen miles, is a vast rich plain, fringed on the shore with towns, and covered with white houses and gardens. Out of this rises the isolated bulk of Vesuvius. This growing mountain is manufactured exactly like an ant-hill.

The northwest side of the bay, keeping a general westerly direction, is very uneven, with headlands, deep bays, and outlying islands. First comes the promontory of Posilipo, pierced by two tunnels, partly natural and partly Greek and Roman work, above the entrance of one of which is the tomb of Virgil, let us believe; then a beautiful bay, the shore of which is incrusted with classic ruins. On this bay stands Pozzuoli, the ancient Puteoli where St. Paul landed one May day, and doubtless walked up this paved road, which leads direct to Rome. At the entrance, near the head of Posilipo, is the volcanic island of "shining Nisida," to which Brutus retired after the assassination of Caesar, and where he bade Portia good-by before he departed for Greece and Philippi: the favorite villa of Cicero, where he wrote many of his letters to Atticus, looked on it. Baiae, epitome of the luxury and profligacy, of the splendor and crime of the most sensual years of the Roman empire, spread there its temples, palaces, and pleasure-gardens, which crowded the low slopes, and extended over the water; and yonder is Cape Misenum, which sheltered the great fleets of Rome.

This region, which is still shaky from fires bubbling under the thin crust, through which here and there the sulphurous vapor breaks out, is one of the most sacred in the ancient world. Here are the Lucrine Lake, the Elysian Fields, the cave of the Cumean Sibyl, and the Lake Avernus. This entrance to the infernal regions was frozen over the day I saw it; so that the profane prophecy of skating on the bottomless pit might have been realized. The islands of Procida and Ischia continue and complete this side of the bay, which is about twenty miles long as the boat sails.

At Castellamare the shore makes a sharp bend, and runs southwest along the side of the Sorrentine promontory. This promontory is a high, rocky, diversified ridge, which extends out between the bays of Naples and Salerno, with its short and precipitous slope towards the latter. Below Castellamare, the mountain range of the Great St. Angelo (an offshoot of the Apennines) runs across the peninsula, and cuts off that portion of it which we have to consider. The most conspicuous of the three parts of this short range is over four thousand seven hundred feet above the Bay of Naples, and the highest land on it. From Great St. Angelo to the point, the Punta di Campanella, it is, perhaps, twelve miles by balloon, but twenty by any other conveyance. Three miles off this point lies Capri.

This promontory has a backbone of rocky ledges and hills; but it has at intervals transverse ledges and ridges, and deep valleys and chains cutting in from either side;

so that it is not very passable in any direction. These little valleys and bays are warm nooks for the olive and the orange; and all the precipices and sunny slopes are terraced nearly to the top. This promontory of rocks is far from being barren.

From Castellamare, driving along a winding, rockcut road by the bay,--one of the most charming in southern Italy,--a distance of seven miles, we reach the Punta di Scutolo. This point, and the opposite headland, the Capo di Sorrento, inclose the Piano di Sorrento, an irregular plain, three miles long, encircled by limestone hills, which protect it from the east and south winds. In this amphitheater it lies, a mass of green foliage and white villages, fronting Naples and Vesuvius.

If nature first scooped out this nook level with the sea, and then filled it up to a depth of two hundred to three hundred feet with volcanic tufa, forming a precipice of that height along the shore, I can understand how the present state of things came about.

This plain is not all level, however. Decided spurs push down into it from the hills; and great chasms, deep, ragged, impassable, split in the tufa, extend up into it from the sea. At intervals, at the openings of these ravines, are little marinas, where the fishermen have their huts' and where their boats land. Little villages, separate from the world, abound on these marinas. The warm volcanic soil of the sheltered plain makes it a paradise of fruits and flowers.

Sorrento, ancient and romantic city, lies at the southwest end of this plain, built along the sheer sea precipice, and running back to the hills,--a city of such narrow streets, high walls, and luxuriant groves that it can be seen only from the heights adjacent. The ancient boundary of the city proper was the famous ravine on the east side, a similar ravine on the south, which met it at right angles, and was supplemented by a high Roman wall, and the same wall continued on the west to the sea. The growing town has pushed away the wall on the west side; but that on the south yet stands as good as when the Romans made it. There is a little attempt at a mall, with double rows of trees, under that wall, where lovers walk, and ragged, handsome urchins play the exciting game of fives, or sit in the dirt, gambling with cards for the Sorrento currency. I do not know what sin it may be to gamble for a bit of printed paper which has the value of one sou.

The great ravine, three quarters of a mile long, the ancient boundary which now cuts the town in two, is bridged where the main street, the Corso, crosses, the bridge resting on old Roman substructions, as everything else about here does. This ravine, always invested with mystery, is the theme of no end of poetry and legend. Demons inhabit it. Here and there, in its perpendicular sides, steps have been cut for descent. Vines and lichens grow on the walls: in one place, at the bottom, an orange grove has taken root. There is even a mill down there, where there is breadth enough for a building; and altogether, the ravine is not so delivered over to the power of darkness as it used to be. It is still damp and slimy, it is true; but from above, it is always beautiful, with its luxuriant growth of vines, and at twilight mysterious. I like as well, however, to look into its entrance from the little marina, where the old fishwives are weaving nets.

These little settlements under the cliff, called marinas, are worlds in themselves, picturesque at a distance, but squalid seen close at hand. They are not very different from the little fishing-stations on the Isle of Wight; but they are more sheltered, and their inhabitants sing at their work, wear bright colors, and bask in the sun a good deal, feeling no sense of responsibility for the world they did not create. To weave nets, to fish in the bay, to sell their fish at the wharves, to eat unexciting vegetables and fish, to drink moderately, to go to the chapel of St. Antonino on Sunday, not to work on fast and feast days, nor more than compelled to any day, this is life at the marinas. Their world is what they can see, and Naples is distant and almost foreign. Generation after generation is content with the same simple life. They have no more idea of the bad way the world is in than bees in their cells.

THE VILLA NARDI

The Villa Nardi hangs over the sea. It is built on a rock, and I know not what Roman and Greek foundations, and the remains of yet earlier peoples, traders, and traffickers, whose galleys used to rock there at the base of the cliff, where the gentle waves beat even in this winter-time with a summer swing and sound of peace.

It was at the close of a day in January that I first knew the Villa Nardi,--a warm, lovely day, at the hour when the sun was just going behind the Capo di Sorrento, in order to disrobe a little, I fancy, before plunging into the Mediterranean off the end of Capri, as is his wont about this time of year. When we turned out of the little piazza, our driver was obliged to take off one of our team of three horses driven abreast, so that we could pass through the narrow and crooked streets, or rather lanes of blank walls. With cracking whip, rattling wheels, and shouting to clear the way, we drove into the Strada di San Francisca, and to an arched gateway. This led down a straight path, between olives and orange and lemon-trees, gleaming with shining leaves and fruit of gold, with hedges of rose-trees in full bloom, to another leafy arch, through which I saw tropical trees, and a terrace with a low wall and battered busts guarding it, and beyond, the blue sea, a white sail or two slanting across the opening, and the whiteness of Naples some twenty miles away on the shore.

The noble family of the Villa did not descend into the garden to welcome us, as we should have liked; in fact, they have been absent now for a long time, so long that even their ghosts, if they ever pace the terrace-walk towards the convent, would appear strange to one who should meet them; and yet our hostess, the Tramontano, did what the ancient occupants scarcely could have done, gave us the choice of rooms in the entire house. The stranger who finds himself in this secluded paradise, at this season, is always at a loss whether to take a room on the sea, with all its changeable loveliness, but no sun, or one overlooking the garden, where the sun all day pours itself into the orange boughs, and where the birds are just beginning to get up a spring twitteration. My friend, whose capacity for taking in the luxurious repose of this region is something extraordinary, has tried, I believe, nearly every room in the house, and has at length gone up to a solitary room on the top, where, like a bird on a tree he looks all ways, and, so to say, swings in the entrancing air. But, wherever you are, you will grow into content with your situation.

At the Villa Nardi we have no sound of wheels, no noise of work or traffic, no suggestion of conflict. I am under the impression that everything that was to have been done has been done. I am, it is true, a little afraid that the Saracens will come here again, and carry off more of the nut-brown girls, who lean over the walls, and look down on us from under the boughs. I am not quite sure that a French Admiral of the Republic will not some morning anchor his three-decker in front, and open fire on us; but nothing else can happen. Naples is a thousand miles away. The boom of the saluting guns of Castel Nuovo is to us scarcely an echo of modern life. Rome does not exist. And as for London and New York, they send their people and their newspapers here, but no pulse of unrest from them disturbs our tranquillity. Hemmed in on the land side by high walls, groves, and gardens, perched upon a rock two hundred feet above the water, how much more secure from invasion is this than any fabled island of the southern sea, or any remote stream where the boats of the lotus-eaters float!

There is a little terrace and flower-plat, where we sometimes sit, and over the wall of which we like to lean, and look down the cliff to the sea. This terrace is the common ground of many exotics as well as native trees and shrubs. Here are the magnolia, the laurel, the Japanese medlar, the oleander, the pepper, the bay, the date-palm, a tree called the plumbago, another from the Cape of Good Hope, the pomegranate, the elder in full leaf, the olive, salvia, heliotrope; close by is a banana-tree.

I find a good deal of companionship in the rows of plaster busts that stand on the wall, in all attitudes of listlessness, and all stages of decay. I thought at first they were penates of the premises; but better acquaintance has convinced me that they never were gods, but the clayey representations of great men and noble dames. The stains of time are on them; some have lost a nose or an ear; and one has parted with a still more important member--his head,--an accident that might profitably have befallen his neighbor, whose curly locks and villainously low forehead proclaim him a Roman emperor. Cut in the face of the rock is a walled and winding way down to the water. I see below the archway where it issues from the underground recesses of our establishment; and there stands a bust, in serious expectation that some one will walk out and saunter down among the rocks; but no one ever does. Just at the right is a little beach, with a few old houses, and a mimic stir of life, a little curve in the cliff, the mouth of the gorge, where the waves come in with a lazy swash. Some fishing-boats ride there; and the shallow water, as I look down this sunny morning, is thickly strewn with floating peels of oranges and lemons, as if some one was brewing a gigantic bowl of punch. And there is an uncommon stir of life; for a schooner is shipping a cargo of oranges, and the entire population is in a clamor. Donkeys are coming down the winding way, with a heavy basket on either flank; stout girls are stepping lightly down with loads on their heads; the drivers shout, the donkeys bray, the people jabber and order each other about; and the oranges, in a continual stream, are poured into the long, narrow vessel, rolling in with a thud, until there is a yellow mass of them. Shouting, scolding, singing, and braying, all come up to me a little mellowed. The disorder is not so great as on the opera stage of San Carlo in Naples; and the effect is much more pleasing.

This settlement, the marina, under the cliff, used to extend along the shore; and a good road ran down there close by the water. The rock has split off, and covered it; and perhaps the shore has sunk. They tell me that those who dig down in the edge of the shallow water find sunken walls, and the remains of old foundations of Roman workmanship. People who wander there pick up bits of marble, serpentine, and malachite,--remains of the palaces that long ago fell into the sea, and have not left even the names of their owners and builders,-the ancient loafers who idled away their days as everybody must in this seductive spot. Not far from here, they point out the veritable caves of the Sirens, who have now shut up house, and gone away, like the rest of the nobility. If I had been a mariner in their day, I should have made no effort to sail by and away from their soothing shore.

I went, one day, through a long, sloping arch, near the sailors' Chapel of St. Antonino, past a pretty shrine of the Virgin, down the zigzag path to this little marina; but it is better to be content with looking at it from above, and imagining how delightful it would be to push off in one of the little tubs of boats. Sometimes, at night, I hear the fishermen coming home, singing in their lusty fashion; and I think it is a good haven to arrive at. I never go down to search for stones on the beach: I like to believe that there are great treasures there, which I might find; and I know that the green and brown and spotty appearance of the water is caused by the showing through of the pavements of courts, and marble floors of palaces, which might vanish if I went nearer, such a place of illusion is this.

The Villa Nardi stands in pleasant relations to Vesuvius, which is just across the bay, and is not so useless as it has been represented; it is our weather-sign and prophet. When the white plume on his top floats inland, that is one sort of weather; when it streams out to sea, that is another. But I can never tell which is which: nor in my experience does it much matter; for it seems impossible for Sorrento to do anything but woo us with gentle weather. But the use of Vesuvius, after all, is to furnish us a background for the violet light at sundown, when the villages at its foot gleam like a silver fringe. I have become convinced of one thing: it is always best when you build a house to have it front toward a volcano, if you can. There is just that lazy activity about a volcano, ordinarily, that satisfies your demand for something that is not exactly dead, and yet does not disturb you.

Sometimes when I wake in the night,--though I don't know why one ever wakes in the night, or the daytime either here,--I hear the bell of the convent, which is in our demesne,--a convent which is suppressed, and where I hear, when I pass in the morning, the humming of a school. At first I tried to count the hour; but when the bell went on to strike seventeen, and even twenty-one o'clock, the absurdity of the thing came over me, and I wondered whether it was some frequent call to prayer for a feeble band of sisters remaining, some reminder of midnight penance and vigil, or whether it was not something more ghostly than that, and was not responded to by shades of nuns, who were wont to look out from their narrow latticed windows upon these same gardens, as long ago as when the beautiful Queen Joanna used to come down here to repent--if she ever did repent--of her wanton ways in Naples.

On one side of the garden is a suppressed monastery. The narrow front towards the sea has a secluded little balcony, where I like to fancy the poor orphaned souls used to steal out at night for a breath of fresh air, and perhaps to see, as I did one dark evening, Naples with its lights like a conflagration on the horizon. Upon the tiles of the parapet are cheerful devices, the crossbones tied with a cord, and the like. How many heavy-hearted recluses have stood in that secluded nook, and been tempted by the sweet, lulling sound of the waves below; how many have paced along this narrow terrace, and felt like prisoners who wore paths in the stone floor where they trod; and how many stupid louts have walked there, insensible to all the charm of it!

If I pass into the Tramontano garden, it is not to escape the presence of history, or to get into the modern world, where travelers are arriving, and where there is the bustle and proverbial discontent of those who travel to enjoy themselves. In the pretty garden, which is a constant surprise of odd nooks and sunny hiding-places, with ruins, and most luxuriant ivy, is a little cottage where, I am told in confidence, the young king of Bavaria slept three nights not very long ago. I hope he slept well. But more important than the sleep, or even death, of a king, is the birth of a poet, I take it; and within this inclosure, on the eleventh day of March, 1541, Torquato Tasso, most melancholy of men, first saw the light; and here was born his noble sister Cornelia, the descendants of whose union with the cavalier Spasiano still live here, and in a manner keep the memory of the poet green with the present generation. I am indebted to a gentleman who is of this lineage for many favors, and for precise information as to the position in the house that stood here of the very room in which Tasso was born. It is also minutely given in a memoir of Tasso and his family, by Bartolommeo Capasso, whose careful researches have disproved the slipshod statements of the guidebooks, that the poet was born in a house which is still standing, farther to the west, and that the room has fallen into the sea. The descendant of the sister pointed out to me the spot on the terrace of the Tramontano where the room itself was, when the house still stood; and, of course, seeing is believing. The sun shone full upon it, as we stood there; and the air was full of the scent of tropical fruit and just-coming blossoms. One could not desire a more tranquil scene of advent into life; and the wandering, broken-hearted author of "Jerusalem Delivered" never found at court or palace any retreat so soothing as that offered him here by his steadfast sister.

If I were an antiquarian, I think I should have had Tasso born at the Villa Nardi, where I like best to stay, and where I find traces of many pilgrims from other countries. Here, in a little corner room on the terrace, Mrs. Stowe dreamed and wrote; and I expect, every morning, as I take my morning sun here by the gate, Agnes of Sorrento will come down the sweet-scented path with a basket of oranges on her head.

SEA AND SHORE

It is not always easy, when one stands upon the highlands which encircle the Piano di Sorrento, in some conditions of the atmosphere, to tell where the sea ends and the sky begins. It seems practicable, at such times, for one to take ship and sail up into heaven. I have often, indeed, seen white sails climbing up there, and fishing-boats, at secure anchor I suppose, riding apparently like balloons in the hazy air. Sea and air and land here are all kin, I suspect, and have certain immaterial qualities in common. The contours of the shores and the outlines of the hills are as graceful as the mobile waves; and if there is anywhere ruggedness and sharpness, the atmosphere throws a friendly veil over it, and tones all that is inharmonious into the repose of beauty.

The atmosphere is really something more than a medium: it is a drapery, woven, one could affirm, with colors, or dipped in oriental dyes. One might account thus for the prismatic colors I have often seen on the horizon at noon, when the sun was pouring down floods of clear golden light. The simple light here, if one could ever represent it by pen, pencil, or brush, would draw the world hither to bathe in it. It is not thin sunshine, but a royal profusion, a golden substance, a transforming quality, a vesture of splendor for all these Mediterranean shores.

The most comprehensive idea of Sorrento and the great plain on which it stands, imbedded almost out of sight in foliage, we obtained one day from our boat, as we put out round the Capo di Sorrento, and stood away for Capri. There was not wind enough for sails, but there were chopping waves, and swell enough to toss us about, and to produce bright flashes of light far out at sea. The red-shirted rowers silently bent to their long sweeps; and I lay in the tossing bow, and studied the high, receding shore. The picture is simple, a precipice of rock or earth, faced with masonry in spots, almost of uniform height from point to point of the little bay, except where a deep gorge has split the rock, and comes to the sea, forming a cove, where a cluster of rude buildings is likely to gather. Along the precipice, which now juts and now recedes a little, are villas, hotels, old convents, gardens, and groves. I can see steps and galleries cut in the face of the cliff, and caves and caverns, natural and artificial: for one can cut this tufa with a knife; and it would hardly seem preposterous to attempt to dig out a cool, roomy mansion in this rocky front with a spade.

As we pull away, I begin to see the depth of the plain of Sorrento, with its villages, walled roads, its groves of oranges, olives, lemons, its figs, pomegranates, almonds, mulberries, and acacias; and soon the terraces above, where the vineyards are planted, and the olives also. These terraces must be a brave sight in the spring, when the masses of olives are white as snow with blossoms, which fill all the plain with their sweet perfume. Above the terraces, the eye reaches the fine outline of the hill; and, to the east, the bare precipice of rock, softened by the purple light; and turning still to the left, as the boat lazily swings, I have Vesuvius, the graceful dip into the plain, and the rise to the heights of Naples, Nisida, the shining houses of Pozzuoli, Cape Misenum, Procida, and rough Ischia. Rounding the headland, Capri is before us, so sharp and clear that we seem close to it; but it is a weary pull before we get under its rocky side.

Returning from Capri late in the afternoon, we had one of those effects which are the despair of artists. I had been told that twilights are short here, and that, when the sun disappeared, color vanished from the sky. There was a wonderful light on all the inner bay, as we put off from shore. Ischia was one mass of violet color, As we got from under the island, there was the sun, a red ball of fire, just dipping into the sea. At once the whole horizon line of water became a bright crimson, which deepened as evening advanced, glowing with more intense fire, and holding a broad band of what seemed solid color for more than three quarters of an hour. The colors, meantime, on the level water, never were on painter's palette, and never were counterfeited by the changeable silks of eastern looms; and this gorgeous spectacle continued till the stars came out, crowding the sky with silver points.

Our boatmen, who had been reinforced at Capri, and were inspired either by the wine of the island or the beauty of the night, pulled with new vigor, and broke out again and again into the wild songs of this coast. A favorite was the Garibaldi song, which invariably ended in a cheer and a tiger, and threw the singers into such a spurt of excitement that the oars forgot to keep time, and there was more splash than speed. The singers all sang one part in minor: there was no harmony, the voices were not rich, and the melody was not remarkable; but there was, after all, a wild pathos in it. Music is very much here what it is in Naples. I have to keep saying to myself that Italy is a land of song; else I should think that people mistake noise for music.

The boatmen are an honest set of fellows, as Italians go; and, let us hope, not unworthy followers of their patron, St. Antonino, whose chapel is on the edge of the gorge near the Villa Nardi. A silver image of the saint, half life-size, stands upon the rich marble altar. This valuable statue has been, if tradition is correct, five times captured and carried away by marauders, who have at different times sacked Sorrento of its marbles, bronzes, and precious things, and each time, by some mysterious providence, has found its way back again,--an instance of constancy in a solid silver image which is worthy of commendation. The little chapel is hung all about with votive offerings in wax of arms, legs, heads, hands, effigies, and with coarse lithographs, in frames, of storms at sea and perils of ships, hung up by sailors who, having escaped the dangers of the deep, offer these tributes to their dear saint. The skirts of the image are worn quite smooth with kissing. Underneath it, at the back of the altar, an oil light is always burning; and below repose the bones of the holy man.

The whole shore is fascinating to one in an idle mood, and is good mousing-ground for the antiquarian. For myself, I am content with one generalization, which I find saves a world of bother and perplexity: it is quite safe to style every excavation, cavern, circular wall, or arch by the sea, a Roman bath. It is the final resort of the antiquarians. This theory has kept me from entering the discussion, whether the substructions in the cliff under the Poggio Syracuse, a royal villa, are temples of the Sirens, or caves of Ulysses. I only know that I descend to the sea there by broad interior flights of steps, which lead through galleries and corridors, and high, vaulted passages, whence extend apartments and caves far reaching into the solid rock. At intervals are landings, where arched windows are cut out to the sea, with stone seats and protecting walls. At the base of the cliff I find a hewn passage, as if there had once been here a way of embarkation; and enormous fragments of rocks, with steps cut in them, which have fallen from above.

Were these anything more than royal pleasure galleries, where one could sit in coolness in the heat of summer and look on the bay and its shipping, in the days when the great Roman fleet used to lie opposite, above the point of Misenum? How many brave and gay retinues have swept down these broad interior stairways, let us say in the picturesque Middle Ages, to embark on voyages of pleasure or warlike forays! The steps are well worn, and must have been trodden for ages, by nobles and robbers, peasants and sailors, priests of more than one religion, and traders of many seas, who have gone, and left no record. The sun was slanting his last rays into the corridors as I musingly looked down from one of the arched openings, quite spell-bound by the strangeness and dead silence of the place, broken only by the plash of waves on the sandy beach below. I had found my way down through a wooden door half ajar; and I thought of the possibility of some one's shutting it for the night, and leaving me a prisoner to await the spectres which I have no doubt throng here when it grows dark. Hastening up out of these chambers of the past, I escaped into the upper air, and walked rapidly home through the narrow orange lanes.

ON TOP OF THE HOUSE

The tiptop of the Villa Nardi is a flat roof, with a wall about it three feet high, and some little turreted affairs, that look very much like chimneys. Joseph, the gray-haired servitor, has brought my chair and table up here to-day, and here I am, established to write.

I am here above most earthly annoyances, and on a level with the heavenly influences. It has always seemed to me that the higher one gets, the easier it must be to write; and that, especially at a great elevation, one could strike into lofty themes, and launch out, without fear of shipwreck on any of the earthly headlands, in his aerial voyages. Yet, after all, he would be likely to arrive nowhere, I suspect; or, to change the figure, to find that, in parting with the taste of the earth, he had produced a flavorless composition. If it were not for the haze in the horizon to-day, I could distinguish the very house in Naples--that of Manso, Marquis of Villa,-- where Tasso found a home, and where John Milton was entertained at a later day by that hospitable nobleman. I wonder, if he had come to the Villa Nardi and written on the roof, if the theological features of his epic would have been softened, and if he would not have received new suggestions for the adornment of the garden. Of course, it is well that his immortal production was not composed on this roof, and in sight of these seductive shores, or it would have been more strongly flavored with classic mythology than it is. But, letting Milton go, it may be necessary to say that my writing to-day has nothing to do with my theory of composition in an elevated position; for this is the laziest place that I have yet found.

I am above the highest olive-trees, and, if I turned that way, should look over the tops of what seems a vast grove of them, out of which a white roof, and an old time-eaten tower here and there, appears; and the sun is flooding them with waves of light, which I think a person delicately enough organized could hear beat. Beyond the brown roofs of the town, the terraced hills arise, in semicircular embrace of the plain; and the fine veil over them is partly the natural shimmer of the heat, and partly the silver duskiness of the olive-leaves. I sit with my back to all this, taking the entire force of this winter sun, which is full of life and genial heat, and does not scorch one, as I remember such a full flood of it would at home. It is putting sweetness, too, into the oranges, which, I observe, are getting redder and softer day by day. We have here, by the way, such a habit of taking up an orange, weighing it in the hand, and guessing if it is ripe, that the test is extending to other things. I saw a gentleman this morning, at breakfast, weighing an egg in the same manner; and some one asked him if it was ripe.

It seems to me that the Mediterranean was never bluer than it is to-day. It has a shade or two the advantage of the sky: though I like the sky best, after all; for it is less opaque, and offers an illimitable opportunity of exploration. Perhaps this is because I am nearer to it. There are some little ruffles of air on the sea, which I do not feel here, making broad spots of shadow, and here and there flecks and sparkles. But the schooners sail idly, and the fishing-boats that have put out from the marina float in the most dreamy manner. I fear that the fishermen who have made a show of industry, and got away from their wives, who are busily weaving nets on shore, are yielding to the seductions of the occasion, and making a day of it. And, as I look at them, I find myself debating which I would rather be, a fisherman there in the boat, rocked by the swell, and warmed by the sun, or a friar, on the terrace of the garden on the summit of Deserto, lying perfectly tranquil, and also soaked in the sun. There is one other person, now that I think of it, who may be having a good time to-day, though I do not know that I envy him. His business is a new one to me, and is an occupation that one would not care to recommend to a friend until he had tried it: it is being carried about in a basket. As I went up the new Massa road the other day, I met a ragged, stout, and rather dirty woman, with a large shallow basket on her head. In it lay her husband, a large man, though I think a little abbreviated as to his legs. The woman asked alms. Talk of Diogenes in his tub! How must the world look to a man in a basket, riding about on his wife's head? When I returned, she had put him down beside the road in the sun, and almost in danger of the passing vehicles. I suppose that the affectionate creature thought that, if he got a new injury in this way, his value in the beggar market would be increased. I do not mean to do this exemplary wife any injustice; and I only suggest the idea in this land, where every beggar who is born with a deformity has something to thank the Virgin for. This custom of carrying your husband on your head in a basket has something to recommend it, and is an exhibition of faith on the one hand, and of devotion on the other, that is seldom met with. Its consideration is commended to my countrywomen at home. It is, at least, a new commentary on the apostolic remark, that the man is the head of the woman. It is, in some respects, a happy division of labor in the walk of life: she furnishes the locomotive power, and he the directing brains, as he lies in the sun and looks abroad; which reminds me that the sun is getting hot on my back. The little bunch of bells in the convent tower is jangling out a suggestion of worship, or of the departure of the hours. It is time to eat an orange.

Vesuvius appears to be about on a level with my eyes and I never knew him to do himself more credit than to-day. The whole coast of the bay is in a sort of obscuration, thicker than an Indian summer haze; and the veil extends almost to the top of Vesuvius. But his summit is still distinct, and out of it rises a gigantic billowy column of white smoke, greater in quantity than on any previous day of our sojourn; and the sun turns it to silver. Above a long line of ordinary looking clouds, float great white masses, formed of the sulphurous vapor. This manufacture of clouds in a clear, sunny day has an odd appearance; but it is easy enough, if one has such a laboratory as Vesuvius. How it tumbles up the white smoke! It is piled up now, I should say, a thousand feet above the crater, straight into the blue sky,--a pillar of cloud by day. One might sit here all day watching it, listening the while to the melodious spring singing of the hundreds of birds which have come to take possession of the garden, receiving southern reinforcements from Sicily and Tunis every morning, and think he was happy. But the morning has gone; and I have written nothing.

THE PRICE OF ORANGES

If ever a northern wanderer could be suddenly transported to look down upon the Piano di Sorrento, he would not doubt that he saw the Garden of the Hesperides. The orange-trees cannot well be fuller: their branches bend with the weight of fruit. With the almond-trees in full flower, and with the silver sheen of the olive leaves, the oranges are apples of gold in pictures of silver. As I walk in these sunken roads, and between these high walls, the orange boughs everywhere hang over; and through the open gates of villas I look down alleys of golden glimmer, roses and geraniums by the walk, and the fruit above,--gardens of enchantment, with never a dragon, that I can see, to guard them.

All the highways and the byways, the streets and lanes, wherever I go, from the sea to the tops of the hills, are strewn with orange-peel; so that one, looking above and below, comes back from a walk with a golden dazzle in his eyes,--a sense that yellow is the prevailing color. Perhaps the kerchiefs of the dark-skinned girls and women, which take that tone, help the impression. The inhabitants are all orange-eaters. The high walls show that the gardens are protected with great care; yet the fruit seems to be as free as apples are in a remote New England town about cider-time.

I have been trying, ever since I have been here, to ascertain the price of oranges; not for purposes of exportation, nor yet for the personal importation that I daily practice, but in order to give an American basis of fact to these idle chapters. In all the paths I meet, daily, girls and boys bearing on their heads large baskets of the fruit, and little children with bags and bundles of the same, as large as they can stagger under; and I understand they are carrying them to the packers, who ship them to New York, or to the depots, where I see them lying in yellow heaps, and where men and women are cutting them up, and removing the peel, which goes to England for preserves. I am told that these oranges are sold for a couple of francs a hundred. That seems to me so dear that I am not tempted into any speculation, but stroll back to the Tramontano, in the gardens of which I find better terms.

The only trouble is to find a sweet tree; for the Sorrento oranges are usually sour in February; and one needs to be a good judge of the fruit, and know the male orange from the female, though which it is that is the sweeter I can never remember (and should not dare to say, if I did, in the present state of feeling on the woman question),--or he might as well eat a lemon. The mercenary aspect of my query does not enter in here. I climb into a tree, and reach out to the end of the branch for an orange that has got reddish in the sun, that comes off easily and is heavy; or I tickle a large one on the top bough with a cane pole; and if it drops readily, and has a fine grain, I call it a cheap one. I can usually tell whether they are good by splitting them open and eating a quarter. The Italians pare their oranges as we do apples; but I like best to open them first, and see the yellow meat in the white casket. After you have eaten a few from one tree, you can usually tell whether it is a good tree; but there is nothing certain about it,--one bough that gets the sun will be better than another that does not, and one half of an orange will fill your mouth with more delicious juices than the other half.

The oranges that you knock off with your stick, as you walk along the lanes, don't cost anything; but they are always sour, as I think the girls know who lean over the wall, and look on with a smile: and, in that, they are more sensible than the lively dogs which bark at you from the top, and wake all the neighborhood with their clamor. I have no doubt the oranges have a market price; but I have been seeking the value the gardeners set on them themselves. As I walked towards the heights, the other morning, and passed an orchard, the gardener, who saw my ineffectual efforts, with a very long cane, to reach the boughs of a tree, came down to me with a basketful he had been picking. As an experiment on the price, I offered him a two-centime piece, which is a sort of satire on the very name of money,-- when he desired me to help myself to as many oranges as I liked. He was a fine-looking fellow, with a spick-span new red Phrygian cap; and I had n't the heart to take advantage of his generosity, especially as his oranges were not of the sweetest. One ought never to abuse generosity.

Another experience was of a different sort, and illustrates the Italian love of bargaining, and their notion of a sliding scale of prices. One of our expeditions to the hills was one day making its long, straggling way through the narrow street of a little village of the Piano, when I lingered behind my companions, attracted by a handcart with several large baskets of oranges. The cart stood untended in the street; and selecting a large orange, which would measure twelve inches in circumference, I turned to look for the owner. After some time a fellow got from the open front of the neighboring cobbler's shop, where he sat with his lazy cronies, listening to the honest gossip of the follower of St. Crispin, and sauntered towards me.

"How much for this?" I ask.

"One franc, signor," says the proprietor, with a polite bow, holding up one finger.

I shake my head, and intimate that that is altogether too much, in fact, preposterous.

The proprietor is very indifferent, and shrugs his shoulders in an amiable manner. He picks up a fair, handsome orange, weighs it in his hand, and holds it up temptingly. That also is one, franc.

I suggest one sou as a fair price, a suggestion which he only receives with a smile of slight pity, and, I fancy, a little disdain. A woman joins him, and also holds up this and that gold-skinned one for my admiration.

As I stand, sorting over the fruit, trying to please myself with size, color, and texture, a little crowd has gathered round; and I see, by a glance, that all the occupations in that neighborhood, including loafing, are temporarily suspended to witness the trade. The interest of the circle visibly increases; and others take such a part in the transaction that I begin to doubt if the first man is, after all, the proprietor.

At length I select two oranges, and again demand the price. There is a little consultation and jabber, when I am told that I can have both for a franc. I, in turn, sigh, shrug my shoulders, and put down the oranges, amid a chorus of exclamations over my graspingness. My offer of two sous is met with ridicule, but not with indifference. I can see that it has made a sensation. These simple, idle children of the sun begin to show a little excitement. I at length determine upon a bold stroke, and resolve to show myself the Napoleon of oranges, or to meet my Waterloo. I pick out four of the largest oranges in the basket, while all eyes are fixed on me intently, and, for the first time, pull out a piece of money. It is a two-sous piece. I offer it for the four oranges.

"No, no, no, no, signor! Ah, signor! ah, signor!" in a chorus from the whole crowd.

I have struck bottom at last, and perhaps got somewhere near the value; and all calmness is gone. Such protestations, such indignation, such sorrow, I have never seen before from so small a cause. It cannot be thought of; it is mere ruin! I am, in turn, as firm, and nearly as excited in seeming. I hold up the fruit, and tender the money.

"No, never, never! The signor cannot be in earnest."

Looking round me for a moment, and assuming a theatrical manner, befitting the gestures of those about me, I fling the fruit down, and, with a sublime renunciation, stalk away.

There is instantly a buzz and a hum that rises almost to a clamor. I have not proceeded far, when a skinny old woman runs after me, and begs me to return. I go back, and the crowd parts to receive me.

The proprietor has a new proposition, the effect of which upon me is intently watched. He proposes to give me five big oranges for four sous. I receive it with utter scorn, and a laugh of derision. I will give two sous for the original four, and not a centesimo more. That I solemnly say, and am ready to depart. Hesitation and renewed conference; but at last the proprietor relents; and, with the look of one who is ruined for life, and who yet is willing to sacrifice himself, he hands me the oranges. Instantly the excitement is dead, the crowd disperses, and the street is as quiet as ever; when I walk away, bearing my hard-won treasures.

A little while after, as I sat upon the outer wall of the terrace of the Camaldoli, with my feet hanging over, these same oranges were taken from my pockets by Americans; so that I am prevented from making any moral reflections upon the honesty of the Italians.

There is an immense garden of oranges and lemons at the village of Massa, through which travelers are shown by a surly fellow, who keeps watch of his trees, and has a bulldog lurking about for the unwary. I hate to see a bulldog in a fruit orchard. I have eaten a good many oranges there, and been astonished at the boughs of immense lemons which bend the trees to the ground. I took occasion to measure one of the lemons, called a citron-lemon, and found its circumference to be twenty-one inches one way by fifteen inches the other,--about as big as a railway conductor's lantern. These lemons are not so sour as the fellow who shows them: he is a mercenary dog, and his prices afford me no clew to the just value of oranges.

I like better to go to a little garden in the village of Meta, under a sunny precipice of rocks overhung by the ruined convent of Camaldoli. I turn up a narrow lane, and push open the wooden door in the garden of a little villa. It is a pretty garden; and, besides the orange and lemon-trees on the terrace, it has other fruit-trees, and a scent of many flowers. My friend, the gardener, is sorting oranges from one basket to another, on a green bank, and evidently selling the fruit to some women, who are putting it into bags to carry away.

When he sees me approach, there is always the same pantomime. I propose to take some of the fruit he is sorting. With a knowing air, and an appearance of great mystery, he raises his left hand, the palm toward me, as one says hush. Having dispatched his business, he takes an empty basket, and with another mysterious flourish, desiring me to remain quiet, he goes to a storehouse in one corner of the garden, and returns with a load of immense oranges, all soaked with the sun, ripe and fragrant, and more tempting than lumps of gold. I take one, and ask him if it is sweet. He shrugs his shoulders, raises his hands, and, with a sidewise shake of the head, and a look which says, How can you be so faithless? makes me ashamed of my doubts.

I cut the thick skin, which easily falls apart and discloses the luscious quarters, plump, juicy, and waiting to melt in the mouth. I look for a moment at the rich pulp in its soft incasement, and then try a delicious morsel. I nod. My gardener again shrugs his shoulders, with a slight smile, as much as to say, It could not be otherwise, and is evidently delighted to have me enjoy his fruit. I fill capacious pockets with the choicest; and, if I have friends with me, they do the same. I give our silent but most expressive entertainer half a franc, never more; and he always seems surprised at the size of the largesse. We exhaust his basket, and he proposes to get more.

When I am alone, I stroll about under the heavily-laden trees, and pick up the largest, where they lie thickly on the ground, liking to hold them in my hand and feel the agreeable weight, even when I can carry away no more. The gardener neither follows nor watches me; and I think perhaps knows, and is not stingy about it, that more valuable to me than the oranges I eat or take away are those on the trees among the shining leaves. And perhaps he opines that I am from a country of snow and ice, where the year has six hostile months, and that I have not money enough to pay for the rich possession of the eye, the picture of beauty, which I take with me.

FASCINATION

There are three places where I should like to live; naming them in the inverse order of preference,--the Isle of Wight, Sorrento, and Heaven. The first two have something in common, the almost mystic union of sky and sea and shore, a soft atmospheric suffusion that works an enchantment, and puts one into a dreamy mood. And yet there are decided contrasts. The superabundant, soaking sunshine of Sorrento is of very different quality from that of the Isle of Wight. On the island there is a sense of home, which one misses on this promontory, the fascination of which, no less strong, is that of a southern beauty, whose charms conquer rather than win.

I remember with what feeling I one day unexpectedly read on a white slab, in the little inclosure of Bonchurch, where the sea whispered as gently as the rustle of the ivy-leaves, the name of John Sterling. Could there be any fitter resting-place for that most, weary, and gentle spirit? There I seemed to know he had the rest that he could not have anywhere on these brilliant historic shores. Yet so impressible was his sensitive nature, that I doubt not, if he had given himself up to the enchantment of these coasts in his lifetime, it would have led him by a spell he could not break.

I am sometimes in doubt what is the spell of Sorrento, and half believe that it is independent of anything visible. There is said to be a fatal enchantment about Capri. The influences of Sorrento are not so dangerous, but are almost as marked. I do not wonder that the Greeks peopled every cove and sea-cave with divinities, and built temples on every headland and rocky islet here; that the Romans built upon the Grecian ruins; that the ecclesiastics in succeeding centuries gained possession of all the heights, and built convents and monasteries, and set out vineyards, and orchards of olives and oranges, and took root as the creeping plants do, spreading themselves abroad in the sunshine and charming air. The Italian of to-day does not willingly emigrate, is tempted by no seduction of better fortune in any foreign clime. And so in all ages the swarming populations have clung to these shores, filling all the coasts and every nook in these almost inaccessible hills with life. Perhaps the delicious climate, which avoids all extremes, sufficiently accounts for this; and yet I have sometimes thought there is a more subtle reason why travelers from far lands are spellbound here, often against will and judgment, week after week, month after month.

However this may be, it is certain that strangers who come here, and remain long enough to get entangled in the meshes which some influence, I know not what, throws around them, are in danger of never departing. I know there are scores of travelers, who whisk down from Naples, guidebook in hand, goaded by the fell purpose of seeing every place in Europe, ascend some height, buy a load of the beautiful inlaid woodwork, perhaps row over to Capri and stay five minutes in the azure grotto, and then whisk away again, untouched by the glamour of the place. Enough that they write "delightful spot" in their diaries, and hurry off to new scenes, and more noisy life. But the visitor who yields himself to the place will soon find his power of will departing. Some satirical people say, that, as one grows strong in body here, he becomes weak in mind. The theory I do not accept: one simply folds his sails, unships his rudder, and waits the will of Providence, or the arrival of some compelling fate. The longer one remains, the more difficult it is to go. We have a fashion--indeed, I may call it a habit--of deciding to go, and of never going. It is a subject of infinite jest among the habitues of the villa, who meet at table, and who are always bidding each other good-by. We often go so far as to write to Naples at night, and bespeak rooms in the hotels; but we always countermand the order before we sit down to breakfast. The good-natured mistress of affairs, the head of the bureau of domestic relations, is at her wits' end, with guests who always promise to go and never depart. There are here a gentleman and his wife, English people of decision enough, I presume, in Cornwall, who packed their luggage before Christmas to depart, but who have not gone towards the end of February,--who daily talk of going, and little by little unpack their wardrobe, as their determination oozes out. It is easy enough to decide at night to go next day; but in the morning, when the soft sunshine comes in at the window, and when we descend and walk in the garden, all our good intentions vanish. It is not simply that we do not go away, but we have lost the motive for those long excursions which we made at first, and which more adventurous travelers indulge in. There are those here who have intended for weeks to spend a day on Capri. Perfect day for the expedition succeeds perfect day, boatload after boatload sails away from the little marina at the base of the cliff, which we follow with eyes of desire, but--to-morrow will do as well. We are powerless to break the enchantment.

I confess to the fancy that there is some subtle influence working this sea-change in us, which the guidebooks, in their enumeration of the delights of the region, do not touch, and which maybe reaches back beyond the Christian era. I have always supposed that the story of Ulysses and the Sirens was only a fiction of the poets, intended to illustrate the allurements of a soul given over to pleasure, and deaf to the call of duty and the excitement of a grapple with the world. But a lady here, herself one of the entranced, tells me that whoever climbs the hills behind Sorrento, and looks upon the Isle of the Sirens, is struck with an inability to form a desire to depart from these coasts. I have gazed at those islands more than once, as they lie there in the Bay of Salerno; and it has always happened that they have been in a half-misty and not uncolored sunlight, but not so draped that I could not see they were only three irregular rocks, not far from shore, one of them with some ruins on it. There are neither sirens there now, nor any other creatures; but I should be sorry to think I should never see them again. When I look down on them, I can also turn and behold on the other side, across the Bay of Naples, the Posilipo, where one of the enchanters who threw magic over them is said to lie in his high tomb at the opening of the grotto. Whether he does sleep in his urn in that exact spot is of no moment. Modern life has disillusioned this region to a great extent; but the romance that the old poets have woven about these bays and rocky promontories comes very easily back upon one who submits himself long to the eternal influences of sky and sea which made them sing. It is all one,--to be a Roman poet in his villa, a lazy friar of the Middle Ages toasting in the sun, or a modern idler, who has drifted here out of the active currents of life, and cannot make up his mind to depart.

MONKISH PERCHES

On heights at either end of the Piano di Sorrento, and commanding it, stood two religious houses: the Convent of the Carnaldoli to the northeast, on the crest of the hill above Meta; the Carthusian Monastery of the Deserto, to the southwest, three miles above Sorrento. The longer I stay here, the more respect I have for the taste of the monks of the Middle Ages. They invariably secured the best places for themselves. They seized all the strategic points; they appropriated all the commanding heights; they knew where the sun would best strike the grapevines; they perched themselves wherever there was a royal view. When I see how unerringly they did select and occupy the eligible places, I think they were moved by a sort of inspiration. In those days, when the Church took the first choice in everything, the temptation to a Christian life must have been strong.

The monastery at the Deserto was suppressed by the French of the first republic, and has long been in a ruinous condition. Its buildings crown the apex of the highest elevation in this part of the promontory: from its roof the fathers paternally looked down upon the churches and chapels and nunneries which thickly studded all this region; so that I fancy the air must have been full of the sound of bells, and of incense perpetually ascending. They looked also upon St. Agata under the hill, with a church bigger than itself; upon more distinct Massa, with its chapels and cathedral and overlooking feudal tower; upon Torca, the Greek Theorica, with its Temple of Apollo, the scene yet of an annual religious festival, to which the peasants of Sorrento go as their ancestors did to the shrine of the heathen god; upon olive and orange orchards, and winding paths and wayside shrines innumerable. A sweet and peaceful scene in the foreground, it must have been, and a whole horizon of enchantment beyond the sunny peninsula over which it lorded: the Mediterranean, with poetic Capri, and Ischia, and all the classic shore from Cape Misenum, Baiae, and Naples, round to Vesuvius; all the sparkling Bay of Naples; and on the other side the Bay of Salerno, covered with the fleets of the commerce of Amalfi, then a republican city of fifty thousand people; and Grecian Paestum on the marshy shore, even then a ruin, its deserted porches and columns monuments of an architecture never equaled elsewhere in Italy. Upon this charming perch, the old Carthusian monks took the summer breezes and the winter sun, pruned their olives, and trimmed their grapevines, and said prayers for the poor sinners toiling in the valleys below.

The monastery is a desolate old shed now. We left our donkeys to eat thistles in front, while we climbed up some dilapidated steps, and entered the crumbling hall. The present occupants are half a dozen monks, and fine fellows too, who have an orphan school of some twenty lads. We were invited to witness their noonday prayers. The flat-roofed rear buildings extend round an oblong, quadrangular space, which is a rich garden, watered from capacious tanks, and coaxed into easy fertility by the impregnating sun. Upon these roofs the brothers were wont to walk, and here they sat at peaceful evening. Here, too, we strolled; and here I could not resist the temptation to lie an unheeded hour or two, soaking in the benignant February sun, above every human concern and care, looking upon a land and sea steeped in romance. The sky was blue above; but in the south horizon, in the direction of Tunis, were the prismatic colors. Why not be a monk, and lie in the sun?

One of the handsome brothers invited us into the refectory, a place as bare and cheerless as the feeding-room of a reform school, and set before us bread and cheese, and red wine, made by the monks. I notice that the monks do not water their wine so much as the osteria keepers do; which speaks equally well for their religion and their taste. The floor of the room was brick, the table plain boards, and the seats were benches; not much luxury. The monk who served us was an accomplished man, traveled, and master of several languages. He spoke English a little. He had been several years in America, and was much interested when we told him our nationality.

"Does the signor live near Mexico?"

"Not in dangerous proximity," we replied; but we did not forfeit his good opinion by saying that we visited it but seldom.

Well, he had seen all quarters of the globe: he had been for years a traveler, but he had come back here with a stronger love for it than ever; it was to him the most delightful spot on earth, he said. And we could not tell him where its equal is. If I had nothing else to do, I think I should cast in my lot with him,--at least for a week.

But the monks never got into a cozier nook than the Convent of the Camaldoli. That also is suppressed: its gardens, avenues, colonnaded walks, terraces, buildings, half in ruins. It is the level surface of a hill, sheltered on the east by higher peaks, and on the north by the more distant range of Great St. Angelo, across the valley, and is one of the most extraordinarily fertile plots of ground I ever saw. The rich ground responds generously to the sun. I should like to have seen the abbot who grew on this fat spot. The workmen were busy in the garden, spading and pruning.

A group of wild, half-naked children came about us begging, as we sat upon the walls of the terrace,--the terrace which overhangs the busy plain below, and which commands the entire, varied, nooky promontory, and the two bays. And these children, insensible to beauty, want centesimi!

In the rear of the church are some splendid specimens of the umbrella-like Italian pine. Here we found, also, a pretty little ruin,--it might be Greek and--it might be Druid for anything that appeared, ivy-clad, and suggesting a religion older than that of the convent. To the east we look into a fertile, terraced ravine; and beyond to a precipitous brown mountain, which shows a sharp outline against the sky; halfway up are nests of towns, white houses, churches, and above, creeping along the slope, the thread of an ancient road, with stone arches at intervals, as old as Caesar.

We descend, skirting for some distance the monastery walls, over which patches of ivy hang like green shawls. There are flowers in profusion, scented violets, daisies, dandelions, and crocuses, large and of the richest variety, with orange pistils, and stamens purple and violet, the back of every alternate leaf exquisitely penciled.

We descend into a continuous settlement, past shrines, past brown, sturdy men and handsome girls working in the vineyards; we descend--but words express nothing--into a wonderful ravine, a sort of refined Swiss scene,--high, bare steps of rock butting over a chasm, ruins, old walls, vines, flowers. The very spirit of peace is here, and it is not disturbed by the sweet sound of bells echoed in the passes. On narrow ledges of precipices, aloft in the air where it would seem that a bird could scarcely light, we distinguish the forms of men and women; and their voices come down to us. They are peasants cutting grass, every spire of which is too precious to waste.

We descend, and pass by a house on a knoll, and a terrace of olives extending along the road in front. Half a dozen children come to the road to look at us as we approach, and then scamper back to the house in fear, tumbling over each other and shouting, the eldest girl making good her escape with the baby. My companion swings his hat, and cries, "Hullo, baby!" And when we have passed the gate, and are under the wall, the whole ragged, brown-skinned troop scurry out upon the terrace, and run along, calling after us, in perfect English, as long as we keep in sight, "Hullo, baby!" "Hullo, baby!" The next traveler who goes that way will no doubt be hailed by the quick-witted natives with this salutation; and, if he is of a philological turn, he will probably benefit his mind by running the phrase back to its ultimate Greek roots.

A DRY TIME

For three years, once upon a time, it did not rain in Sorrento. Not a drop out of the clouds for three years, an Italian lady here, born in Ireland, assures me. If there was an occasional shower on the Piano during all that drought, I have the confidence in her to think that she would not spoil the story by noticing it.

The conformation of the hills encircling the plain would be likely to lead any shower astray, and discharge it into the sea, with whatever good intentions it may have started down the promontory for Sorrento. I can see how these sharp hills would tear the clouds asunder, and let out all their water, while the people in the plain below watched them with longing eyes. But it can rain in Sorrento. Occasionally the northeast wind comes down with whirling, howling fury, as if it would scoop villages and orchards out of the little nook; and the rain, riding on the whirl-wind, pours in drenching floods. At such times I hear the beat of the waves at the foot of the rock, and feel like a prisoner on an island. Eden would not be Eden in a rainstorm.

The drought occurred just after the expulsion of the Bourbons from Naples, and many think on account of it. There is this to be said in favor of the Bourbons: that a dry time never had occurred while they reigned,--a statement in which all good Catholics in Sorrento will concur. As the drought went on, almost all the wells in the place dried up, except that of the Tramontano and the one in the suppressed convent of the Sacred Heart,--I think that is its name.

It is a rambling pile of old buildings, in the center of the town, with a court-yard in the middle, and in it a deep well, boring down I know not how far into the rock, and always full of cold sweet water. The nuns have all gone now; and I look in vain up at the narrow slits in the masonry, which served them for windows, for the glance of a worldly or a pious eye. The poor people of Sorrento, when the public wells and fountains had gone dry, used to come and draw at the Tramontano; but they were not allowed to go to the well of the convent, the gates were closed. Why the government shut them I cannot see: perhaps it knew nothing of it, and some stupid official took the pompous responsibility. The people grumbled, and cursed the government; and, in their simplicity, probably never took any steps to revoke the prohibitory law. No doubt, as the government had caused the drought, it was all of a piece, the good rustics thought.

For the government did indirectly occasion the dry spell. I have the information from the Italian lady of whom I have spoken. Among the first steps of the new government of Italy was the suppression of the useless convents and nunneries. This one at Sorrento early came under the ban. It always seemed to me almost a pity to rout out this asylum of praying and charitable women, whose occupation was the encouragement of beggary and idleness in others, but whose prayers were constant, and whose charities to the sick of the little city were many. If they never were of much good to the community, it was a pleasure to have such a sweet little hive in the center of it; and I doubt not that the simple people felt a genuine satisfaction, as they walked around the high walls, in believing that pure prayers within were put up for them night and day; and especially when they waked at night, and heard the bell of the convent, and knew that at that moment some faithful soul kept her vigils, and chanted prayers for them and all the world besides; and they slept the sounder for it thereafter. I confess that, if one is helped by vicarious prayer, I would rather trust a convent of devoted women (though many of them are ignorant, and some of them are worldly, and none are fair to see) to pray for me, than some of the houses of coarse monks which I have seen.

But the order came down from Naples to pack off all the nuns of the Sacred Heart on a day named, to close up the gates of the nunnery, and hang a flaming sword outside. The nuns were to be pulled up by the roots, so to say, on the day specified, and without postponement, and to be transferred to a house prepared for them at Massa, a few miles down the promontory, and several hundred feet nearer heaven. Sorrento was really in mourning: it went about in grief. It seemed as if something sacrilegious were about to be done. It was the intention of the whole town to show its sense of it in some way.

The day of removal came, and it rained! It poured: the water came down in sheets, in torrents, in deluges; it came down with the wildest tempest of many a year. I think, from accurate reports of those who witnessed it, that the beginning of the great Deluge was only a moisture compared to this. To turn the poor women out of doors such a day as this was unchristian, barbarous, impossible. Everybody who had a shelter was shivering indoors. But the officials were inexorable. In the order for removal, nothing was said about postponement on account of weather; and go the nuns must.

And go they did; the whole town shuddering at the impiety of it, but kept from any demonstration by the tempest. Carriages went round to the convent; and the women were loaded into them, packed into them, carried and put in, if they were too infirm to go themselves. They were driven away, cross and wet and bedraggled. They found their dwelling on the hill not half prepared for them, leaking and cold and cheerless. They experienced very rough treatment, if I can credit my informant, who says she hates the government, and would not even look out of her lattice that day to see the carriages drive past.

And when the Lady Superior was driven away from the gate, she said to the officials, and the few faithful attendants, prophesying in the midst of the rain that poured about her, "The day will come shortly, when you will want rain, and shall not have it; and you will pray for my return."

And it did not rain, from that day for three years.

And the simple people thought of the good Superior, whose departure had been in such a deluge, and who had taken away with her all the moisture of the land; and they did pray for her return, and believed that the gates of heaven would be again opened if only the nunnery were repeopled. But the government could not see the connection between convents and the theory of storms, and the remnant of pious women was permitted to remain in their lodgings at Massa. Perhaps the government thought they could, if they bore no malice, pray as effectually for rain there as anywhere.

I do not know, said my informant, that the curse of the Lady Superior had anything to do with the drought, but many think it had; and those are the facts.

CHILDREN OF THE SUN

The common people of this region are nothing but children; and ragged, dirty, and poor as they are, apparently as happy, to speak idiomatically, as the day is long. It takes very little to please them; and their easily-excited mirth is contagious. It is very rare that one gets a surly return to a salutation; and, if one shows the least good-nature, his greeting is met with the most jolly return. The boatman hauling in his net sings; the brown girl, whom we meet descending a steep path in the hills, with an enormous bag or basket of oranges on her head, or a building-stone under which she stands as erect as a pillar, sings; and, if she asks for something, there is a merry twinkle in her eye, that says she hardly expects money, but only puts in a "beg" at a venture because it is the fashion; the workmen clipping the olive-trees sing; the urchins, who dance about the foreigner in the street, vocalize their petitions for un po' di moneta in a tuneful manner, and beg more in a spirit of deviltry than with any expectation of gain. When I see how hard the peasants labor, what scraps and vegetable odds and ends they eat, and in what wretched, dark, and smoke-dried apartments they live, I wonder they are happy; but I suppose it is the all-nourishing sun and the equable climate that do the business for them. They have few artificial wants, and no uneasy expectation--bred by the reading of books and newspapers--that anything is going to happen in the world, or that any change is possible. Their fruit-trees yield abundantly year after year; their little patches of rich earth, on the built-up terraces and in the crevices of the rocks, produce four-fold. The sun does it all.

Every walk that we take here with open mind and cheerful heart is sure to be an adventure. Only yesterday, we were coming down a branch of the great gorge which splits the plain in two. On one side the path is a high wall, with garden trees overhanging. On the other, a stone parapet; and below, in the bed of the ravine, an orange orchard. Beyond rises a precipice; and, at its foot, men and boys were quarrying stone, which workmen raised a couple of hundred feet to the platform above with a windlass. As we came along, a handsome girl on the height had just taken on her head a large block of stone, which I should not care to lift, to carry to a pile in the rear; and she stopped to look at us. We stopped, and looked at her. This attracted the attention of the men and boys in the quarry below, who stopped work, and set up a cry for a little money. We laughed, and responded in English. The windlass ceased to turn. The workmen on the height joined in the conversation. A grizzly beggar hobbled up, and held out his greasy cap. We nonplussed him by extending our hats, and beseeching him for just a little something. Some passers on the road paused, and looked on, amused at the transaction. A boy appeared on the high wall, and began to beg. I threatened to shoot him with my walkingstick, whereat he ran nimbly along the wall in terror The workmen shouted; and this started up a couple of yellow dogs, which came to the edge of the wall and barked violently. The girl, alone calm in the confusion, stood stock still under her enormous load looking at us. We swung out hats, and hurrahed. The crowd replied from above, below, and around us, shouting, laughing, singing, until the whole little valley was vocal with a gale of merriment, and all about nothing. The beggar whined; the spectators around us laughed; and the whole population was aroused into a jolly mood. Fancy such a merry hullaballoo in America. For ten minutes, while the funny row was going on, the girl never moved, having forgotten to go a few steps and deposit her load; and when we disappeared round a bend of the path, she was still watching us, smiling and statuesque.

As we descend, we come upon a group of little children seated about a door-step, black-eyed, chubby little urchins, who are cutting oranges into little bits, and playing "party," as children do on the other side of the Atlantic. The instant we stop to speak to them, the skinny hand of an old woman is stretched out of a window just above our heads, the wrinkled palm itching for money. The mother comes forward out of the house, evidently pleased with our notice of the children, and shows us the baby in her arms. At once we are on good terms with the whole family. The woman sees that there is nothing impertinent in our cursory inquiry into her domestic concerns, but, I fancy, knows that we are genial travelers, with human sympathies. So the people universally are not quick to suspect any imposition, and meet frankness with frankness, and good-nature with good-nature, in a simple-hearted, primeval manner. If they stare at us from doorway and balcony, or come and stand near us when we sit reading or writing by the shore, it is only a childlike curiosity, and they are quite unconscious of any breach of good manners. In fact, I think travelers have not much to say in the matter of staring. I only pray that we Americans abroad may remember that we are in the presence of older races, and conduct ourselves with becoming modesty, remembering always that we were not born in Britain.

Very likely I am in error; but it has seemed to me that even the funerals here are not so gloomy as in other places. I have looked in at the churches when they are in progress, now and then, and been struck with the general good feeling of the occasion. The real mourners I could not always distinguish; but the seats would be filled with a motley gathering of the idle and the ragged, who seemed to enjoy the show and the ceremony. On one occasion, it was the obsequies of an officer in the army. Guarding the gilded casket, which stood upon a raised platform before the altar, were four soldiers in uniform. Mass was being said and sung; and a priest was playing the organ. The church was light and cheerful, and pervaded by a pleasant bustle. Ragged boys and beggars, and dirty children and dogs, went and came wherever they chose--about the unoccupied spaces of the church. The hired mourners, who are numerous in proportion to the rank of the deceased, were clad in white cotton,--a sort of nightgown put on over the ordinary clothes, with a hood of the same drawn tightly over the face, in which slits were cut for the eyes and mouth. Some of them were seated on benches near the front; others were wandering about among the pillars, disappearing in the sacristy, and reappearing with an aimless aspect, altogether conducting themselves as if it were a holiday, and if there was anything they did enjoy, it was mourning at other people's expense. They laughed and talked with each other in excellent spirits; and one varlet near the coffin, who had slipped off his mask, winked at me repeatedly, as if to inform me that it was not his funeral. A masquerade might have been more gloomy and depressing.

SAINT ANTONINO

The most serviceable saint whom I know is St. Antonino. He is the patron saint of the good town of Sorrento; he is the good genius of all sailors and fishermen; and he has a humbler office,--that of protector of the pigs. On his day the pigs are brought into the public square to be blessed; and this is one reason why the pork of Sorrento is reputed so sweet and wholesome. The saint is the friend, and, so to say, companion of the common people. They seem to be all fond of him, and there is little of fear in their confiding relation. His humble origin and plebeian appearance have something to do with his popularity, no doubt. There is nothing awe-inspiring in the brown stone figure, battered and cracked, that stands at one corner of the bridge, over the chasm at the entrance of the city. He holds a crosier in one hand, and raises the other, with fingers uplifted, in act of benediction. If his face is an indication of his character, he had in him a mixture of robust good-nature with a touch of vulgarity, and could rough it in a jolly manner with fishermen and peasants. He may have appeared to better advantage when he stood on top of the massive old city gate, which the present government, with the impulse of a vandal, took down a few years ago. The demolition had to be accomplished in the night, under a guard of soldiers, so indignant were the populace. At that time the homely saint was deposed; and he wears now, I think, a snubbed and cast-aside aspect. Perhaps he is dearer to the people than ever; and I confess that I like him much better than many grander saints, in stone, I have seen in more conspicuous places. If ever I am in rough water and foul weather, I hope he will not take amiss anything I have here written about him.

Sunday, and it happened to be St. Valentine's also, was the great fete-day of St. Antonino. Early in the morning there was a great clanging of bells; and the ceremony of the blessing of the pigs took place,--I heard, but I was not abroad early enough to see it,--a laziness for which I fancy I need not apologize, as the Catholic is known to be an earlier religion than the Protestant. When I did go out, the streets were thronged with people, the countryfolk having come in for miles around. The church of the patron saint was the great center of attraction. The blank walls of the little square in front, and of the narrow streets near, were hung with cheap and highly-colored lithographs of sacred subjects, for sale; tables and booths were set up in every available space for the traffic in pre-Raphaelite gingerbread, molasses candy, strings of dried nuts, pinecone and pumpkin seeds, scarfs, boots and shoes, and all sorts of trumpery. One dealer had preempted a large space on the pavement, where he had spread out an assortment of bits of old iron, nails, pieces of steel traps, and various fragments which might be useful to the peasants. The press was so great, that it was difficult to get through it; but the crowd was a picturesque one, and in the highest good humor. The occasion was a sort of Fourth of July, but without its worry and powder and flowing bars.

The spectacle of the day was the procession bearing the silver image of the saint through the streets. I think there could never be anything finer or more impressive; at least, I like these little fussy provincial displays,--these tag-rags and ends of grandeur, in which all the populace devoutly believe, and at which they are lost in wonder,--better than those imposing ceremonies at the capital, in which nobody believes. There was first a band of musicians, walking in more or less disorder, but blowing away with great zeal, so that they could be heard amid the clangor of bells the peals of which reverberate so deafeningly between the high houses of these narrow streets. Then follow boys in white, and citizens in black and white robes, carrying huge silken banners, triangular like sea-pennants, and splendid silver crucifixes which flash in the sun. Then come ecclesiastics, walking with stately step, and chanting in loud and pleasant unison. These are followed by nobles, among whom I recognize, with a certain satisfaction, two descendants of Tasso, whose glowing and bigoted soul may rejoice in the devotion of his posterity, who help to bear to-day the gilded platform upon which is the solid silver image of the saint. The good old bishop walks humbly in the rear, in full canonical rig, with crosier and miter, his rich robes upborne by priestly attendants, his splendid footman at a respectful distance, and his roomy carriage not far behind.

The procession is well spread out and long; all its members carry lighted tapers, a good many of which are not lighted, having gone out in the wind. As I squeeze into a shallow doorway to let the cortege pass, I am sorry to say that several of the young fellows in white gowns tip me the wink, and even smile in a knowing fashion, as if it were a mere lark, after all, and that the saint must know it. But not so thinks the paternal bishop, who waves a blessing, which I catch in the flash of the enormous emerald on his right hand. The procession ends, where it started, in the patron's church; and there his image is set up under a gorgeous canopy of crimson and gold, to hear high mass, and some of the choicest solos, choruses, and bravuras from the operas.

In the public square I find a gaping and wondering crowd of rustics collected about one of the mountebanks whose trade is not peculiar to any country. This one might be a clock-peddler from Connecticut. He is mounted in a one-seat vettura, and his horse is quietly eating his dinner out of a bag tied to his nose. There is nothing unusual in the fellow's dress; he wears a shiny silk hat, and has one of those grave faces which would be merry if their owner were not conscious of serious business on hand. On the driver's perch before him are arranged his attractions,--a box of notions, a grinning skull, with full teeth and jaws that work on hinges, some vials of red liquid, and a closed jar containing a most disagreeable anatomical preparation. This latter he holds up and displays, turning it about occasionally in an admiring manner. He is discoursing, all the time, in the most voluble Italian. He has an ointment, wonderfully efficacious for rheumatism and every sort of bruise: he pulls up his sleeve, and anoints his arm with it, binding it up with a strip of paper; for the simplest operation must be explained to these grown children. He also pulls teeth, with an ease and expedition hitherto unknown, and is in no want of patients among this open-mouthed crowd. One sufferer after another climbs up into the wagon, and goes through the operation in the public gaze. A stolid, good-natured hind mounts the seat. The dentist examines his mouth, and finds the offending tooth. He then turns to the crowd and explains the case. He takes a little instrument that is neither forceps nor turnkey, stands upon the seat, seizes the man's nose, and jerks his head round between his knees, pulling his mouth open (there is nothing that opens the mouth quicker than a sharp upward jerk of the nose) with a rude jollity that sets the spectators in a roar. Down he goes into the cavern, and digs away for a quarter of a minute, the man the while as immovable as a stone image, when he holds up the bloody tooth. The patient still persists in sitting with his mouth stretched open to its widest limit, waiting for the operation to begin, and will only close the orifice when he is well shaken and shown the tooth. The dentist gives him some yellow liquid to hold in his mouth, which the man insists on swallowing, wets a handkerchief and washes his face, roughly rubbing his nose the wrong way, and lets him go. Every step of the process is eagerly watched by the delighted spectators.

He is succeeded by a woman, who is put through the same heroic treatment, and exhibits like fortitude. And so they come; and the dentist after every operation waves the extracted trophy high in air, and jubilates as if he had won another victory, pointing to the stone statue yonder, and reminding them that this is the glorious day of St. Antonino. But this is not all that this man of science does. He has the genuine elixir d'amour, love-philters and powders which never fail in their effects. I see the bashful girls and the sheepish swains come slyly up to the side of the wagon, and exchange their hard-earned francs for the hopeful preparation. O my brown beauty, with those soft eyes and cheeks of smothered fire, you have no need of that red philter! What a simple, childlike folk! The shrewd fellow in the wagon is one of a race as old as Thebes and as new as Porkopolis; his brazen face is older than the invention of bronze, but I think he never had to do with a more credulous crowd than this. The very cunning in the face of the peasants is that of the fox; it is a sort of instinct, and not an intelligent suspicion.

This is Sunday in Sorrento, under the blue sky. These peasants, who are fooled by the mountebank and attracted by the piles of adamantine gingerbread, do not forget to crowd the church of the saint at vespers, and kneel there in humble faith, while the choir sings the Agnus Dei, and the priests drone the service. Are they so different, then, from other people? They have an idea on Capri that England is such another island, only not so pleasant; that all Englishmen are rich and constantly travel to escape the dreariness at home; and that, if they are not absolutely mad, they are all a little queer. It was a fancy prevalent in Hamlet's day. We had the English service in the Villa Nardi in the evening. There are some Englishmen staying here, of the class one finds in all the sunny spots of Europe, ennuye and growling, in search of some elixir that shall bring back youth and enjoyment. They seem divided in mind between the attractions of the equable climate of this region and the fear of the gout which lurks in the unfermented wine. One cannot be too grateful to the sturdy islanders for carrying their prayers, like their drumbeat, all round the globe; and I was much edified that night, as the reading went on, by a row of rather battered men of the world, who stood in line on one side of the room, and took their prayers with a certain British fortitude, as if they were conscious of performing a constitutional duty, and helping by the act to uphold the majesty of English institutions.

PUNTA DELLA CAMPANELLA

There is always a mild excitement about mounting donkeys in the morning here for an excursion among the hills. The warm sun pouring into the garden, the smell of oranges, the stimulating air, the general openness and freshness, promise a day of enjoyment. There is always a doubt as to who will go; generally a don-key wanting; somebody wishes to join the party at the last moment; there is no end of running up and downstairs, calling from balconies and terraces; some never ready, and some waiting below in the sun; the whole house in a tumult, drivers in a worry, and the sleepy animals now and then joining in the clatter with a vocal performance that is neither a trumpet-call nor a steam-whistle, but an indescribable noise, that begins in agony and abruptly breaks down in despair. It is difficult to get the train in motion. The lady who ordered Succarina has got a strange donkey, and Macaroni has on the wrong saddle. Succarina is a favorite, the kindest, easiest, and surest-footed of beasts,--a diminutive animal, not bigger than a Friesland sheep; old, in fact grizzly with years, and not unlike the aged, wizened little women who are so common here: for beauty in this region dries up; and these handsome Sor-rento girls, if they live, and almost everybody does live, have the prospect, in their old age, of becoming mummies, with parchment skins. I have heard of climates that preserve female beauty; this embalms it, only the beauty escapes in the process. As I was saying, Succarina is little, old, and grizzly; but her head is large, and one might be contented to be as wise as she looks.

The party is at length mounted, and clatters away through the narrow streets. Donkey-riding is very good for people who think they cannot walk. It looks very much like riding, to a spectator; and it deceives the person undertaking it into an amount of exercise equal to walking. I have a great admiration for the donkey character. There never was such patience under wrong treatment, such return of devotion for injury. Their obstinacy, which is so much talked about, is only an exercise of the right of private judgment, and an intelligent exercise of it, no doubt, if we could take the donkey point of view, as so many of us are accused of doing in other things. I am certain of one thing: in any large excursion party there will be more obstinate people than obstinate donkeys; and yet the poor brutes get all the thwacks and thumps. We are bound to-day for the Punta della Campanella, the extreme point of the promontory, and ten miles away. The path lies up the steps from the new Massa carriage-road, now on the backbone of the ridge, and now in the recesses of the broken country. What an animated picture is the donkeycade, as it mounts the steeps, winding along the zigzags! Hear the little bridlebells jingling, the drivers groaning their "a-e-ugh, a-e-ugh," the riders making a merry din of laughter, and firing off a fusillade of ejaculations of delight and wonder.

The road is between high walls; round the sweep of curved terraces which rise above and below us, bearing the glistening olive; through glens and gullies; over and under arches, vine-grown,--how little we make use of the arch at home!--round sunny dells where orange orchards gleam; past shrines, little chapels perched on rocks, rude villas commanding most extensive sweeps of sea and shore. The almond trees are in full bloom, every twig a thickly-set spike of the pink and white blossoms; daisies and dandelions are out; the purple crocuses sprinkle the ground, the petals exquisitely varied on the reverse side, and the stamens of bright salmon color; the large double anemones have come forth, certain that it is spring; on the higher crags by the wayside the Mediterranean heather has shaken out its delicate flowers, which fill the air with a mild fragrance; while blue violets, sweet of scent like the English, make our path a perfumed one. And this is winter.

We have made a late start, owing to the fact that everybody is captain of the expedition, and to the Sorrento infirmity that no one is able to make up his mind about anything. It is one o'clock when we reach a high transverse ridge, and find the headlands of the peninsula rising before us, grim hills of limestone, one of them with the ruins of a convent on top, and no road apparent thither, and Capri ahead of us in the sea, the only bit of land that catches any light; for as we have journeyed the sky has thickened, the clouds of the sirocco have come up from the south; there has been first a mist, and then a fine rain; the ruins on the peak of Santa Costanza are now hid in mist. We halt for consultation. Shall we go on and brave a wetting, or ignominiously retreat? There are many opinions, but few decided ones. The drivers declare that it will be a bad time. One gentleman, with an air of decision, suggests that it is best to go on, or go back, if we do not stand here and wait. The deaf lady, from near Dublin, being appealed to, says that, perhaps, if it is more prudent, we had better go back if it is going to rain. It does rain. Waterproofs are put on, umbrellas spread, backs turned to the wind; and we look like a group of explorers under adverse circumstances, "silent on a peak in Darien," the donkeys especially downcast and dejected. Finally, as is usual in life, a compromise prevails. We decide to continue for half an hour longer and see what the weather is. No sooner have we set forward over the brow of a hill than it grows lighter on the sea horizon in the southwest, the ruins on the peak become visible, Capri is in full sunlight. The clouds lift more and more, and still hanging overhead, but with no more rain, are like curtains gradually drawn up, opening to us a glorious vista of sunshine and promise, an illumined, sparkling, illimitable sea, and a bright foreground of slopes and picturesque rocks. Before the half hour is up, there is not one of the party who does not claim to have been the person who insisted upon going forward.

We halt for a moment to look at Capri, that enormous, irregular rock, raising its huge back out of the sea, its back broken in the middle, with the little village for a saddle. On the farther summit, above Anacapri, a precipice of two thousand feet sheer down to the water on the other side, hangs a light cloud. The east elevation, whence the playful Tiberius used to amuse his green old age by casting his prisoners eight hundred feet down into the sea, has the strong sunlight on it; and below, the row of tooth-like rocks, which are the extreme eastern point, shine in a warm glow. We descend through a village, twisting about in its crooked streets. The inhabitants, who do not see strangers every day, make free to stare at and comment on us, and even laugh at something that seems very comical in our appearance; which shows how ridiculous are the costumes of Paris and New York in some places. Stalwart girls, with only an apology for clothes, with bare legs, brown faces, and beautiful eyes, stop in their spinning, holding the distaff suspended, while they examine us at leisure. At our left, as we turn from the church and its sunny piazza, where old women sit and gabble, down the ravine, is a snug village under the mountain by the shore, with a great square medieval tower. On the right, upon rocky points, are remains of round towers, and temples perhaps.

We sweep away to the left round the base of the hill, over a difficult and stony path. Soon the last dilapidated villa is passed, the last terrace and olive-tree are left behind; and we emerge upon a wild, rocky slope, barren of vegetation, except little tufts of grass and a sort of lentil; a wide sweep of limestone strata set on edge, and crumbling in the beat of centuries, rising to a considerable height on the left. Our path descends toward the sea, still creeping round the end of the promontory. Scattered here and there over the rocks, like conies, are peasants, tending a few lean cattle, and digging grasses from the crevices. The women and children are wild in attire and manner, and set up a clamor of begging as we pass. A group of old hags begin beating a poor child as we approach, to excite our compassion for the abused little object, and draw out centimes.

Walking ahead of the procession, which gets slowly down the rugged path, I lose sight of my companions, and have the solitude, the sun on the rocks, the glistening sea, all to myself. Soon I espy a man below me sauntering down among the rocks. He sees me and moves away, a solitary figure. I say solitary; and so it is in effect, although he is leading a little boy, and calling to his dog, which runs back to bark at me. Is this the brigand of whom I have read, and is he luring me to his haunt? Probably. I follow. He throws his cloak about his shoulders, exactly as brigands do in the opera, and loiters on. At last there is the point in sight, a gray wall with blind arches. The man disappears through a narrow archway, and I follow. Within is an enormous square tower. I think it was built in Spanish days, as an outlook for Barbary pirates. A bell hung in it, which was set clanging when the white sails of the robbers appeared to the southward; and the alarm was repeated up the coast, the towers were manned, and the brown-cheeked girls flew away to the hills, I doubt not, for the touch of the sirocco was not half so much to be dreaded as the rough importunity of a Saracen lover. The bell is gone now, and no Moslem rovers are in sight. The maidens we had just passed would be safe if there were.

My brigand disappears round the tower; and I follow down steps, by a white wall, and lo! a house,--a red stucco, Egyptian-looking building,--on the very edge of the rocks. The man unlocks a door and goes in. I consider this an invitation, and enter. On one side of the passage a sleeping-room, on the other a kitchen,--not sumptuous quarters; and we come then upon a pretty circular terrace; and there, in its glass case, is the lantern of the point. My brigand is a lighthouse-keeper, and welcomes me in a quiet way, glad, evidently, to see the face of a civilized being. It is very solitary, he says. I should think so. It is the end of everything. The Mediterranean waves beat with a dull thud on the worn crags below. The rocks rise up to the sky behind. There is nothing there but the sun, an occasional sail, and quiet, petrified Capri, three miles distant across the strait. It is an excellent place for a misanthrope to spend a week, and get cured. There must be a very dispiriting influence prevailing here; the keeper refused to take any money, the solitary Italian we have seen so affected.

We returned late. The young moon, lying in the lap of the old one, was superintending the brilliant sunset over Capri, as we passed the last point commanding it; and the light, fading away, left us stumbling over the rough path among the hills, darkened by the high walls. We were not sorry to emerge upon the crest above the Massa road. For there lay the sea, and the plain of Sorrento, with its darkening groves and hundreds of twinkling lights. As we went down the last descent, the bells of the town were all ringing, for it was the eve of the fete of St. Antonino.

CAPRI

"CAP, signor? Good day for Grott." Thus spoke a mariner, touching his Phrygian cap. The people here abbreviate all names. With them Massa is Mas, Meta is Met, Capri becomes Cap, the Grotta Azzurra is reduced familiarly to Grott, and they even curtail musical Sorrento into Serent.

Shall we go to Capri? Should we dare return to the great Republic, and own that we had not been into the Blue Grotto? We like to climb the steeps here, especially towards Massa, and look at Capri. I have read in some book that it used to be always visible from Sorrento. But now the promontory has risen, the Capo di Sorrento has thrust out its rocky spur with its ancient Roman masonry, and the island itself has moved so far round to the south that Sorrento, which fronts north, has lost sight of it.

We never tire of watching it, thinking that it could not be spared from the landscape. It lies only three miles from the curving end of the promontory, and is about twenty miles due south of Naples. In this atmosphere distances dwindle. The nearest land, to the northwest, is the larger island of Ischia, distant nearly as far as Naples; yet Capri has the effect of being anchored off the bay to guard the entrance. It is really a rock, three miles and a half long, rising straight out of the water, eight hundred feet high at one end, and eighteen hundred feet at the other, with a depression between. If it had been chiseled by hand and set there, it could not be more sharply defined. So precipitous are its sides of rock, that there are only two fit boat-landings, the marina on the north side, and a smaller place opposite. One of those light-haired and freckled Englishmen, whose pluck exceeds their discretion, rowed round the island alone in rough water, last summer, against the advice of the boatman, and unable to make a landing, and weary with the strife of the waves, was in considerable peril.

Sharp and clear as Capri is in outline, its contour is still most graceful and poetic. This wonderful atmosphere softens even its ruggedness, and drapes it with hues of enchanting beauty. Sometimes the haze plays fantastic tricks with it,--a cloud-cap hangs on Monte Solaro, or a mist obscures the base, and the massive summits of rock seem to float in the air, baseless fabrics of a vision that the rising wind will carry away perhaps. I know now what Homer means by "wandering islands." Shall we take a boat and sail over there, and so destroy forever another island of the imagination? The bane of travel is the destruction of illusions.

We like to talk about Capri, and to talk of going there. The Sorrento people have no end of gossip about the wild island; and, simple and primitive as they are, Capri is still more out of the world. I do not know what enchantment there is on the island; but--whoever sets foot there, they say, goes insane or dies a drunkard. I fancy the reason of this is found in the fact that the Capri girls are raving beauties. I am not sure but the monotony of being anchored off there in the bay, the monotony of rocks and precipices that goats alone can climb, the monotony of a temperature that scarcely ever, winter and summer, is below 55 or above 75 Fahrenheit indoors, might drive one into lunacy. But I incline to think it is due to the handsome Capri girls.

There are beautiful girls in Sorrento, with a beauty more than skin deep, a glowing, hidden fire, a ripeness like that of the grape and the peach which grows in the soft air and the sun. And they wither, like grapes that hang upon the stem. I have never seen a handsome, scarcely a decent-looking, old woman here. They are lank and dry, and their bones are covered with parchment. One of these brown-cheeked girls, with large, longing eyes, gives the stranger a start, now and then, when he meets her in a narrow way with a basket of oranges on her head. I hope he has the grace to go right by. Let him meditate what this vision of beauty will be like in twenty ears.

The Capri girls are famed as magnificent beauties, but they fade like their mainland sisters. The Saracens used to descend on their island, and carry them off to their harems. The English, a very adventurous people, who have no harems, have followed the Saracens. The young lords and gentlemen have a great fondness for Capri. I hear gossip enough about elopements, and not seldom marriages, with the island girls,--bright girls, with the Greek mother-wit, and surpassingly handsome; but they do not bear transportation to civilized life (any more than some of the native wines do): they accept no intellectual culture; and they lose their beauty as they grow old. What then? The young English blade, who was intoxicated by beauty into an injudicious match and might, as the proverb says, have gone insane if he could not have made it, takes to drink now, and so fulfills the other alternative. Alas! the fatal gift of beauty.

But I do not think Capri is so dangerous as it is represented. For (of course we went to Capri) neither at the marina, where a crowd of bare-legged, vociferous maidens with donkeys assailed us, nor in the village above, did I see many girls for whom and one little isle a person would forswear the world. But I can believe that they grow here. One of our donkey girls was a handsome, dark-skinned, black-eyed girl; but her little sister, a mite of a being of six years, who could scarcely step over the small stones in the road, and was forced to lead the donkey by her sister in order to establish another lien on us for buona mano, was a dirty little angel in rags, and her great soft black eyes will look somebody into the asylum or the drunkard's grave in time, I have no doubt. There was a stout, manly, handsome little fellow of five years, who established himself as the guide and friend of the tallest of our party. His hat was nearly gone; he was sadly out of repair in the rear; his short legs made the act of walking absurd; but he trudged up the hill with a certain dignity. And there was nothing mercenary about his attachment: he and his friend got upon very cordial terms: they exchanged gifts of shells and copper coin, but nothing was said about pay.

Nearly all the inhabitants, young and old, joined us in lively procession, up the winding road of three quarters of a mile, to the town. At the deep gate, entering between thick walls, we stopped to look at the sea. The crowd and clamor at our landing had been so great that we enjoyed the sight of the quiet old woman sitting here in the sun, and the few beggars almost too lazy to stretch out their hands. Within the gate is a large paved square, with the government offices and the tobacco-shop on one side, and the church opposite; between them, up a flight of broad stone steps, is the Hotel Tiberio. Our donkeys walk up them and into the hotel. The church and hotel are six hundred years old; the hotel was a villa belonging to Joanna II. of Naples. We climb to the roof of the quaint old building, and sit there to drink in the strange oriental scene. The landlord says it is like Jaffa or Jerusalem. The landlady, an Irish woman from Devonshire, says it is six francs a day. In what friendly intercourse the neighbors can sit on these flat roofs! How sightly this is, and yet how sheltered! To the east is the height where Augustus, and after him Tiberius, built palaces. To the west, up that vertical wall, by means of five hundred steps cut in the face of the rock, we go to reach the tableland of Anacapri, the primitive village of that name, hidden from view here; the medieval castle of Barbarossa, which hangs over a frightful precipice; and the height of Monte Solaro. The island is everywhere strewn with Roman ruins, and with faint traces of the Greeks.

Capri turns out not to be a barren rock. Broken and picturesque as it is, it is yet covered with vegetation. There is not a foot, one might say a point, of soil that does not bear something; and there is not a niche in the rock, where a scrap of dirt will stay, that is not made useful. The whole island is terraced. The most wonderful thing about it, after all, is its masonry. You come to think, after a time, that the island is not natural rock, but a mass of masonry. If the labor that has been expended here, only to erect platforms for the soil to rest on, had been given to our country, it would have built half a dozen Pacific railways, and cut a canal through the Isthmus.

But the Blue Grotto? Oh, yes! Is it so blue? That depends upon the time of day, the sun, the clouds, and something upon the person who enters it. It is frightfully blue to some. We bend down in our rowboat, slide into the narrow opening which is three feet high, and passing into the spacious cavern, remain there for half an hour. It is, to be sure, forty feet high, and a hundred by a hundred and fifty in extent, with an arched roof, and clear water for a floor. The water appears to be as deep as the roof is high, and is of a light, beautiful blue, in contrast with the deep blue of the bay. At the entrance the water is illuminated, and there is a pleasant, mild light within: one has there a novel subterranean sensation; but it did not remind me of anything I have seen in the "Arabian Nights." I have seen pictures of it that were much finer.

As we rowed close to the precipice in returning, I saw many similar openings, not so deep, and perhaps only sham openings; and the water-line was fretted to honeycomb by the eating waves. Beneath the water-line, and revealed here and there when the waves receded, was a line of bright red coral.

THE STORY OF FIAMMETTA

At vespers on the fete of St. Antonino, and in his church, I saw the Signorina Fiammetta. I stood leaning against a marble pillar near the altar-steps, during the service, when I saw the young girl kneeling on the pavement in act of prayer. Her black lace veil had fallen a little back from her head; and there was something in her modest attitude and graceful figure that made her conspicuous among all her kneeling companions, with their gay kerchiefs and bright gowns. When she rose and sat down, with folded hands and eyes downcast, there was something so pensive in her subdued mien that I could not take my eyes from her. To say that she had the rich olive complexion, with the gold struggling through, large, lustrous black eyes, and harmonious features, is only to make a weak photograph, when I should paint a picture in colors and infuse it with the sweet loveliness of a maiden on the way to sainthood. I was sure that I had seen her before, looking down from the balcony of a villa just beyond the Roman wall, for the face was not one that even the most unimpressible idler would forget. I was sure that, young as she was, she had already a history; had lived her life, and now walked amid these groves and old streets in a dream. The story which I heard is not long.

In the drawing-room of the Villa Nardi was shown, and offered for sale, an enormous counterpane, crocheted in white cotton. Loop by loop, it must have been an immense labor to knit it; for it was fashioned in pretty devices, and when spread out was rich and showy enough for the royal bed of a princess. It had been crocheted by Fiammetta for her marriage, the only portion the poor child could bring to that sacrament. Alas! the wedding was never to be; and the rich work, into which her delicate fingers had knit so many maiden dreams and hopes and fears, was offered for sale in the resort of strangers. It could not have been want only that induced her to put this piece of work in the market, but the feeling, also, that the time never again could return when she would have need of it. I had no desire to purchase such a melancholy coverlet, but I could well enough fancy why she would wish to part with what must be rather a pall than a decoration in her little chamber.

Fiammetta lived with her mother in a little villa, the roof of which is in sight from my sunny terrace in the Villa Nardi, just to the left of the square old convent tower, rising there out of the silver olive-boughs,--a tumble-down sort of villa, with a flat roof and odd angles and parapets, in the midst of a thrifty but small grove of lemons and oranges. They were poor enough, or would be in any country where physical wants are greater than here, and yet did not belong to that lowest class, the young girls of which are little more than beasts of burden, accustomed to act as porters, bearing about on their heads great loads of stone, wood, water, and baskets of oranges in the shipping season. She could not have been forced to such labor, or she never would have had the time to work that wonderful coverlet.

Giuseppe was an honest and rather handsome young fellow of Sorrento, industrious and good-natured, who did not bother his head much about learning. He was, however, a skillful workman in the celebrated inlaid and mosaic woodwork of the place, and, it is said, had even invented some new figures for the inlaid pictures in colored woods. He had a little fancy for the sea as well, and liked to pull an oar over to Capri on occasion, by which he could earn a few francs easier than he could saw them out of the orangewood. For the stupid fellow, who could not read a word in his prayer-book, had an idea of thrift in his head, and already, I suspect, was laying up liras with an object. There are one or two dandies in Sorrento who attempt to dress as they do in Naples. Giuseppe was not one of these; but there was not a gayer or handsomer gallant than he on Sunday, or one more looked at by the Sorrento girls, when he had on his clean suit and his fresh red Phrygian cap. At least the good Fiammetta thought so, when she met him at church, though I feel sure she did not allow even his handsome figure to come between her and the Virgin. At any rate, there can be no doubt of her sentiments after church, when she and her mother used to walk with him along the winding Massa road above the sea, and stroll down to the shore to sit on the greensward over the Temple of Hercules, or the Roman Baths, or the remains of the villa of C. Fulvius Cunctatus Cocles, or whatever those ruins subterranean are, there on the Capo di Sorrento. Of course, this is mere conjecture of mine. They may have gone on the hills behind the town instead, or they may have stood leaning over the garden-wall of her mother's little villa, looking at the passers-by in the deep lane, thinking about nothing in the world, and talking about it all the sunny afternoon, until Ischia was purple with the last light, and the olive terraces behind them began to lose their gray bloom. All I do know is, that they were in love, blossoming out in it as the almond-trees do here in February; and that all the town knew it, and saw a wedding in the future, just as plain as you can see Capri from the heights above the town.

It was at this time that the wonderful counterpane began to grow, to the continual astonishment of Giuseppe, to whom it seemed a marvel of skill and patience, and who saw what love and sweet hope Fiammetta was knitting into it with her deft fingers. I declare, as I think of it, the white cotton spread out on her knees, in such contrast to the rich olive of her complexion and her black shiny hair, while she knits away so merrily, glancing up occasionally with those liquid, laughing eyes to Giuseppe, who is watching her as if she were an angel right out of the blue sky, I am tempted not to tell this story further, but to leave the happy two there at the open gate of life, and to believe that they entered in.

This was about the time of the change of government, after this region had come to be a part of the Kingdom of Italy. After the first excitement was over, and the simple people found they were not all made rich, nor raised to a condition in which they could live without work, there began to be some dissatisfaction. Why the convents need have been suppressed, and especially the poor nuns packed off, they couldn't see; and then the taxes were heavier than ever before; instead of being supported by the government, they had to support it; and, worst of all, the able young fellows must still go for soldiers. Just as one was learning his trade, or perhaps had acquired it, and was ready to earn his living and begin to make a home for his wife, he must pass the three best years of his life in the army. The conscription was relentless.

The time came to Giuseppe, as it did to the others. I never heard but he was brave enough; there was no storm on the Mediterranean that he dare not face in his little boat; and he would not have objected to a campaign with the red shirts of Garibaldi. But to be torn away from his occupations by which he was daily laying aside a little for himself and Fiammetta, and to leave her for three years,--that seemed dreadful to him. Three years is a longtime; and though he had no doubt of the pretty Fiammetta, yet women are women, said the shrewd fellow to himself, and who knows what might happen, if a gallant came along who could read and write, as Fiammetta could, and, besides, could play the guitar?

The result was, that Giuseppe did not appear at the mustering-office on the day set; and, when the file of soldiers came for him, he was nowhere to be found. He had fled to the mountains. I scarcely know what his plan was, but he probably trusted to some good luck to escape the conscription altogether, if he could shun it now; and, at least, I know that he had many comrades who did the same, so that at times the mountains were full of young fellows who were lurking in them to escape the soldiers. And they fared very roughly usually, and sometimes nearly perished from hunger; for though the sympathies of the peasants were undoubtedly with the quasi-outlaws rather than with the carbineers, yet the latter were at every hamlet in the hills, and liable to visit every hut, so that any relief extended to the fugitives was attended with great danger; and, besides, the hunted men did not dare to venture from their retreats. Thus outlawed and driven to desperation by hunger, these fugitives, whom nobody can defend for running away from their duties as citizens, became brigands. A cynical German, who was taken by them some years ago on the road to Castellamare, a few miles above here, and held for ransom, declared that they were the most honest fellows he had seen in Italy; but I never could see that he intended the remark as any compliment to them. It is certain that the inhabitants of all these towns held very loose ideas on the subject of brigandage: the poor fellows, they used to say, only robbed because they were hungry, and they must live somehow.

What Fiammetta thought, down in her heart, is not told: but I presume she shared the feelings of those about her concerning the brigands, and, when she heard that Giuseppe had joined them, was more anxious for the safety of his body than of his soul; though I warrant she did not forget either, in her prayers to the Virgin and St. Antonino. And yet those must have been days, weeks, months, of terrible anxiety to the poor child; and if she worked away at the counterpane, netting in that elaborate border, as I have no doubt she did, it must have been with a sad heart and doubtful fingers. I think that one of the psychological sensitives could distinguish the parts of the bedspread that were knit in the sunny days from those knit in the long hours of care and deepening anxiety.

It was rarely that she received any message from him and it was then only verbal and of the briefest; he was in the mountains above Amalfi; one day he had come so far round as the top of the Great St. Angelo, from which he could look down upon the piano of Sorrento, where the little Fiammetta was; or he had been on the hills near Salerno, hunted and hungry; or his company had descended upon some travelers going to Paestum, made a successful haul, and escaped into the steep mountains beyond. He didn't intend to become a regular bandit, not at all. He hoped that something might happen so that he could steal back into Sorrento, unmarked by the government; or, at least, that he could escape away to some other country or island, where Fiammetta could join him. Did she love him yet, as in the old happy days? As for him, she was now everything to him; and he would willingly serve three or thirty years in the army, if the government could forget he had been a brigand, and permit him to have a little home with Fiammetta at the end of the probation. There was not much comfort in all this, but the simple fellow could not send anything more cheerful; and I think it used to feed the little maiden's heart to hear from him, even in this downcast mood, for his love for her was a dear certainty, and his absence and wild life did not dim it.

My informant does not know how long this painful life went on, nor does it matter much. There came a day when the government was shamed into new vigor against the brigands. Some English people of consequence (the German of whom I have spoken was with them) had been captured, and it had cost them a heavy ransom. The number of the carbineers was quadrupled in the infested districts, soldiers penetrated the fastnesses of the hills, there were daily fights with the banditti; and, to show that this was no sham, some of them were actually shot, and others were taken and thrown into prison. Among those who were not afraid to stand and fight, and who would not be captured, was our Giuseppe. One day the Italia newspaper of Naples had an account of a fight with brigands; and in the list of those who fell was the name of Giuseppe---, of Sorrento, shot through the head, as he ought to have been, and buried without funeral among the rocks.

This was all. But when the news was read in the little post office in Sorrento, it seemed a great deal more than it does as I write it; for, if Giuseppe had an enemy in the village, it was not among the people; and not one who heard the news did not think at once of the poor girl to whom it would be more than a bullet through the heart. And so it was. The slender hope of her life then went out. I am told that there was little change outwardly, and that she was as lovely as before; but a great cloud of sadness came over her, in which she was always enveloped, whether she sat at home, or walked abroad in the places where she and Giuseppe used to wander. The simple people respected her grief, and always made a tender-hearted stillness when the bereft little maiden went through the streets,--a stillness which she never noticed, for she never noticed anything apparently. The bishop himself when he walked abroad could not be treated with more respect.

This was all the story of the sweet Fiammetta that was confided to me. And afterwards, as I recalled her pensive face that evening as she kneeled at vespers, I could not say whether, after all, she was altogether to be pitied, in the holy isolation of her grief, which I am sure sanctified her, and, in some sort, made her life complete. For I take it that life, even in this sunny Sorrento, is not alone a matter of time.

ST. MARIA A CASTELLO

The Great St. Angelo and that region are supposed to be the haunts of brigands. From those heights they spy out the land, and from thence have, more than once, descended upon the sea-road between Castellamare and Sorrento, and caught up

English and German travelers. This elevation commands, also, the Paestum way. We have no faith in brigands in these days; for in all our remote and lonely explorations of this promontory we have never met any but the most simple-hearted and good-natured people, who were quite as much afraid of us as we were of them. But there are not wanting stories, every day, to keep alive the imagination of tourists.

We are waiting in the garden this sunny, enticing morning-just the day for a tramp among the purple hills--for our friend, the long Englishman, who promised, over night, to go with us. This excellent, good-natured giant, whose head rubs the ceiling of any room in the house, has a wife who is fond of him, and in great dread of the brigands. He comes down with a sheepish air, at length, and informs us that his wife won't let him go.

"Of course I can go, if I like," he adds. "But the fact is, I have n't slept much all night: she kept asking me if I was going!" On the whole, the giant don't care to go. There are things more to be feared than brigands.

The expedition is, therefore, reduced to two unarmed persons. In the piazza we pick up a donkey and his driver for use in case of accident; and, mounting the driver on the donkey,--an arrangement that seems entirely satisfactory to him,--we set forward. If anything can bring back youth, it is a day of certain sunshine and a bit of unexplored country ahead, with a whole day in which to wander in it without a care or a responsibility. We walk briskly up the walled road of the piano, striking at the overhanging golden fruit with our staves; greeting the orange-girls who come down the side lanes; chaffing with the drivers, the beggars, the old women who sit in the sun; looking into the open doors of houses and shops upon women weaving, boys and girls slicing up heaps of oranges, upon the makers of macaroni, the sellers of sour wine, the merry shoemakers, whose little dens are centers of gossip here, as in all the East: the whole life of these people is open and social; to be on the street is to be at home.

We wind up the steep hill behind Meta, every foot of which is terraced for olive-trees, getting, at length, views over the wayside wall of the plain and bay and rising into the purer air and the scent of flowers and other signs of coming spring, to the little village of Arola, with its church and bell, its beggars and idlers,--just a little street of houses jammed in between the hills of Camaldoli and Pergola, both of which we know well.

Upon the cliff by Pergola is a stone house, in front of which I like to lie, looking straight down a thousand or two feet upon the roofs of Meta, the map of the plain, and the always fascinating bay. I went down the backbone of the limestone ridge towards the sea the other afternoon, before sunset, and unexpectedly came upon a group of little stone cottages on a ledge, which are quite hidden from below. The inhabitants were as much surprised to see a foreigner break through their seclusion as I was to come upon them. However, they soon recovered presence of mind to ask for a little money. Half a dozen old hags with the parchment also sat upon the rocks in the sun, spinning from distaffs, exactly as their ancestors did in Greece two thousand years ago, I doubt not. I do not know that it is true, as Tasso wrote, that this climate is so temperate and serene that one almost becomes immortal in it. Since two thousand years all these coasts have changed more or less, risen and sunk, and the temples and palaces of two civilizations have tumbled into the sea. Yet I do not know but these tranquil old women have been sitting here on the rocks all the while, high above change and worry and decay, gossiping and spinning, like Fates. Their yarn must be uncanny.

But we wander. It is difficult to go to any particular place here; impossible to write of it in a direct manner. Our mulepath continues most delightful, by slopes of green orchards nestled in sheltered places, winding round gorges, deep and ragged with loose stones, and groups of rocks standing on the edge of precipices, like medieval towers, and through village after village tucked away in the hills. The abundance of population is a constant surprise. As we proceed, the people are wilder and much more curious about us, having, it is evident, seen few strangers lately. Women and children, half-dressed in dirty rags which do not hide the form, come out from their low stone huts upon the windy terraces, and stand, arms akimbo, staring at us, and not seldom hailing us in harsh voices. Their sole dress is often a single split and torn gown, not reaching to the bare knees, evidently the original of those in the Naples ballet (it will, no doubt, be different when those creatures exchange the ballet for the ballot); and, with their tangled locks and dirty faces, they seem rather beasts than women. Are their husbands brigands, and are they in wait for us in the chestnut-grove yonder?

The grove is charming; and the men we meet there gathering sticks are not so surly as the women. They point the way; and when we emerge from the wood, St.

Maria a Castello is before us on a height, its white and red church shining in the sun. We climb up to it. In front is a broad, flagged terrace; and on the edge are deep wells in the rock, from which we draw cool water. Plentifully victualed, one could stand a siege here, and perhaps did in the gamey Middle Ages. Monk or soldier need not wish a pleasanter place to lounge. Adjoining the church, but lower, is a long, low building with three rooms, at once house and stable, the stable in the center, though all of them have hay in the lofts. The rooms do not communicate. That is the whole of the town of St. Maria a Castello.

In one of the apartments some rough-looking peasants are eating dinner, a frugal meal: a dish of unclean polenta, a plate of grated cheese, a basket of wormy figs, and some sour red wine; no bread, no meat. They looked at us askance, and with no sign of hospitality. We made friends, however, with the ragged children, one of whom took great delight in exhibiting his litter of puppies; and we at length so far worked into the good graces of the family that the mother was prevailed upon to get us some milk and eggs. I followed the woman into one of the apartments to superintend the cooking of the eggs. It was a mere den, with an earth floor. A fire of twigs was kindled against the farther wall, and a little girl, half-naked, carrying a baby still more economically clad, was stooping down to blow the smudge into a flame. The smoke, some of it, went over our heads out at the door. We boiled the eggs. We desired salt; and the woman brought us pepper in the berry. We insisted on salt, and at length got the rock variety, which we pounded on the rocks. We ate our eggs and drank our milk on the terrace, with the entire family interested spectators. The men were the hardest-looking ruffians we had met yet: they were making a bit of road near by, but they seemed capable of turning their hands to easier money-getting; and there couldn't be a more convenient place than this.

When our repast was over, and I had drunk a glass of wine with the proprietor, I offered to pay him, tendering what I knew was a fair price in this region. With some indignation of gesture, he refused it, intimating that it was too little. He seemed to be seeking an excuse for a quarrel with us; so I pocketed the affront, money and all, and turned away. He appeared to be surprised, and going indoors presently came out with a bottle of wine and glasses, and followed us down upon the rocks, pressing us to drink. Most singular conduct; no doubt drugged wine; travelers put into deep sleep; robbed; thrown over precipice; diplomatic correspondence, flattering, but no compensation to them. Either this, or a case of hospitality. We declined to drink, and the brigand went away.

We sat down upon the jutting ledge of a precipice, the like of which is not in the world: on our left, the rocky, bare side of St. Angelo, against which the sunshine dashes in waves; below us, sheer down two thousand feet, the city of Positano, a nest of brown houses, thickly clustered on a conical spur, and lying along the shore, the home of three thousand people,--with a running jump I think I could land in the midst of it,--a pygmy city, inhabited by mites, as we look down upon it; a little beach of white sand, a sailboat lying on it, and some fishermen just embarking; a long hotel on the beach; beyond, by the green shore, a country seat charmingly situated amid trees and vines; higher up, the ravine-seamed hill, little stone huts, bits of ruin, towers, arches. How still it is! All the stiller that I can, now and then, catch the sound of an axe, and hear the shouts of some children in a garden below. How still the sea is! How many ages has it been so? Does the purple mist always hang there upon the waters of Salerno Bay, forever hiding from the gaze Paestum and its temples, and all that shore which is so much more Grecian than Roman?

After all, it is a satisfaction to turn to the towering rock of St. Angelo; not a tree, not a shrub, not a spire of grass, on its perpendicular side. We try to analyze the satisfaction there is in such a bald, treeless, verdureless mass. We can grasp it intellectually, in its sharp solidity, which is undisturbed by any ornament: it is, to the mind, like some complete intellectual performance; the mind rests on it, like a demonstration in Euclid. And yet what a color of beauty it takes on in the distance!

When we return, the bandits have all gone to their road-making: the suspicious landlord is nowhere to be seen. We call the woman from the field, and give her money, which she seemed not to expect, and for which she shows no gratitude. Life appears to be indifferent to these people. But, if these be brigands, we prefer them to those of Naples, and even to the innkeepers of England. As we saunter home in the pleasant afternoon, the vesper-bells are calling to each other, making the sweetest echoes of peace everywhere in the hills, and all the piano is jubilant with them, as we come down the steeps at sunset.

"You see there was no danger," said the giant to his wife that evening at the supper-table.

"You would have found there was danger, if you had gone," returned the wife of the giant significantly.

THE MYTH OF THE SIRENS

I like to walk upon the encircling ridge behind Sorrento, which commands both bays. From there I can look down upon the Isles of the Sirens. The top is a broad, windy strip of pasture, which falls off abruptly to the Bay of Salerno on the south: a regular embankment of earth runs along the side of the precipitous steeps, towards Sorrento. It appears to be a line of defence for musketry, such as our armies used to throw up: whether the French, who conducted siege operations from this promontory on Capri, under Murat, had anything to do with it, does not appear.

Walking there yesterday, we met a woman shepherdess, cowherd, or siren--standing guard over three steers while they fed; a scantily-clad, brown woman, who had a distaff in her hand, and spun the flax as she watched the straying cattle, an example of double industry which the men who tend herds never imitate. Very likely her ancestors so spun and tended cattle on the plains of Thessaly. We gave the rigid woman good-morning, but she did not heed or reply; we made some inquiries as to paths, but she ignored us; we bade her good-day, and she scowled at us: she only spun. She was so out of tune with the people, and the gentle influences of this region, that we could only regard her as an anomaly,--the representative of some perversity and evil genius, which, no doubt, lurks here as it does elsewhere in the world. She could not have descended from either of the groups of the Sirens; for she was not fascinating enough to be fatal.

I like to look upon these islets or rocks of the Sirens, barren and desolate, with a few ruins of the Roman time and remains of the Middle-Age prisons of the doges of Amalfi; but I do not care to dissipate any illusions by going to them. I remember how the Sirens sat on flowery meads by the shore and sang, and are vulgarly supposed to have allured passing mariners to a life of ignoble pleasure, and then let them perish, hungry with all unsatisfied longings. The bones of these unfortunates, whitening on the rocks, of which Virgil speaks, I could not see. Indeed, I think any one who lingers long in this region will doubt if they were ever there, and will come to believe that the characters of the Sirens are popularly misconceived.

Allowing Ulysses to be only another name for the sun-god, who appears in myths as Indra, Apollo, William Tell, the sure-hitter, the great archer, whose arrows are sunbeams, it is a degrading conception of him that he was obliged to lash himself to the mast when he went into action with the Sirens, like Farragut at Mobile, though for a very different reason. We should be forced to believe that Ulysses was not free from the basest mortal longings, and that he had not strength of mind to resist them, but must put himself in durance; as our moderns who cannot control their desires go into inebriate asylums.

Mr. Ruskin says that "the Sirens are the great constant desires, the infinite sicknesses of heart, which, rightly placed, give life, and, wrongly placed, waste it away; so that there are two groups of Sirens, one noble and saving, as the other is fatal." Unfortunately we are all, as were the Greeks, ministered unto by both these groups, but can fortunately, on the other hand, choose which group we will listen to the singing of, though the strains are somewhat mingled; as, for instance, in the modern opera, where the music quite as often wastes life away, as gives to it the energy of pure desire. Yet, if I were to locate the Sirens geographically, I should place the beneficent desires on this coast, and the dangerous ones on that of wicked Baiae; to which group the founder of Naples no doubt belonged.

Nowhere, perhaps, can one come nearer to the beautiful myths of Greece, the springlike freshness of the idyllic and heroic age, than on this Sorrentine promontory. It was no chance that made these coasts the home of the kind old monarch Eolus, inventor of sails and storm-signals. On the Telegrafo di Mare Cuccola is a rude signal-apparatus for communication with Capri,--to ascertain if wind and wave are propitious for entrance to the Blue Grotto,--which probably was not erected by Eolus, although he doubtless used this sightly spot as one of his stations. That he dwelt here, in great content, with his six sons and six daughters, the Months, is nearly certain; and I feel as sure that the Sirens, whose islands were close at hand, were elevators and not destroyers of the primitive races living here.

It seems to me this must be so; because the pilgrim who surrenders himself to the influences of these peaceful and sun-inundated coasts, under this sky which the bright Athena loved and loves, loses, by and by, those longings and heart-sicknesses which waste away his life, and comes under the dominion, more and more, of those constant desires after that which is peaceful and enduring and has the saving quality of purity. I know, indeed, that it is not always so; and that, as Boreas is a better nurse of rugged virtue than Zephyr, so the soft influences of this clime only minister to the fatal desires of some: and such are likely to sail speedily back to Naples.

The Sirens, indeed, are everywhere; and I do not know that we can go anywhere that we shall escape the infinite longings, or satisfy them. Here, in the purple twilight of history, they offered men the choice of good and evil. I have a fancy, that, in stepping out of the whirl of modern life upon a quiet headland, so blessed of two powers, the air and the sea, we are able to come to a truer perception of the drift of the eternal desires within us. But I cannot say whether it is a subtle fascination, linked with these mythic and moral influences, or only the physical loveliness of this promontory, that lures travelers hither, and detains them on flowery meads.

The Codes Of Hammurabi And Moses
W. W. Davies

QTY

The discovery of the Hammurabi Code is one of the greatest achievements of archaeology, and is of paramount interest, not only to the student of the Bible, but also to all those interested in ancient history...

Religion   **ISBN:** *1-59462-338-4*   **Pages:132**
MSRP $12.95

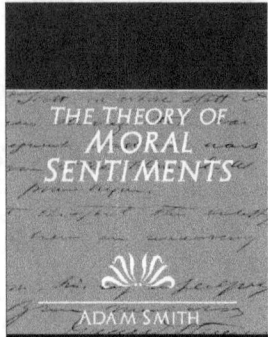

The Theory of Moral Sentiments
Adam Smith

QTY

This work from 1749. contains original theories of conscience amd moral judgment and it is the foundation for systemof morals.

Philosophy   **ISBN:** *1-59462-777-0*   **Pages:536**
MSRP $19.95

Jessica's First Prayer
Hesba Stretton

QTY

In a screened and secluded corner of one of the many railway-bridges which span the streets of London there could be seen a few years ago, from five o'clock every morning until half past eight, a tidily set-out coffee-stall, consisting of a trestle and board, upon which stood two large tin cans, with a small fire of charcoal burning under each so as to keep the coffee boiling during the early hours of the morning when the work-people were thronging into the city on their way to their daily toil...

Childrens   **ISBN:** *1-59462-373-2*

Pages:84
MSRP $9.95

My Life and Work
Henry Ford

QTY

Henry Ford revolutionized the world with his implementation of mass production for the Model T automobile. Gain valuable business insight into his life and work with his own auto-biography... "We have only started on our development of our country we have not as yet, with all our talk of wonderful progress, done more than scratch the surface. The progress has been wonderful enough but..."

Biographies/   **ISBN:** *1-59462-198-5*

Pages:300
MSRP $21.95

The Art of Cross-Examination
Francis Wellman

I presume it is the experience of every author, after his first book is published upon an important subject, to be almost overwhelmed with a wealth of ideas and illustrations which could readily have been included in his book, and which to his own mind, at least, seem to make a second edition inevitable. Such certainly was the case with me; and when the first edition had reached its sixth impression in five months, I rejoiced to learn that it seemed to my publishers that the book had met with a sufficiently favorable reception to justify a second and considerably enlarged edition. ..

QTY

Pages:412

Reference   **ISBN:** *1-59462-647-2*   *MSRP $19.95*

On the Duty of Civil Disobedience
Henry David Thoreau

Thoreau wrote his famous essay, On the Duty of Civil Disobedience, as a protest against an unjust but popular war and the immoral but popular institution of slave-owning. He did more than write—he declined to pay his taxes, and was hauled off to gaol in consequence. Who can say how much this refusal of his hastened the end of the war and of slavery ?

QTY

Pages:48

Law   **ISBN:** *1-59462-747-9*   *MSRP $7.45*

Dream Psychology Psychoanalysis for Beginners
Sigmund Freud

Sigmund Freud, born Sigismund Schlomo Freud (May 6, 1856 - September 23, 1939), was a Jewish-Austrian neurologist and psychiatrist who co-founded the psychoanalytic school of psychology. Freud is best known for his theories of the unconscious mind, especially involving the mechanism of repression; his redefinition of sexual desire as mobile and directed towards a wide variety of objects; and his therapeutic techniques, especially his understanding of transference in the therapeutic relationship and the presumed value of dreams as sources of insight into unconscious desires.

QTY

Pages:196

Psychology   **ISBN:** *1-59462-905-6*   *MSRP $15.45*

The Miracle of Right Thought
Orison Swett Marden

Believe with all of your heart that you will do what you were made to do. When the mind has once formed the habit of holding cheerful, happy, prosperous pictures, it will not be easy to form the opposite habit. It does not matter how improbable or how far away this realization may see, or how dark the prospects may be, if we visualize them as best we can, as vividly as possible, hold tenaciously to them and vigorously struggle to attain them, they will gradually become actualized, realized in the life. But a desire, a longing without endeavor, a yearning abandoned or held indifferently will vanish without realization.

QTY

Pages:360

Self Help   **ISBN:** *1-59462-644-8*   *MSRP $25.45*

QTY

☐ **The Rosicrucian Cosmo-Conception Mystic Christianity** *by Max Heindel*　ISBN: *1-59462-188-8*　**$38.95**
The Rosicrucian Cosmo-conception is not dogmatic, neither does it appeal to any other authority than the reason of the student. It is: not controversial, but is: sent forth in the, hope that it may help to clear...　New Age/Religion Pages 646

☐ **Abandonment To Divine Providence** *by Jean-Pierre de Caussade*　ISBN: *1-59462-228-0*　**$25.95**
"The Rev. Jean Pierre de Caussade was one of the most remarkable spiritual writers of the Society of Jesus in France in the 18th Century. His death took place at Toulouse in 1751. His works have gone through many editions and have been republished...　Inspirational/Religion Pages 400

☐ **Mental Chemistry** *by Charles Haanel*　ISBN: *1-59462-192-6*　**$23.95**
Mental Chemistry allows the change of material conditions by combining and appropriately utilizing the power of the mind. Much like applied chemistry creates something new and unique out of careful combinations of chemicals the mastery of mental chemistry...　New Age Pages 354

☐ **The Letters of Robert Browning and Elizabeth Barret Barrett 1845-1846 vol II**　ISBN: *1-59462-193-4*　**$35.95**
by Robert Browning and Elizabeth Barrett　Biographies Pages 596

☐ **Gleanings In Genesis (volume I)** *by Arthur W. Pink*　ISBN: *1-59462-130-6*　**$27.45**
Appropriately has Genesis been termed "the seed plot of the Bible" for in it we have, in germ form, almost all of the great doctrines which are afterwards fully developed in the books of Scripture which follow...　Religion/Inspirational Pages 420

☐ **The Master Key** *by L. W. de Laurence*　ISBN: *1-59462-001-6*　**$30.95**
In no branch of human knowledge has there been a more lively increase of the spirit of research during the past few years than in the study of Psychology, Concentration and Mental Discipline. The requests for authentic lessons in Thought Control, Mental Discipline and...　New Age/Business Pages 422

☐ **The Lesser Key Of Solomon Goetia** *by L. W. de Laurence*　ISBN: *1-59462-092-X*　**$9.95**
This translation of the first book of the "Lemegton" which is now for the first time made accessible to students of Talismanic Magic was done, after careful collation and edition, from numerous Ancient Manuscripts in Hebrew, Latin, and French...　New Age/Occult Pages 92

☐ **Rubaiyat Of Omar Khayyam** *by Edward Fitzgerald*　ISBN:*1-59462-332-5*　**$13.95**
Edward Fitzgerald, whom the world has already learned, in spite of his own efforts to remain within the shadow of anonymity, to look upon as one of the rarest poets of the century, was born at Bredfield, in Suffolk, on the 31st of March, 1809. He was the third son of John Purcell...　Music Pages 172

☐ **Ancient Law** *by Henry Maine*　ISBN: *1-59462-128-4*　**$29.95**
The chief object of the following pages is to indicate some of the earliest ideas of mankind, as they are reflected in Ancient Law, and to point out the relation of those ideas to modern thought.　Religiom/History Pages 452

☐ **Far-Away Stories** *by William J. Locke*　ISBN: *1-59462-129-2*　**$19.45**
"Good wine needs no bush," but a collection of mixed vintages does. And this book is just such a collection. Some of the stories I do not want to remain buried for ever in the museum files of dead magazine-numbers an author's not unpardonable vanity..."　Fiction Pages 272

☐ **Life of David Crockett** *by David Crockett*　ISBN: *1-59462-250-7*　**$27.45**
"Colonel David Crockett was one of the most remarkable men of the times in which he lived. Born in humble life, but gifted with a strong will, an indomitable courage, and unremitting perseverance...　Biographies/New Age Pages 424

☐ **Lip-Reading** *by Edward Nitchie*　ISBN: *1-59462-206-X*　**$25.95**
Edward B. Nitchie, founder of the New York School for the Hard of Hearing, now the Nitchie School of Lip-Reading, Inc, wrote "LIP-READING Principles and Practice". The development and perfecting of this meritorious work on lip-reading was an undertaking...　How-to Pages 400

☐ **A Handbook of Suggestive Therapeutics, Applied Hypnotism, Psychic Science**　ISBN: *1-59462-214-0*　**$24.95**
by Henry Munro　Health/New Age/Health/Self-help Pages 376

☐ **A Doll's House: and Two Other Plays** *by Henrik Ibsen*　ISBN: *1-59462-112-8*　**$19.95**
Henrik Ibsen created this classic when in revolutionary 1848 Rome. Introducing some striking concepts in playwriting for the realist genre, this play has been studied the world over.　Fiction/Classics/Plays 308

☐ **The Light of Asia** *by sir Edwin Arnold*　ISBN: *1-59462-204-3*　**$13.95**
In this poetic masterpiece, Edwin Arnold describes the life and teachings of Buddha. The man who was to become known as Buddha to the world was born as Prince Gautama of India but he rejected the worldly riches and abandoned the reigns of power when...　Religion/History/Biographies Pages 170

☐ **The Complete Works of Guy de Maupassant** *by Guy de Maupassant*　ISBN: *1-59462-157-8*　**$16.95**
"For days and days, nights and nights, I had dreamed of that first kiss which was to consecrate our engagement, and I knew not on what spot I should put my lips..."　Fiction/Classics Pages 240

☐ **The Art of Cross-Examination** *by Francis L. Wellman*　ISBN: *1-59462-309-0*　**$26.95**
Written by a renowned trial lawyer, Wellman imparts his experience and uses case studies to explain how to use psychology to extract desired information through questioning.　How-to/Science/Reference Pages 408

☐ **Answered or Unanswered?** *by Louisa Vaughan*　ISBN: *1-59462-248-5*　**$10.95**
Miracles of Faith in China　Religion Pages 112

☐ **The Edinburgh Lectures on Mental Science (1909)** *by Thomas*　ISBN: *1-59462-008-3*　**$11.95**
This book contains the substance of a course of lectures recently given by the writer in the Queen Street Hail, Edinburgh. Its purpose is to indicate the Natural Principles governing the relation between Mental Action and Material Conditions...　New Age/Psychology Pages 148

☐ **Ayesha** *by H. Rider Haggard*　ISBN: *1-59462-301-5*　**$24.95**
Verily and indeed it is the unexpected that happens! Probably if there was one person upon the earth from whom the Editor of this, and of a certain previous history, did not expect to hear again...　Classics Pages 380

☐ **Ayala's Angel** *by Anthony Trollope*　ISBN: *1-59462-352-X*　**$29.95**
The two girls were both pretty, but Lucy who was twenty-one who supposed to be simple and comparatively unattractive, whereas Ayala was credited, as her Bombwhat romantic name might show, with poetic charm and a taste for romance. Ayala when her father died was nineteen...　Fiction Pages 484

☐ **The American Commonwealth** *by James Bryce*　ISBN: *1-59462-286-8*　**$34.45**
An interpretation of American democratic political theory. It examines political mechanics and society from the perspective of Scotsman James Bryce　Politics Pages 572

☐ **Stories of the Pilgrims** *by Margaret P. Pumphrey*　ISBN: *1-59462-116-0*　**$17.95**
This book explores pilgrims religious oppression in England as well as their escape to Holland and eventual crossing to America on the Mayflower, and their early days in New England...　History Pages 268

QTY

The Fasting Cure *by Sinclair Upton*   ISBN: *1-59462-222-1*   **$13.95**
In the Cosmopolitan Magazine for May, 1910, and in the Contemporary Review (London) for April, 1910, I published an article dealing with my experi-
ences in fasting. I have written a great many magazine articles, but never one which attracted so much attention... New Age/Self Help/Health Pages 164

Hebrew Astrology *by Sepharial*   ISBN: *1-59462-308-2*   **$13.45**
In these days of advanced thinking it is a matter of common observation that we have left many of the old landmarks behind and that we are now pressing
forward to greater heights and to a wider horizon than that which represented the mind-content of our progenitors...   Astrology Pages 144

Thought Vibration or The Law of Attraction in the Thought World   ISBN: *1-59462-127-6*   **$12.95**

by William Walker Atkinson   *Psychology/Religion Pages 144*

Optimism *by Helen Keller*   ISBN: *1-59462-108-X*   **$15.95**
Helen Keller was blind, deaf, and mute since 19 months old, yet famously learned how to overcome these handicaps, communicate with the world, and
spread her lectures promoting optimism. An inspiring read for everyone...   Biographies/Inspirational Pages 84

Sara Crewe *by Frances Burnett*   ISBN: *1-59462-360-0*   **$9.45**
In the first place, Miss Minchin lived in London. Her home was a large, dull, tall one, in a large, dull square, where all the houses were alike, and all the
sparrows were alike, and where all the door-knockers made the same heavy sound...   Childrens/Classic Pages 88

The Autobiography of Benjamin Franklin *by Benjamin Franklin*   ISBN: *1-59462-135-7*   **$24.95**
The Autobiography of Benjamin Franklin has probably been more extensively read than any other American historical work, and no other book of its kind
has had such ups and downs of fortune. Franklin lived for many years in England, where he was agent...   Biographies/History Pages 332

Name	
Email	
Telephone	
Address	
City, State ZIP	

☐ **Credit Card**   ☐ **Check / Money Order**

Credit Card Number	
Expiration Date	
Signature	

Please Mail to: Book Jungle
PO Box 2226
Champaign, IL 61825
or Fax to: 630-214-0564

ORDERING INFORMATION

web: *www.bookjungle.com*
email: *sales@bookjungle.com*
fax: *630-214-0564*
mail: *Book Jungle PO Box 2226 Champaign, IL 61825*
or PayPal *to sales@bookjungle.com*

Please contact us for bulk discounts

DIRECT-ORDER TERMS

**20% Discount if You Order
Two or More Books**
Free Domestic Shipping!
Accepted: Master Card, Visa,
Discover, American Express

www.ingramcontent.com/pod-product-compliance
Lightning Source LLC
Chambersburg PA
CBHW080905020726
47502CB00008B/2361